THE
BUZZER

THE
BUZZER
DAVID MASON

The Book Guild Ltd

First published in Great Britain in 2017 by
The Book Guild Ltd
9 Priory Business Park
Wistow Road, Kibworth
Leicestershire, LE8 0RX
Freephone: 0800 999 2982
www.bookguild.co.uk
Email: info@bookguild.co.uk
Twitter: @bookguild

Typeset in Minion Pro

Printed and bound in Great Britain by CPI Group (UK) Ltd, Croydon, CR0 4YY

ISBN 978 1911320 951

British Library Cataloguing in Publication Data.
A catalogue record for this book is available from the British Library.

For my wife and our special girls.

PREFACE

To this day the radio signal UVB-76, 'The Buzzer', is a transmission that is broadcast constantly around the world. It can be received on any short-wave radio or heard on the Internet on a frequency of 4625 kHz. Despite its obvious nature, no person or organisation has ever claimed responsibility for it. Its purpose is truly unknown. Many of the locations and events in this story are real. By piecing together this information, the story provides a theory to finally explain the mystery surrounding 'The Buzzer'.

PROLOGUE

19 September 2010, Povarovo Military Base, Russia

Two men stood solemnly in a forest clearing. The storm surrounding them was like nothing either had seen before. Sheets of water, whipped up by a ferocious swirling wind, fell relentlessly from the black night sky. They stood firm as they watched huge raindrops smashing against the metal bodywork of thirty trucks lined up in front of them. With each impact, the water scattered into dull sparkles, reflecting what little artificial light there was. Competing with the deluge, the ancient pine trees of the surrounding forest groaned against the ferocity of the storm.

Captain Malinov, the younger and taller of the men, shouted to his colleague. Even in full voice, the sound was barely audible over the continuous symphony of nature. 'Sir, it looks as if this place doesn't want us to leave.'

The older man said nothing. Rain drove into his face, stinging his skin, and yet he remained motionless. Behind his stony expression, he knew what had to be done. The base was no longer efficient in this location. It had to be relocated, and then back online before the deadline. If they failed, the protection it provided from one of Russia's deadliest secrets would cease, and the weapon would once again be unleashed on the world.

Ahead of him, an army of staff swarmed over the assembled trucks, loading large wooden crates of precious cargo and strapping them securely into the loading bays. He looked behind him towards a large square concrete building standing three floors high. On its flat roof, three tall, white cylinders stood proudly, shrouding the parabolic antenna responsible for the base's communications. Inside the building, a few lights remained lit, twinkling through the watery glass. He knew there wouldn't be anyone going back in to turn them off.

General Valentin knew this day would arrive. He had been building towards this dauntless inevitability for years. All that time to plan and prepare the perfect scenario, and now it was to end like this. Reports had come through, bringing forward the relocation years ahead of schedule. They had no choice; they were dealing with powers way beyond their control. Tonight was the last opportunity. He had not expected it to arrive so soon.

A hooded figure scurried up to the pair; his head bowed low, braced against the elements. His feet slipped on the thick mud as he struggled to gain enough purchase to stand straight, while the howling wind thrashed against his saturated coat. He offered both men a brisk salute before dropping his head once more. The wind whipped up even stronger for a moment, trying to steal the man's words away before they had barely passed his lips.

'We have just dropped offline, sir. We have twenty-three hours before we need to initiate recommencement. The charges have been set in accordance to your orders and await your command.'

General Valentin looked at the messenger and nodded his dismissal. The man gratefully accepted, scampering back towards the limited cover of the trucks, with one hand raised to hold his hood in position.

Captain Malinov stood thoughtful for a while before

speaking. 'We've got one chance to get this right, sir. May I ask, do you think we'll make it?'

General Valentin didn't respond with words, but fixed his colleague straight in the eye with a stare that could have melted lead.

Captain Malinov felt ashamed for asking, for showing weakness in requesting empty reassurance. How could the general answer that? Contemplating failure would serve only to waste time and make the chances of success far more unlikely. Diverting his gaze, he looked at the ground. Huge raindrops continued to smash into mud-filled pools at their feet. He glanced at his watch, knowing full well that they were only a few minutes into their twenty-three hour deadline. Considering the conditions, they seemed to be making good progress.

Teams of people were still hauling crates out of smaller buildings, dragging them across the mud to load them onto the convoy, although many of the trucks were now loaded to capacity. Figures hauled heavy tarpaulins down from their rolled-up positions to conceal the shipment within. Each time a roll of canvas was released, it was quickly followed by a gush of water that had gathered in the folds, soaking the men below. Numerous straps were pulled tight, fastened, and locked into position, securing the billowing sails to enclose the cargo area of each truck.

Finally, as each team completed their tasks, they stood in a line at the side of their assigned vehicle. It was plain to see the effort it took to stand to attention, as wave upon wave of water hammered down from the heavens. Once the final truck had been secured, a row of over one hundred people had assembled, awaiting orders.

Captain Malinov winced as a vivid streak of light shot out from the sky and into the nearby forest. The thunderclap that accompanied it reverberated off every surface, shaking the very foundations of the earth.

'That was a bit too close for comfort, sir.' They had the only source of metal for miles around. Should it attract a lightning strike to one of the vehicles, it would be game over.

Another messenger scuttled forwards, approaching as quickly as he dared in order to keep his footing. He stood inches away from the general and barked something into his ear. Despite standing close by, the captain couldn't make out a single word over the cacophony of the storm. The messenger returned to join the ranks.

General Valentin turned to his colleague. 'It's time to leave, Captain.'

The younger man gave a single nod. He would be pleased to get on the road, but something was playing on his mind. He knew they had little time to waste and that the general was not a man that enjoyed being questioned, even at the best of times, but this he couldn't ignore. A task still had not been completed.

'Sir...' he began cautiously.

A sudden echoing boom stopped him in his tracks. The general didn't flinch.

The noise wasn't thunder. It came specifically from a location a little way across the clearing. The ground shook, and numerous people in the line turned to locate the source of the sound. For a few seconds, nothing happened, and then a silent flash of orange light ripped through the darkness.

Two hundred metres away, a domed concrete outbuilding erupted into a raging fireball. For a few seconds, it burned brightly as the flames blasted out of its tall steel entrance doors. Fuelled by fresh oxygen streaming in from the open air, the flames ballooned upwards, reaching as high as the surrounding trees. The orange glow bathed the whole clearing in light before being sucked back into the opening from which it came. As quickly as it had appeared, the fire was gone.

Captain Malinov composed himself. 'Sir...' he began again, 'have you considered what we are to do with the other... projects?'

General Valentin turned to face his second in command with cold, dark eyes, his level voice projecting easily through the background noise.

'They are your responsibility, Captain. They are of no use to us now, and they are unsuitable for transportation. You will need to dispose of them.'

Captain Malinov turned away, the general had only ever concentrated on the transmission; he had never shared Malinov's passion for his project, or appreciated its brilliance. He trudged across the saturated grass and looked down into the darkness of the first exercise pit: a huge concrete circle, twenty metres in diameter, and sunken five metres into the earth. Below him, a flicker of movement caught his eye. A movement that represented five years of research and development into the production of a new biological weapon.

The project was to design a perfect predator, superior to humans, which could be manufactured and unleashed behind enemy lines. Creating the physical attributes was relatively straightforward, as nature had already provided the weapons needed. It was merely the case of combining them. Each version of the project improved upon the last, providing greater strength and stamina, greater sensory capacities. However, one problem remained: the projects always acted like animals – animals that acted upon instincts to kill only when necessary.

The pack that hid in the darkness below Captain Malinov's feet, however, was different. He was most proud of this latest version. In a moment of brilliance, he had instructed his development team to include components from a different animal in the genetic sequencing, and one they had not dared use before: the only animal on the planet that kills for fun. All he needed was a little more time to test them, to put them through their paces and prove their worth. This pack was perfect. He couldn't destroy them now, not when he was so close. General Valentin was being hasty. Once this night was through, Malinov would reconsider his order. In the meantime, to leave them here to survive alone would act as their final test. They would be stored safely, locked in their underground complex. The exercise pits were the only access they had to the open air, but the smooth, vertical walls ensured they were unable to leave their subterranean prison. They were suited to the darkness of the tunnels, designed to function at their optimum at night when humans were at their weakest.

If they were still alive by the time Malinov returned, then he would know that they were ready.

1

Twenty-six-year-old Natalya Kovalski looked around her shabby rented apartment with dismay. Black smudged dust stains formed shadow patterns on the tired walls. There never seemed to be any point in brightening it up. It was always meant to be a temporary stop, one lasting four years longer than planned.

It had been five years since she had left the family farm to live in Moscow. To some, life in an isolated village in the Sverdlovsk region of rural central Russia was a comfort. To a girl like Natalya, it was stifling. She wasn't the first to want to leave. Most people slotted into village life, finding a comfortable place amongst the community. But Natalya had found herself huddled around the family radio for hours, listening to reports on the world and its people, daring to imagine what it would be like to be out there, exploring its mysteries. As a farmer's daughter, she could fix machines, drive a tractor, and fire a gun, but her family always knew that one day she would leave.

After relocating to Moscow city centre, she had fallen into her current position at NTV almost straight away. That first step towards her media ambitions had been easy. Since then, progress had been slow. Five years of delivering reports and making coffee in one of Russia's most popular TV stations, when

1

all she wanted was to become a journalist. Initially, her manager, Anderi, had taken her under his wing. He had shown her the ropes, offering fantastic promises of promotions that he could guide her towards. Unfortunately, it wasn't long before reality caught up with his empty words. It wasn't just Natalya's skills as a journalist he was interested in.

There'd been another one in the waiting room today, looking as if she didn't have a care in the world. A petite young girl filled with innocence, her long blonde hair flowing down her back, shimmering each time she moved. Despite Anderi's presence on the interview panel, Natalya knew she would be his choice, not her, as he swore blindly it would be, every time an opening for a trainee journalist arose.

Like her life, her home was a mess. Oddments and unfinished projects, second-hand furniture, carpet offcuts, walls still the plain white generously provided by the landlord. But she still let herself dream of success. She would give Anderi an ultimatum: to give her an assignment or she would make an official complaint. The idea made her feel better. She rooted down the back of her great black sofa and found a half-empty bottle of wine, then sifted through the room for a suitable glass.

In front of her, stood a low iron coffee table, with a cracked glass top, that she'd found in a skip. It was now the store for a mountain of clothes where a cascade of socks and pants erupted onto the floor. Underneath, she found a glass. One of the advantages of living alone was that she knew her own system. Nothing was lost. She slumped onto the sofa as she considered her next move.

Despite her dreams of journalism, she would always be Natalya who could mend a fence, Natalya who could service an engine. It was who she was, and who she would remain, despite the new world in which she now chose to live. That experience of real life, of the practical problems faced by so many people every day, would be her edge. Should anyone ever decide to give her a chance, she could use it to relate to people outside of the city in a way that many journalists could not.

***

The following morning, Natalya approached her work building after a night of restless sleep. Today, she would be told the outcome of the job interview. Anderi could make this easy on himself and just give her the position, but that was unlikely to happen. She would confront him. She had already left this far too long, and it was time for make or break.

The staffroom was as sterile and lifeless as the rest of the NTV offices. The harsh fluorescent lighting shone off endless white walls studded with lines of coat hooks below a row of metal shelving. Natalya selected her usual spot to store her bag and hung her coat on the hook underneath. A hook that had been used for far too long.

Natalya had taken only a few steps out of the staffroom before she caught sight of Anderi. He was a puffy little man on the wrong side of sixty, with slicked-back hair and a flushed red face. His purple striped suit with straining buttons did his portly physique no favours as he pointed his finger at Natalya, beckoning her towards him. Normally, she would have stood her ground, and made him walk to her. Today was different; today she actually wanted to hear what he had to say.

'Natalya, just the person. Could I invite you for a quick liaison in my office?'

She smiled at him through gritted teeth, choosing not to reply.

Anderi didn't care. He turned, assuming she would do as she was told, and follow him.

The building had miles of halls. Some were embellished by various works of art or tired-looking faux potted plants. Those, however, were reserved for the corridors frequented by the more privileged members of staff. This passageway was totally void of all decorations. The only distraction to occupy Natalya's mind from her imminent judgement was the echo of their footsteps on the hard tiled floor.

Focusing ahead on Anderi's short, rolling wobble, Natalya slowed her pace, choosing to stay a few steps behind. He waddled like a penguin in a nature documentary as it shuffled across the glaciers – more specifically, the penguins that were carrying eggs on their feet. Her pulse quickened as they approached his office door.

Anderi entered first, flinging the door wide so that it slammed into the wall. Natalya rolled her eyes at her manager's back. In the five years of working at NTV, she was all too familiar with her manager's chest-pounding efforts to prove his macho masculinity.

Anderi switched on the lights, which responded with a buzz and a flicker before illuminating the tiny windowless room with a bright white glare.

In the centre stood a small desk with a smattering of folders strewn haphazardly over the surface, and on either side, a reception chair. The walls were home to several items that displayed Anderi's modest life achievements. Behind his desk hung a college graduation certificate, below which was a shelf – its sole purpose to house a collection of three small trophies. He spun around to the far side of the desk. 'Make yourself comfortable,' he smirked.

Natalya sat in the opposite chair. It was impossible to be comfortable when in such close proximity to Anderi, but she did her best. Her heartbeat quickened in anticipation of the news she hoped to hear. The result was always going to be the same, but a tiny glimmer of hope in the back of her mind refused to go away.

Anderi must have sensed it. He grinned like a hyena through yellowed teeth, resulting from years of chain-smoking. 'I have some very good news for you, Natalya. I hope you'll be able to control your excitement.'

Natalya's stomach leapt. Leaning forwards, a rush of heat coursed up her body causing her face to flush a bright red.

Anderi continued. 'I'm pleased to tell you that you will be having the pleasure of my company for a little longer, as unfortunately you didn't get the job.'

Natalya felt a knot of anger churn inside her. Anderi had deliberately given her that second of success before crushing it. Some kind of sick joke. Tears of frustration started to well up as her vision began to smear. Determined not to give him the satisfaction, Natalya used all of her will power to force them away.

Anderi continued to grin. 'I tried the best I could to convince them that you were the right candidate for the job. I gave you my vote, but in the end, it came down to your lack of experience. They wanted someone with more... credentials. I'm sorry.'

With the smile still plastered across his face, he didn't look sorry. It was true that Natalya didn't have the paper certificate that they put so much value on, or a wealth of experience. But due to the age of the other candidates, they wouldn't have experience either.

Anderi stopped smiling. An awkward silence hung between them as he simply sat staring at her. His face had changed; he looked solemn, sympathetic.

'Thank you for trying...' Natalya began as another wave of tears crept over her, cutting her off mid flow.

Anderi sidled round his desk and placed his arm round her shoulder. 'Don't thank me. All I told them was the truth. I think very highly of you. If you ever need to talk, you know where I am. Even after work one day, maybe?'

Natalya stood, forcing Anderi to break his attempt of a comforting embrace. She sucked in her disappointment. 'Thank you, again. I'm sure you tried your best, but I'm afraid I really must insist...'

'Insist?' Anderi repeated, taking a step back.

'Yes, insist that you give me a chance. A chance to prove my worth. You've promised me so many times and yet this always happens.'

'I'm really sorry, Natalya, but it's out of my hands. I did my best for you.'

'Well, I'm afraid that isn't good enough this time. I know what sort of credentials you look for in the people you promote. It isn't hard to see a pattern. Who did get the job, by the way?'

Anderi stared back at Natalya. 'I... erm... am not at liberty to divulge that at the moment.'

'Oh aren't you? So, it wouldn't be that blonde skirt that followed me, by any chance? Maybe it was one of the two male candidates that got the job?' Natalya stared intensely into Anderi's dumbstruck face.

'What is it that you're saying, Natalya?'

'What I'm saying is that I need a trial assignment, today. That or I start to talk about your favouritism amongst certain members of the female staff. I'm sure NTV won't look too kindly on that sort of inappropriate behaviour in the work place.'

'Now hang on,' began Anderi, 'there's no need for this sort of talk, no need at all. You know I've always been there for you, to help when you needed it. I tell you what – leave this with me. You head off back to work and we'll talk later, how's that?'

Natalya nodded. 'You've promised for so long. I can't waste any more time, I need this job...'

'I understand. Leave it with me; I'll see what I can do.' He walked over to the door and opened it for her.

As Natalya left the room, she could feel Anderi's eyes burning into her back. The second she heard the door close behind her, her face contorted into a sob. She didn't register the walk back to her workstation. She moved through the corridors as if trapped inside a bubble. Concerned faces of her colleagues peered at her as she passed by, offering sympathetic questions, but she didn't recall the answers that she gave them. Ahead lay a cruel day of tedious boredom, as Anderi once again fell short on one of his infamous promises.

Natalya's workstation was in the corner of one of the larger communal offices at NTV. It was a huge room, divided up by low grey screens creating smaller workstations, each containing a desk and computer next to a storage cabinet. This was where the researchers worked, the junior journalists, the team leaders, the 'useful' people. There were no screens around her area. She sat in the corner on a worn-out office chair at what was little more than a shelf. On it was an old desktop computer; a hand-me-down from when the main central workstations had been revamped.

Natalya stared mindlessly at her blank computer monitor as the rest of the office continued their normal routines around her. Occasionally, people gave her an odd look as they walked by, but nobody bothered her. Trapped in a punishing daydream of failure, she didn't notice the stubby form of her boss standing behind her, until he cleared his throat.

The little man crouched down and carefully placed his arm around the back of her chair. 'I've come to see how you're bearing up.' His voice was soft and sensitive, yet his face still managed to wear a sly smile.

The distance between them was uncomfortably close, and Natalya had no way to increase it. His casual arm seemed to be constricting her. 'That's very kind of you, Anderi. I'm just fine… really.' Her final word was as much to convince herself as it was him.

Anderi's voice dropped even quieter as he leant in further to Natalya. 'That's good; that's really good. I was worried about you.' His eyes made a quick glance left and right before returning to

Natalya. 'You see, at the risk of showing you favouritism, I have an idea that maybe you would be interested in?' He paused to give her a chance to appreciate his generosity.

'What's your idea?' she prompted, unable to resist rising to the bait.

'Well, I thought that since NTV weren't willing to give you a chance, that maybe I could make one for you. I thought perhaps a short assignment. A bit of research, some fieldwork and then a short article. A chance to show what you're made of.'

She shot him a smile. 'Absolutely. That sounds fantastic. But really, as easy as that?'

Anderi's eyes flitted around the room once more, as he stood up and leaned in even closer. His chin almost rested on her shoulder as he flashed his yellow-toothed grin. 'Just don't mention it to the others. I don't want them knowing that you're my favourite. It's not... professional.'

As far as Natalya was concerned, nothing about Anderi was professional, but it had never stopped him before. She instinctively recoiled as he reached towards her with his free hand, bumping her head against his loitering arm. His hand was still outstretched towards her, clutching a small piece of folded paper.

'Meet me here tonight, after work,' he said. 'We'll go over the details then.'

Gingerly, she took the scrap from between Anderi's nicotine-stained fingers. His hand brushed along hers for far longer than necessary. She turned the note over and unfolded its crumpled edges. Anderi's familiar handwriting was scrawled across its centre.

Toba Restaurant
6.00 p.m.
X X X

Finally, he had managed it. How long had he been threatening this? More to the point, how long had he been planning it? Still, despite how repulsive Natalya thought Anderi was, maybe finally he would deliver on one of his promises.

2

The Toba Restaurant glowed warmly against the chilly darkness of the evening. Internal lights blazed down upon rows of tables with diners eating busily within.

Despite this being strictly a business meeting, the thought of meeting Anderi here turned her stomach. The question was, would he see it that way? The plan was to be quick and polite. After all, she did want to hear him out, but under no circumstances was she to say or do anything that may be... misinterpreted. It wouldn't take long, and even though she had not been offered the promotion that she had hoped for, this was an opportunity, none the less.

Despite the situation, the soft burgundy carpet under her feet, and the waist-high panels that created the small private dining areas, made the restaurant feel welcoming. The portly form of Anderi was unmissable. He sat, facing Natalya, halfway along the room, on a small table seated for two. The tension in the straining fabric of his lime-green shirt looked almost painful as the buttons clung on, exposing small diamond-shaped holes through to a white vest underneath. He had clearly ordered a bottle of wine, the bottle now empty on the table. As Natalya approached, he speedily quaffed his way through the remains of the large glass in his hand. She mentally steadied herself for the final time.

During what seemed like hours of tedious small talk, Natalya tried desperately to steer the conversation in the direction of the opportunity that brought her here.

As the meal ended, Anderi finally relented. 'So, I suppose you'd like to know more about what I have in mind for you?'

Natalya winced. The question was ambiguous and, no doubt, another toe-curling innuendo would follow. She agreed, bracing herself for the response.

'What I have in mind is an opportunity for you to produce a short article on film for me. I can lend you all the equipment you'll need, but all the content will be entirely your own work. I shall oversee you personally, and we will need to meet up regularly so that you can keep me updated on your progress, as we are tonight. I could allow you two weeks' absence from your normal duties, but I would insist that if you were to have that time out, you continue to meet me after hours to report your progress. Is that something you'd be interested in?'

Natalya wasn't naïve: Anderi's ulterior motive couldn't be any more obvious. Normally, she would have declined the offer outright, but after five years as a runner, she had made no progress, her life still on hold. Despite its dubious nature, this was her best chance. She smiled sweetly at the purple, puffy-faced man sitting opposite. 'I'd be delighted.'

Anderi parted his lips, sucking in a long breath. 'Wonderful, absolutely wonderful. I have the topic of the article all lined up. Just to reiterate, I will need regular updates on your progress in order to give you the time you'll need. Let's say a meeting here in four days – that's Monday. You understand the importance of that, don't you?'

'Of course. I won't be shirking off on any two-week long holidays in the sun, if that's what you're worried about.'

It was wrong to play along, but life was becoming desperate.

The content of her article would be irrelevant to Anderi, but if she could get it right… if she could produce something brilliant, then that work would be hers. She could take a copy. It could be an opportunity to prove herself, not necessarily to Anderi, but to anybody else willing to listen who may give her a chance.

Natalya continued to smile. She leant forwards, putting her elbows on the table, and cupped her chin casually on her fingers. 'So what subject matter did you have in mind?'

An hour later, Natalya was heading home, having refused a lift from a very insistent Anderi. He had explained the content of her assignment. It was a joke.

As an initiation, a new journalist would often be given a brief such as this. A hopeless, dead-end article where the witless newcomer, who had been told their job was on the line, would stumble and panic to create a newsworthy article out of nothing. The end result would then be distributed for the amusement of the rest of the office.

This particular assignment was regarding a flower that grew on the Lotus Lake of Eastern Russia. A sample of the ancient Komarov lotus had been taken from the lakes and propagated in the Moscow Botanical Gardens, where any day now, it would bloom for the first time.

Anderi did not intend to give Natalya an opportunity. What he had given her was a fool's errand. She would give him his flower story, but this wouldn't be the project to prove herself as a journalist. For that, she would need to find her own story, one a little more ground-breaking.

Back in her apartment, Natalya sat at her computer and drained another mug of cold coffee. With an aching back and tired eyes, she persevered to search for the content of her promotion-winning masterpiece.

Two hours passed, and despite her best efforts, success had

continued to elude her. She stood and retrieved the empty coffee mug from the desk. She didn't really want another mug, but it gave her a good excuse to take a break from her efforts.

After refilling, she returned to her computer to continue her search. She had established that the paranormal was a popular area for general interest leading her to study her current list of 'Russian Urban Legends'.

Number 1: 'The Well to Hell'. In the 1990s, a drilling team working in Siberia claimed to have found a direct passage to hell, recording screams of the damned and witnessing a talking demon. It had later been found, not surprisingly, to be a hoax. The whole story being based on an article appearing in a Jewish-Christian newsletter called *Jewels of Jericho*. It sounded a little too far-fetched to be taken seriously, particularly now that the story had been categorically unproven.

Number 2: UVB-76, a short-wave radio broadcast first noticed in the 1970s. Possibly originating from the Russian military, but the exact origins and purpose were unknown. To this day, the government has neither acknowledged nor denied its existence. More commonly known as the Buzzer.

The website she had found containing various Buzzer-related facts offered an audio sample of the transmission. The sound emitted from the speakers made her skin crawl. It was nothing more than a two-second buzz, followed by a brief silence before repeating. It was layered with the crackle of interference, similar to the background noise when playing an old vinyl record. To Natalya, it was the sound of intrigue, the sound of an unsolved puzzle.

For several more hours, she trawled through endless pages of blogs and conspiracy websites – anything that contained information on the Buzzer. From each different page, she noted the contact details and sent an enquiry email, until she could manage no more.

3

The cutting buzz of the alarm shook Natalya's unconscious mind from its peaceful slumber. In her shocked state, it took a moment for her brain to recollect the previous night's activities. Eventually, it all flooded back. The project, the people she had contacted...

Eagerly, she checked her emails and found two replies: the first from a female blogger. In her excitement, she struggled to slow her eyes down enough to read and register its contents, but she managed to get the gist. The lady was interested and willing to help as much as possible. Unfortunately, it seemed as if she was located in Paris for the foreseeable future.

The second reply was from the administrator of a website known as Doomsday Conspiracy. The email was positive, and obviously from someone well aware of the Buzzer.

Natalya skimmed through the lengthy reply:

Very interested in researching 'The Buzzer' further... Looking forward to hearing about any developments you uncover... The website would be delighted to publish any articles you produce... If Doomsday Conspiracy can be of any further assistance, please don't hesitate to contact again.

Doomsday Conspiracy hadn't actually given any new information, but Natalya composed her reply. To kick-start the project, she would need to organise an interview.

***

Later that evening, Natalya returned to her computer after a day's worth of tedious research. She had to be seen to be entertaining Anderi's Lotus Flower assignment. He always made it one of his regular routines to remind the office of how he monitored all the workstations for personal projects and the zero-tolerance policy if anyone were ever caught. He would almost certainly be monitoring her now.

At her feet lay a large black holdall. This was the recording equipment provided by Anderi – his final insult. The camera itself was tiny, more suited to taking still shots than video. Although digital, it was an early model with a chipped black cover surrounding a small LED viewing screen. Audio recording would be through a microphone, almost as tiny as the camera. As an afterthought, it was attached by a short wire and taped securely to the side of the camera with electrical insulation tape. The rest of the bag was filled with a telescopic tripod and a small laptop with video editing software. The level of sophistication of the equipment seemed to mirror perfectly Anderi's faith in Natalya's ability.

Checking her email, she had received one new message. It was from the Doomsday Conspiracy's website administrator. Natalya stumbled quickly through its contents. It seemed he would be willing to do an interview, based on two conditions: first, that his face would be obscured from view – that was OK; it may even add to the interview's mysterious nature – and second, it must be that evening.

As much as she needed the interview, tonight was too soon. The reply had come through while she was at work, but being

15

unable to check her emails meant that now she had to leave almost immediately to make it in time. She needed at least a day before shooting the first footage to prepare the interview. Yet, if her plan was going to work, she had no choice – it had to be tonight.

The website administrator had specified to meet up in a popular bar in Moscow centre. It was a terrible place to record an interview. They would need to move on, but there was no doubt that the location had been picked for a reason. Whatever that was, the most important thing was that they had agreed to meet. Yet, still, the administrator's identity was a mystery. It wasn't even obvious what the gender of the person was. There was no time to think, it was now or never. Natalya shot a hurried email back in reply, agreeing to their terms, before grabbing her bag of recording gear and rushing out of the door.

The journey would take twenty minutes on the Moscow Metro. The time sitting in the cramped metal carriage gave her a chance to gather her thoughts as the darkness of the tunnel funnelled past the grime-covered window of the carriage. She looked down at the black bag of recording equipment at her feet. She wasn't even sure how it all worked yet. This would be a one-shot chance. It needed to be right, and she had absolutely nothing prepared. The journey couldn't be over quickly enough as her mind raced furiously through the basic research she had done so far, frantically trying to assemble a collection of questions that maybe somehow strung together to form some sort of coherent interview. She would need to improvise.

The bar was heaving with crowds of people celebrating the start of their weekend. The majority of them were sitting on tightly packed wooden tables surrounded by low wicker chairs. The rest were along the long shining bar that dominated the whole of one side of the room. Some seated on plump pink bar stools, others standing, shuffling constantly as new customers wriggled their way forwards to place their orders.

Everyone was young and fashionably dressed. Natalya hated places like this. There was a bar in the village where she grew up. She could drink and shoot pool with the best of them, but that was different. Here people lent casually on one arm, while the other was twirling through the air, emphasising the climax of a witty anecdote. The only whirling arms at home would be the result of a brawl.

The entrance to the bar was elevated with five steps descending to the main floor. Natalya took advantage of the view across the room, scanning for anybody who might look like her interviewee. Nobody seemed to be obviously looking out for her. A small group of people had followed her in and were now colliding with her recording bag as they squeezed past to go down the steps. She couldn't linger up here for long. She reached for her mobile, to let the Doomsday administrator know that she had arrived.

She kept one eye on the entrance the whole time as she made her way towards the bar. A young lady entered, quickly followed by another. Most likely early twenties, but it was hard to tell through that much make-up. Unlikely to be Doomsday.

The bartender took her order as she checked her phone. No new emails. At least this delay would give more time to consider interview questions. Other customers were forcing their way forwards to be served as Natalya stepped back with her drink. More people entered. A small group of four, enthralled in loud conversation. None of them so much as looked up before joining the ranks. Doomsday was late. The bag of recording equipment was making standing in the churning swirl of people very uncomfortable. It was heavy to hold, but Natalya dare not put it down. Even if its contents were basic, having to explain to Anderi how she had damaged it, or worse, lost it, would be too awful to contemplate.

Natalya kept her eye on the entrance door. Occasionally, new arrivals would pause before descending the steps, studying the room. Natalya's heartbeat would skip in anticipation, but it soon became obvious that she was not the target of their search. Time passed slowly as the evening crawled by. Natalya checked her phone again. Still nothing. The later it became, the more obvious it appeared that Doomsday wasn't late, but not coming at all. She scanned the room one last time, hoping desperately to see someone that she had missed. She knew it was useless. Angry at spending the whole evening standing, waiting for nothing, she placed her empty glass down heavily on the bar and decided to head home.

It was almost midnight by the time Natalya stumbled back into her apartment. Her only relief coming from her aching shoulder as she swung the heavy bag down into a corner. Despite the hour, she wouldn't be able to sleep until she had a way to vent her frustration. Tomorrow was Saturday: her day off. A day usually spent wasted anyway. There was plenty of time now to email Doomsday. She wouldn't expect a reply. Just the knowledge that they had been given a piece of her mind would be enough.

She clicked through to the main email options. The inbox indicated one new message, received ten minutes ago. Natalya went to open it, expecting an excuse and an apology from Doomsday as to why she'd been stood up. To her surprise, it was someone else: Stepan Litvin, Chairman of the Moscow Short-wave Radio Club. Natalya tutted as she ignored the message, and began composing her email to Doomsday. Even though she hadn't written it yet, she already felt significantly more satisfied. The pressures of the last two days poured easily onto the screen as the lengthy letter grew ever longer down the page. Doomsday would get more than they bargained for when they received this essay of frustration.

As Natalya continued to write, she realised that she was starting to repeat herself. That didn't matter; it would only go to emphasise her points. Sending her out at night, alone, in

Moscow could have been dangerous. Although, in reality, it would take a lot more than that to make Natalya feel vulnerable. But Doomsday didn't know that. It would go in the email too.

The name from her unopened email popped into her head: Stepan Litvin. She paused. She used to know someone called Stepan. His surname wasn't Litvin though. She returned to typing her rant; soon back into full flow. It wasn't just the fact she had been stood up. It was everything over the last few days. Especially Anderi and the lousy equipment he arranged for her. Tonight, Doomsday had let her down, so they were fair game to be the target of her emotional outburst.

Soon, she was running out of things to write. As her anger had begun to subside, her curiosity about Stepan's email peaked. Carefully saving her composition into the draft folder, she opened the new mail.

The email that faced Natalya was long. Stepan wrote warmly about his love of his hobby and his enthusiasm to promote it, stating how his support would extend to any project that would promote interest into the field of amateur radio. It appeared he would be more than willing to help. It also appeared that he was fully researched into the subject of the Buzzer. She couldn't afford to make the same mistake again, but an interview with Stepan would be perfect. The length of his reply alone was enough to convince her that his intentions were genuine. He'd also given full contact details, no vague email address this time. His full name, address, and a mobile phone number – a number that Natalya had already began to text.

4

At 10.00 a.m. Saturday morning, Natalya sat patiently in the back seat of a slow-moving taxi. It seemed that Stepan Litvin was as keen to get started on the project as she was. After several hurried text messages, he had extended an invitation to his home to discuss the Buzzer further. The address he had sent her was just a short drive away, and the taxi finally drew up outside a huge apartment block.

Emerging from the car's warm embrace, into the freezing temperatures of an early spring day, threw Natalya's body into a torrent of uncontrollable shivers. Fighting to stifle her chattering teeth, the last of her body's warmth was stolen by an icy wind causing her cheeks to flush a bright red. She forced herself forwards on taut legs and approached the four stone steps that led to the plate glass doors of the entrance. Her footsteps crunched on a layer of salt scattered liberally to melt the ice. A small gesture, but one never undertaken by the maintenance workers of her own building.

Inside the lobby was an expanse of highly polished ceramic surfaces. Natalya made her way across the floor towards the open doors of a waiting lift. Standing in its mirrored cell, she began scrunching her toes inside her shoes, in anticipation of being only moments away from recording the first interview of her project. She arrived at Stepan's door, and stood fumbling with her bag for nothing in particular; the action just giving herself a few more seconds to steady her excitement.

The front door opened, revealing a man in his early thirties with wide shining brown eyes. The bridge of his nose looked twisted slightly, as if it had once been broken and not quite set properly. He was smartly dressed in a tailored blue shirt and black trousers, yet, on his feet he wore a pair of dirty white trainers. He smiled as he introduced himself.

'Natalya, I assume? I'm Stepan, and it's a pleasure to meet you. Please come in.'

He stepped back, and with an overly grand sweep of his arm guided her through to a room beyond.

'I have to admit,' he continued, 'I was very excited to receive your email. It's wonderful to have someone showing an interest in short-wave radio listening. It's been my hobby for a long time, but our numbers have been dwindling over recent years. Any exposure in the media is good news. People need to know that it's not just listening to static for hours on end.'

Natalya found herself in a small sitting room, in stark contrast to her own. Not an item out of place; the furniture positioned perfectly to optimise every inch of the room's modest proportions. She made her way across soft grey carpet to a black sofa. Its four stumpy chrome legs shone brightly in the sunlight entering through a huge full-length window.

'Please sit and be comfortable,' said Stepan. 'This sounds like a very interesting project you have going on. How long have you been short-wave radio listening, may I ask?'

Natalya felt a rush of heat to her face. 'Erm… well…'

'I'm guessing not long then.'

She looked down at her shoes and flicked the handle of her bag with her thumbnail. 'I'm here to be enlightened. I'm a quick learner. Anyway, I was hoping to start with a short interview to camera. Maybe on the sofa here. Only…'

She turned towards the seat, studying its proximity to the large window opposite. A shaft of sunlight blazed in through the window, lighting up nearly half the room, but leaving the other half in shadow. She shook her head. 'The lighting here is terrible for recording. The sunlight will play havoc with the light adaptation settings.'

Stepan smiled, but said nothing. He picked up a small black box from the top of the television unit, aimed it at the window, and pressed a single central button. Instantly, the glass changed from transparent to frosted.

'I'm no cameraman, but is that any better?' he asked, thrilled to be given the opportunity to demonstrate his toy. 'Electrochromic,' he continued. 'Apply a small current through and it becomes opaque. It saves dusting a blind.'

'Much better,' Natalya said, smiling at Stepan's comment before unzipping her bag of recording equipment. She pulled out the sorry-looking camera with taped-on microphone.

'I must apologise for the state of my current equipment, it's only temporary...' Natalya started to explain as Stepan settled himself down into position, having given the camera no more than a fleeting glance.

'So, where would you like me to start?' Stepan began as Natalya took position behind the tripod. 'I must warn you, I could talk all day if you let me.'

'Firstly, the Buzzer. I was hoping you could give me a bit of background. An introduction into what it is and where it came from?'

Stepan took a deep breath. 'OK, where to start... Well, it's commonly known as the Buzzer because of the tone it uses as a channel marker. The transmission was first recorded in the 1980s, but it is rumoured to have started many years before. It's a Russian-based AM radio broadcast on 4625 kilohertz. It runs twenty-four hours a day as a buzzing tone that lasts just over a second. In the world of short-wave radio listening it has the call sign 'UVB-76', but it has been changed more recently to 'MDZhB'. The mystery is that nobody knows why it exists and what it's used for. We know the station is in constant use, due to subtle changes to its transmission over the years, so therefore it must have a purpose. The tone itself has evolved from a short pip in the earliest recordings to, more recently, a longer, more pronounced buzz. It changed most noticeably in 2010 to extend to just over a second...'

Natalya felt a yawn coming on. She managed to stifle it before it was too late. 'So what draws so many people to pay any attention to the station?'

'That would be the coded messages.'

'Messages?' Natalya repeated, leaning forwards.

'Very occasionally, the buzzing tone stops, and a live voice announces a sequence of letters and numbers: a call sign and a code word. It's very rare, happening once in 1997 – Christmas Eve, in fact – then 2002 and 2006. Recently, there have been more; the activity levels have dramatically increased. Once, they even broadcast music: 'Dance of the Little Swans', from the ballet *Swan Lake*.'

'That's crazy! What does that have to do with anything? Has anyone ever cracked any of the codes?'

Stepan shrugged his shoulders. 'Not to my knowledge. People have tried for years, but nobody has had any success, especially not with the *Swan Lake* broadcast. It's widely suspected to be related to the Russian military, but theories range from mundane weather monitoring to aliens. A popular theory is that the transmission is a Russian nuclear dead man's switch, a relic from the Cold War. If it were ever to stop transmitting, then the whole of Russia's nuclear arsenal would be unleashed on predetermined targets around the world.'

Natalya considered Stepan's last statement. 'So for over thirty years, the transmission has never stopped?'

'That's not entirely true,' Stepan said. 'In 2010, the source of the transmission was tracked to a broadcasting station in a military base near to Povarovo, nineteen miles outside Moscow. Locals say that one night, a terrible storm rolled in bringing with it a thick fog that covered the entire area. They say the whole base was totally evacuated in ninety minutes. During that time the Buzzer did stop, but quickly restarted again very shortly after in new locations as if nothing had happened.'

'So does anyone know where the signal is based now?'

'Not exactly. It seems to be broadcast from multiple locations. Triangulation attempts have been made on the new signals, and their locations have been narrowed down to three areas: Pskov Oblast, Kolpino, and Kirsino, which is a tiny village with a population of only thirty-nine people. All the locations seem to be clustered together in western Russia.'

'But why was it moved from Povarovo? Was it to hide its location if people knew where it was? I guess if they started to visit the location of the secret transmission, it would only be a matter of time before it wasn't secret anymore.'

Stepan replied with a shrug. 'I would guess so, but again it remains a mystery. After it was moved, the original broadcast site was investigated by a group of urban explorers. They found it hastily abandoned. They even found logs of the coded transmitted messages and other documents left lying around.'

Natalya's mind was racing ahead, formulating a plan. Footage from an abandoned military base would look great on camera. 'Do you know where the old transmission site is?'

Stepan's cheerful expression hardened immediately. 'I do, yes, but if you're thinking about paying it a visit, you might want to rethink.'

Natalya gave Stepan a little smile. 'What makes you think I would want to do a crazy thing like that?'

He fixed her straight in the eye with a steely stare. 'Really, trust me. It's not a pleasant place.'

'You say that as if you've already been. Have you?'

Stepan nodded. 'A few years ago now. After the first explorers had been in. I found coordinates for the base on the Internet, and out of sheer curiosity, decided to go and check it out. It's only about an hour and a half drive from here. The site was huge, but seemed totally abandoned. It's surrounded by fences, walls and gates, all marked with military warning signs restricting access. I drove up to the main gates expecting to be turned away, but nothing – no guards – and the gates were unlocked. I've never known a place so eerie. Anybody could just drive on in.'

'And did you?'

'I had spoken to a local lady who lived in the village next to the base on the way through. The whole site seems steeped in local legend. She told me about weird goings-on around the area. They say strange creatures stalk the forest at night. Nobody goes near the trees after darkness falls. A mysterious lady has been seen regularly walking the perimeter fence with a pushchair loaded with meat. People say she feeds the creatures so that they don't leave the forest looking for food. I know they are just silly stories, but when I stood there at those iron gates, going in alone didn't seem like a good idea. The lady told me I would find them open. She said they didn't need to be kept locked. "Nobody ever strays though the gates," she said.'

Natalya felt a shudder of excitement running up her back. 'So if the gates are unlocked, is it trespassing to go in and have a look around? It's certainly not breaking and entering. What if a lost hiker inadvertently wondered in by mistake?'

Stepan shook his head. 'Be very careful. The whole place just seemed... I don't know... rotten.'

'But you did say those urban explorers went in and had a look around. They must have been OK. Maybe it's a bit spooky, but you'll have me with you this time. What do you say? Up for a trip?'

Stepan looked into Natalya's excited blue eyes as she popped her head around the camera. He had always imagined exploring through those menacing gates. Sometimes it even seemed like a good idea from the comfort of his safe apartment. 'I don't know. I mean it's been abandoned for years. I really don't think you'll find anything worth going in for.'

'All we need to do is drive in and take some footage of what's left of the base, that's all. We'll be done in minutes and we don't even need to get out of the car. Besides, I need you to show me where it is.'

Stepan knew that was true. The base wasn't marked on any map. Natalya seemed so filled with enthusiasm, and she needed his help. If he refused, she would leave today and that would be it. He didn't want that. He wanted to see her again. He sighed. 'Maybe if I drive us up to the gates, we can play it by ear. As long as we don't have to go any further.'

'To the gates, and then we'll play it by ear,' Natalya repeated, beaming a broad grin.

5

Natalya followed Stepan out of his apartment block and into a large car park. The wind whipped over frost-covered tarmac causing flurries of ice crystals to spiral, as if dancing into the air.

Stepan strode quickly towards a large royal-blue Jeep. Its heavy sides rose higher than other cars as it sat on top of four chunky off-road tyres.

'Throw your bag in the back and jump in,' he said as he unlocked the doors. 'First, I'll take you back to your apartment so you can grab some warmer clothes.'

From under the driver's seat, Stepan produced a large map book.

Natalya glanced across. Maps weren't her strong point, but he didn't know that. 'I hope you can remember where you're going?' she laughed. 'I don't think we can just type it into a satnav.'

Stepan pointed at a green, forested area, north-west of the huge intricate blob that marked Moscow city centre. 'This is Lozhki. It's the closest town to the base. South of it is a small village. It's only a short drive from there. It may have been a few years since I last went, but I've got a good memory for detail. You ready?'

'Absolutely,' Natalya replied.

With a smooth surge, Stepan pulled away. 'It's lovely to get out into the countryside; I never seem to leave the city anymore. I do a lot of my work from home. Sometimes, I don't leave my apartment for days.'

Natalya tried to picture herself working amongst the chaos of her own apartment. 'I don't think I could do that. What is it that you do?'

'I work in computer security, designing virus protection and firewall software. My company doesn't mind where I do my work, just so long as I get results. I do enjoy it, it's just a bit isolating sometimes. Communication is all so distant these days, never face-to-face with a person. Maybe that's what attracted me to short-wave radio listening. It's like a pre-Internet social network of friends that you never meet. After spending all day designing software for the latest technology, sometimes it's a relief to go old school.'

Despite her best efforts, Natalya still wasn't entirely savvy with short-wave radio listening, but she did understand about social media.

It took an hour and a half to reach the small rural village that bordered the forest in which the Povarovo base was hidden. As they travelled through, they could have been in a different world to the one that contained the mighty structures of Moscow city centre. Most of the houses were low, single-floor buildings made from a mixture of stone and wooden walls. Many had crudely assembled timber and corrugated iron extensions patched on to their sides.

They passed a small row of shops set back from the road. Natalya swallowed hard as a swell of emotion washed over her. This place was so similar to home – her real home. After living in Moscow for so long, she was worried about losing touch with who she was. She didn't want that to happen. She was proud of her roots, but a place like this seemed so foreign now.

Her thoughts were cut short as Stepan suddenly heaved the Jeep off the main road and on to a tarmac path. A few metres ahead stood a dense evergreen forest stretching as far as the eye could see. The trunks of its mighty fir trees stood like a regimented army barring the way ahead, save a small, battered track that wound its way into the darkness beneath the tight needle canopy.

Stepan slowed to a stop. 'Well, we're here.'

Natalya's stomach jumped. 'Really, this is it?'

'This is the access road to the gate, yes. It's not what you expected?'

'I guess I thought there would be a few more buildings about. You know, bunkers and things?' Natalya glanced in the wing mirror at the traffic passing behind them. 'And maybe somewhere a bit more secretive?'

Stepan laughed. 'Don't you worry, that access road goes on for quite a way. It's in there, I promise.'

'I thought it would have barriers up or something to stop people just wandering in. It just seems a bit, obvious,' Natalya continued.

'If I hadn't stopped here, do you think you would have noticed this road at all?'

'I guess not.'

'If it had barriers across it or fencing, the first thing people would wonder was what was on the other side. Anyway, it doesn't need anything like that. People just don't go in.'

'But we are, right?' Natalya questioned, hopeful that Stepan wouldn't go back on his promise. 'You did say as far as the gates. Are they further in?'

Stepan shuffled awkwardly at the reminder. 'They are, yes.' He ran his fingers through his hair. 'Are you sure you want to carry on?'

Natalya looked at him questionably. 'Of course. We can't see much from here.'

'OK, but we should be careful,' Stepan replied, moving the Jeep onwards.

'Be careful of what?' Natalya shot back. 'I thought you said the base had been deserted for years?'

Stepan twisted the steering wheel as he tried to avoid the worst of some enormous potholes. 'It has been – I mean, it is deserted. I'm just saying,' he said through gritted teeth.

'You wouldn't really come all this way only to turn around now, would you? Where's your sense of adventure?' Natalya smiled.

'Where's your sense of self-preservation?' Stepan muttered quietly.

Amongst the silent trees, darkness reigned. The mighty firs stole almost every morsel of daylight, leaving only a faint glimmer behind at the forest boundary, not daring to follow. It was as if the trees had something to hide and didn't want to give up their secrets lightly.

Stepan turned the headlights on, creating long dancing shadows that spiralled forwards as they moved. Ahead, the road cut deeper through huge columns of tree trunks rising up from a carpet of discarded golden brown needles. Stepan leaned forwards, the steering wheel touching his chest as he maintained the car's steady crawl deeper into the forest. Refusing to let his guard down for even a second, his eyes remained fixed on the road ahead.

'We should be coming up to the gates soon. We can see them from the Jeep; there's no need to get out.'

'It's only a forest, Stepan,' said Natalya, getting a little frustrated. 'It doesn't look dangerous. Unless there's something you're not telling me...'

'No, of course not. I just thought I'd say... to save you getting out.'

'But there's no reason *not* to get out, is there?' Natalya prompted.

'No, no, it's just there's no need. You can see everything from inside.'

'Thanks, that's very kind.' replied Natalya. She'd heard him the first time.

The path straightened slightly, extending the view ahead. Either side of the road were two enormous gateposts: huge, square, concrete pillars almost three metres high, and riddled with cracks, some so deep they exposed the metal reinforcing rods within. Despite the damage, they had lost none of their structural integrity, standing guard, looking as they had done for an eternity. The gates between the pillars stood just as high, fashioned from a tangle of twisted iron bars, and covered with sharpened barbed spikes protruding at all angles through coils of tightly wrapped razor wire.

Stepan slowed the Jeep to a stop, and released a slow sigh. 'Well, what do you think? This is as far as I came last time.'

Through the perfect silence, the gates seemed to scream, 'Turn back!'

Natalya had no choice; to go back now would be the end of the assignment before it had even begun. Turning to Stepan, she nonchalantly shrugged her shoulders. 'I think I should get the camera and start recording. It looks as if you're right, though; I can't see a lock on the gates.'

'You still want to go in? You're not even slightly nervous, are you?'

Natalya smiled. 'I've driven through plenty of gates in my time. That's what they're for; otherwise, it would be a fence.'

Stepan scratched his head. 'I'm not sure whether you're brave or crazy.'

With a click of the door handle, Natalya was outside and making her way to the gates for a closer look. She paused to listen. All she could hear was a cold lifeless silence. There was no bird song, not even the rustle of the trees in the wind. It was unnatural. She moved in front of the Jeep, giving Stepan a confident wave. Should she show any hesitation, it would be just the excuse he needed to turn around and head for home, and she needed him to carry on.

From the driver's seat, he raised a hand in reply.

As expected, the gates were unlocked. Natalya gripped at them with gloved fingers and heaved at the metal. Both gates flung wide. It had taken far less force than it should have.

Stepan looked on as the small figure standing in the road ahead of him waved her arms to beckon him forwards. He shook his head in disbelief as he drove through and stopped to let her jump back in.

The road beyond was little more than a three-foot-wide path that continued arrow-straight into the distance. On both sides, the branches of towering pine trees formed a long tunnel of permanent gloom, while dilapidated street lights, long out of use, leaned at precarious angles after years of nature had taken its toll.

As they trundled on, Natalya said, 'Do you have any idea how long this road is? It seems to go on forever.'

'I've seen satellite photos of the area. I would guess this goes on for a couple of kilometres, give or take. It's hard to tell.'

Natalya turned to the back seat and retrieved the camera from her holdall. She aimed it forwards and flicked it onto record. The little viewing screen remained black for a second before it cleared into focus, adjusting to the low light levels. She aimed the camera as far down the path as she could and extended the zoom to its maximum. It looked a little brighter ahead.

'We might be getting somewhere now,' Stepan announced.

Natalya concentrated on the camera. 'Is this the transmission base you were talking about?'

'I don't think so. The footage I've seen online shows that the base is surrounded by a number of outbuildings, but we'll soon see.'

Stepan drew the Jeep to a steady halt as they entered a large clearing. It was the size of a football pitch, filled with tall wild rye grass. Surrounding the area, the huge pine trees stood guard as eager sunlight streamed through the rare break in the trees.

In the centre of the grass, was a low, single-storey brick building, painted entirely in a soft shade of pink. Given its age and neglect, its corrugated iron roof and row of four low ground floor windows looked in remarkably good condition.

Natalya panned her camera across the scene. 'Unusual colour for a guardhouse, don't you think?'

'I couldn't agree more, but I don't think that's what it is. Look over there, behind the building, at the edge of the grass.'

On the far side of the clearing stood a thin metal radio tower made from a criss-cross of slender metal rods, and held upright by a network of guide wires.

Stepan leant across to get a better view of it on the camera's LCD screen. His movement caught Natalya unaware as she sat awkwardly with Stepan's head inches from her shoulder.

He pointed at the screen. 'Can you see that comb aerial on the top of the mast?'

Natalya looked closer, glad to be given the excuse to move the camera to a more central position. 'I think I can, yes. Do you think this was the transmission antenna for the Buzzer?'

'I doubt it. I know amateur radio enthusiasts who have that level of equipment. With that arrangement, the tower is a receiver, not a transmitter.'

Natalya leant forwards in her seat, trying to change the camera angle. It was difficult to get a clear shot of the scene without also recording any of the car's interior or Stepan himself. Filming over the roof would be a much better shot. She reached for the door handle. 'I'm going out for a better view. Don't drive off or anything.'

Before Stepan had a chance to reply, Natalya thrust herself out of the door and stood on the Jeep's side step. He waited for her to turn her body around so that she faced the right direction, but she kept her back to him. 'Everything OK?' he called.

Natalya popped her head back inside. 'I think you need to look at this. I can't believe we missed it.'

6

A little way into the trees, emerging well above the forest canopy, stood an enormous metal radio tower. It was constructed in a similar design to the smaller version only made from huge metal girders held together by massive bolts. A precarious rusted ladder wrapped itself around the slowly disintegrating metal framework like a giant bronzed python, leading all the way to a tiny platform at the summit. Occasional dishes were dotted up its length, but the radio transmission equipment had been long since removed.

Natalya panned her camera upwards. 'This is huge. I can't believe we didn't see it until now. What do you think?'

'Well that's definitely the main transmission tower,' said Stepan, standing in front of the Jeep. 'Trees are very good at hiding things from view, but also at blocking transmission signals. If you wanted to send a radio broadcast within a forest like this in the 1980s that is what you needed.'

The pair stood in silence for a moment, 'Right, well, ready to carry on and get this over with?' said Stepan.

'I suppose so. I'm guessing there's a lot more to see.'

They returned inside and Stepan moved the vehicle forwards, slowly gathering speed past the clearing and back into the forest. The dense tree canopy once again formed a long dark tunnel, but here the road was wider. An unused strip of tarmac ran either side of the Jeep's chunky tyres allowing for extra speed, and it didn't take long to reach the next break in the forest.

Stepan slowed the Jeep to a crawl. The second clearing was much larger than the first, and circular. The entrance way was separated from the edge of the surrounding forest by a chain-link fence, supported by thick concrete posts. It curved away from them on both sides, into the distance. Thick metal tracks were embedded into the tarmac where a sliding gate should have been, but that was long gone.

Lying next to the road was a red rectangular metal sign. Across its centre in bold white lettering were the words 'Authorised Access Only'.

Natalya looked at Stepan. 'What do you think? Are we authorised?' She asked.

Stepan grinned. For the first time since they arrived, he looked more relaxed, the roadmap of wrinkles on his forehead finally cleared. 'I think we have all the authorisation we need,' he said, revving the engine and shooting the Jeep forwards, the tyres bumping twice in quick succession as he drove over the gate track.

A rectangular concrete building, standing three floors high, dominated the second clearing. Its featureless grey walls were dotted with many windows. On its flat roof, stood three tall white cylinders, while on the ground floor, a pair of large double doors stood enticingly ajar. At the front of the building, a paved area of square slabs was surrounded by more wild rye grass that reached four feet high in places.

Natalya let out a short breath. 'I wasn't expecting to find anything like this. It's huge. It looks as if someone has picked up an office block straight out of the city and dropped it off here, in the middle of nowhere.'

Stepan drew the Jeep closer and parked on the forecourt.

'This must have been some place in its day. Imagine what it would have been like here when it was fully staffed.'

'Yes, and all this was just to transmit a radio signal?'

'All of this, officially, doesn't exist. The Buzzer was suspected to have originated from here, but whether that was the only thing that was done...' Stepan's voice trailed off.

Away from the main building, to the left, dotted in amongst coppices of pine trees and long grass stood a number of small outbuildings. They were all single storey, varying in size from little more than a shed to a small bungalow. All were in various states of dilapidation. Some of the wooden structures had been reduced to little more than stakes in the ground, but the concrete had fared better.

Stepan gestured towards them. 'I think we should check out some of these first. I've watched a lot of footage taken by the urban explorers from inside that main building, but they didn't make it to any of these.'

Natalya thought about Stepan's last statement before replying. 'Why d'you think they didn't *make it* to them?'

'I...erm...I'm not sure. Maybe they just ran out of time?'

'Ran out of time...? Stepan, look at me. Were they really that rushed?'

An awkward silence hung in the air between them. Stepan turned to face her; however, his eyes chose to focus on the glove box. 'It is a very big area.'

'Stepan, I'm not buying it. There's something you're not telling me, and I'm not asking you again. What is it?'

Stepan looked into Natalya's blue eyes. Her expression the same as the one that had made him come back here in the first place. 'The explorers...I mean, these are guys that spend every hour they can running around creepy old buildings or charging down sinister abandoned tunnels. They're not soft. I've seen all their videos, always so carefree, always larking around, but the video they took from this place...it was totally different to the others. Something about this place seriously spooked them. They seemed to think there were other people around, as if they were being watched. They left in a hurry after that.'

'And you're only telling me this now because…?'

'Well they didn't actually see anybody. They analysed the footage they took afterwards frame by frame. The only sign they saw was a very hazy silhouette at one of the windows up there in the main building. If you look at it closely, though, it really could have been the shadow of anything, most likely old furniture. I couldn't see it as a person myself.'

'Who was watching them Stepan? The military? Squatters…?'

'It's not like I knew them personally. They said that they didn't actually see anyone. It's probably just something they wrote to get more people to read their blog.'

'And do you have any idea which window the photo was of? If it's only furniture maybe it's still there?'

'I've got no idea; it could have been any of them. It was zoomed right in and low quality.'

Natalya scanned the building, beginning from the top, checking each window. It was impossible to see anything except reflections of the low sun glinting off the grime-covered glass. It was unusual for all the glass to be intact after so long, as the rest of the building fell into disrepair around it. The surrounding grey walls had started to crumble badly, exposing areas of white masonry underneath like a reptile wriggling out of its skin.

Stepan regretted mentioning the photograph. He shouldn't have told her about the explorers either. He had brought her here to record a documentary, built up her hopes, and now he had dropped this on her. She'd be so disappointed if they left now. She'd hate him for letting her down.

'I wouldn't worry,' Stepan lied, 'there hasn't been anyone around here for years. There's nothing here. Anyway, if there were, wouldn't there be another vehicle? It's a long way to walk.'

Natalya considered this for a second. It was a good point.

'Also, look...' Stepan continued. 'With the trees gone, everything, including the ground is covered in frost. We would see footprints.'

It was true. The road and slabs surrounding the entrance were all coated in a layer of perfect shimmering white. Small puddles of frozen rainwater had formed in the centre of some of the slabs, their delicate surfaces unbroken, reflecting the glorious light of the clear blue sky.

Natalya started to feel better; she could see Stepan's point. 'I suppose it's time to go and have a look around then?'

7

With her hand on the door handle, Natalya waited. Something in the back of her mind told her to check again before stepping out. Straining her eyes, she scanned across the windows, looking for movement. Nothing. The hairs on the back of her neck bristled as she drew a long breath preparing to leave the safety of the Jeep.

Jumping down she landed with a crunch on the frost-covered ground, her first step leaving a dark, unmistakable footprint in the sparkling white surface. Her brain told her body to relax, that logically they had to be alone. Yet, despite the reassurance, she stood taut, like a coiled spring, ready to react. Stepan walked around to her and touched her lightly on her shoulder, motioning for them to walk. He spoke in barely a whisper.

'There's something I've seen online that I would like to check out first. I think it's this way.'

Natalya tried to voice her agreement quietly, but the whisper caught in her throat and failed to pass her lips. Instead, she replied with a nod.

The silence filling the base was stifling, disorientating, even claustrophobic to be surrounded by air so still and heavy, yet filled with nothing. They walked on, crunching past the side of the main building and off into the wild rye. The sound of their movements was muffled, but even the rustle of their trousers seemed to be too loud.

Stepan slowed his approach, allowing Natalya to draw level. 'Careful, it's just up here,' he whispered, putting an arm out to guide her.

In front of them, sunk into the ground, were two wide, circular pits. Each one had featureless walls of thick concrete descending several metres down, broken only at one point by the mouth of a dark tunnel that led further into the earth.

Taking an intuitive step back, Natalya turned to Stepan. 'What are they? If you fell in there, you wouldn't be getting out in a hurry.'

Stepan stood staring down into the closest pit. The bottom had started to fill with forest debris, enabling a number of small stunted pine trees to take hold.

'Maybe that was the idea?' he said. 'I've seen these on satellite photos, but nobody knows what they were used for. The most popular theory online is that they were cooling tanks, but seeing them here for myself...'

'Cooling tanks? I thought this base was used to transmit a radio signal. What would need cooling?'

'Exactly. It doesn't make a lot of sense, does it? I've never seen a cooling tank that looks like this before. Whatever they were designed to contain has long gone now anyway.'

'I think I'm glad of that,' Natalya replied.

'Come on,' Stepan said, turning around. 'Let's move on before one of us ends up down there with a broken leg. We need to have a look at some of these smaller buildings. I think they're our best chance of finding something new.'

Stepan changed his direction, towards the smaller outbuildings they had spotted previously.

Natalya followed closely in the path of flattened grass that he left behind him, to where they came across a smaller concrete structure with a domed roof. Partly buried in the earth and cloaked by foliage, nature shrouded its presence from all but those who stumbled upon it. It resembled a small aircraft hangar, only big enough to contain one room, with solid windowless walls. In front of the building, resting on chunks of perished concrete, lay a pair of, once impenetrable, reinforced steel doors.

Natalya carefully picked her way closer to where Stepan was standing at the edge of the open doorway and peered inside. Peeling green paint lined the walls, which, every so often, were coated in spiralling shadows of ash. The room was littered with effects all ravaged by fire. Most of them were indistinguishable piles of charcoal with only some larger items of furniture surviving what must have been a fierce blaze. It was soon obvious why the small building once had such high security armoured doors. At the far side of the room, sloping away and down into inky darkness was the unmistakable mouth of a tunnel. Natayla slowly made her way towards it, negotiating lumps of fallen masonry that made each footstep crunch loudly.

She edged forwards to get a better view, and peered down into the gloom. Walls covered in peeling twisted whitewash descended into the decaying dark. On the bare concrete floor, pools of ice formed around reels of hastily discarded copper cabling. An overwhelming aroma of rancid air rose up out of the passage to greet her.

Stepan made his way closer to her, turning to check behind him as something inside beckoned his attention back towards the empty doorway before he spoke.

'I've never seen anything like this in any notes on the base before. The other buildings are wrecked for sure, but there has never been any sign of a fire. Maybe it was an accident, or happened after the base was abandoned? Or maybe it was just the quickest way to cleanse the place of any evidence of any projects undertaken here.'

Swallowing hard, Natalya stared down into the darkness of the tunnel. Stepan was right, but it wasn't going to disclose any of its secrets from ground level.

Stepan shuffled closer until his coat brushed up against her shoulder. 'It's been rumoured that the base continued underground, but the other explorers only found a small basement in the main building. They didn't go down.'

'They didn't go down? That sounds very strange... I don't suppose you have any idea why a group of fearless thrill seekers might pass on a chance to explore a mysterious basement filled with all sorts of hidden secrets, do you?'

Stepan looked at the ground as he spoke. 'They heard animal noises coming from the darkness before they ran...'

'Oh great, and I don't suppose it was a nest of chirping baby birds, by any chance?'

'Not exactly... but there's going to be all sorts of animals living in the forest. It was most likely just a lynx. So long as we stay away, it won't bother us.'

'Right... that makes me feel a lot better. So are there any other revelations you think I should know about from this explorer blog, or is this the last of them?'

'No, that's it now. There's nothing else.'

'Right,' Natalya replied, finding her gaze drawn over Stepan's shoulder back through the doorway towards the main building. She nonchalantly shrugged her shoulders. 'Well, after all that, I think there's only one way to go on from here.'

Stepan wrung his hands. 'I... erm... maybe I should stay up here. To let you know if anything happens. Just in case...' He ran out of words as he slowly started to back away from the darkness.

Natalya fought hard to resist rolling her eyes. 'Good idea... You stay up here and call me if you need anything.'

Stepan didn't reply. He knew he should be going down there with her.

8

Natalya edged forwards, being careful to avoid the snakes of cable at her feet as she slowly made her way down into the square black hole. She turned her camera on to record, and switched the flash on permanently to act as a torch, but it did little to lighten her mood. The light from the tiny lamp was hungrily consumed by the dark. Cracks through the thick walls spread like a network of blood vessels upwards and across the ceiling. The heat had been much more intense down here; the whitewash was totally stripped, leaving only bare concrete.

She was not normally bothered by confined spaces, but as she trudged reluctantly down the slope, deeper into the earth, her breathing started to turn shallow. Summoning up all of her courage, she pushed the fear from her mind, and forced her taut legs to continue. She crept on, following the coils of copper wire down still further. Following these was the most logical approach, as they would always lead to the way out. The thought of being lost was not one Natalya wanted to dwell upon. Every sensible part of her being wanted her to turn around, but her overwhelming curiosity urged her on.

Up ahead was a ninety-degree turn. Once around this corner, her view of the surface would be gone and all comfort would be left behind. She turned round to look at Stepan, but all she could see was his silhouette, his body outlined by a square of daylight. Plunging further into the darkness, she reached the turn and swung the camera around the bend, flashing it through the darkness. A concrete corridor stretched out as far as the small light would allow her to see.

She took a final glance back up the slope towards the glorious daylight above, then stepped forwards and around the corner. The air was cool. All was silent, besides the echoing drip of far distant water. Natalya ventured on, following the cabling deeper into the underground tunnels as her heart began to pound faster. Every so often, a burnt-out doorway led off either side. In most of them, only the frames remained, but some still contained shards of blackened wood, clinging to crooked hinges. The roof of the corridor was interrupted at regular intervals by light fixtures, now jagged glass shards covered in thick dust.

She passed door after burnt-out door, winding her way through the maze of darkened tunnels. The image of Stepan's silhouette seemed like a long way away, yet she kept on going, following the cabling around each turn. The smell of damp and putrid decay stuck in her throat, and her stomach twisted at the thought of the rancid air she was now breathing. The little camera light worked hard to fight against the smothering blackness, but its beam stretched only as far as the next bend leaving her mind free to invent unimaginable horrors lurking in the darkness.

The tangle of copper wire disappeared through a wall ahead, her way blocked by a heavy steel door with an electronic key pad embedded into the crumbling wall next to it. She cast her light over it. No sign of life. She tried the buttons – totally dead. The chances of her guessing the code anyway were practically impossible.

She tried the door with the faintest of pushes, feeling stupid for doing so. To her amazement, it moved. She pushed again, a little harder. The door slowly creaked inwards, scraping across the floor. Flashing the camera light around the room, she realised it was an office, but unlike everything else she had seen, was untouched by fire.

The office was sparse with white walls and a low ceiling. The copper wire she had been following continued across the bottom of the floor and disappeared through the far wall, impossible to follow. The majority of the space was dominated by a large wooden desk on which lay a blue folder, but it was what stood behind it that held Natalya's gaze. Facing her was the reverse of a high-backed black chair. She knew it had to be empty, but her imagination ran wild. Taking a deep breath, she summoned up every drop of courage, demanding herself to step into the room. Slowly she entered, never once taking her eyes away from the chair. She willed logic to overcome fear. It will be empty, she told herself. The floor felt softer in here, maybe carpet, but she was not prepared to look down to see. She edged forwards, taking one small step at a time, until her brain alerted her with a flash of reality. Her current position was not good. She was deep underground, alone and vulnerable. But this seemed to be the only room within the tunnel that was intact. She needed to investigate. She didn't know what she was looking for, or what she wanted to find, but this room could be the making of her project.

She reached the desk and slowly raised her arm, stretching out to the chair. With the sickening taste of dust in her mouth and the gushing of her pulse in her ears, she pushed it just enough to spin it slowly round to face her. As its high sides and arms steadily came into view, Natalya's fought hard to maintain control, forcing her legs from running out the door. Suddenly, eventually, it was all the way around, facing her.

The chair was empty.

Natalya felt very silly. What did she expect? A villain waiting for years in the dark for an unsuspecting researcher? Relaxing, she released the breath she had been holding seemingly forever and inhaled back in deeply. The smell of damp and mould hit the back of her throat hard, and it suddenly tightened, sending her into a spasm of violent coughing.

The sound echoed through the passageways, cutting through the silence. Her mind raced as the sound awoke all the horrors she had imagined lying in wait for her in the shadows of her camera light. At that moment, her curiosity failed. Her heart pumped hard as blood shot to her muscles. She scooped up the folder from the desk and turned, leaping through the open door behind her and back into the tunnel.

This time she ran along the passageways, camera light swinging wildly across the floor, desperately trained on the copper cabling, her mind clinging to the logic that it would lead to the exit. The corridors stretched out in front of her. In her panic, nothing looked familiar. She was lost and trapped deep underground. Her head began to spin wildly throwing her off balance, but her legs continued to run. Veering off to the side, her shoulder met heavily with the wall of the tunnel sending her bouncing off, nearly tripping. Its sharp surface cut deeply into her skin. Still nothing looked familiar, but the cabling was still there at her feet. Her shoulder started to sting, and instinctively, Natalya put her hand up to the wound. She swayed off centre again, smashing into the concrete on the other side. Another bolt of pain lashed at her. The impact sent her falling forwards as her arms spun wildly through the air. Balanced only on the very tips of her toes, somehow she remained upright. Her legs continued running, carrying her quickly through the maze, following the cables around the twists and turns. The pain in her shoulders had cleared her head, concentrating her thoughts. The cable would lead to the exit; she was going in the right direction.

She rounded another corner, stumbling as her feet found the start of the uphill slope. At the top was a square of daylight offering blessed relief from the frightful dark. There it was: the way out. She picked up speed, so grateful to be soon at ground level.

As Natalya burst back into the concrete hangar, she flew past Stepan like a whirlwind and then sunk to her knees, panting heavily, fighting the cramps in her chest as she struggled to regain her breath.

Stepan stood over her. 'What…?'

'I don't…' Natalya drew a huge breath as her lungs strained for air. 'I don't want to be here anymore.'

'What happened? And what's that folder?'

'Nothing happened. I just spooked myself, that's all.' Her breathing started to slow. 'It's horrible down there. I found this in an office. Most of the rooms seem to be burned out, but this one had steel doors, so must have escaped the flames.'

'I could see it was horrible from here, but do you think we should have another scout around to make sure we haven't missed anything? Maybe shoot some more footage?'

Natalya got up and thrust her camera into Stepan's hands before heading for the exit. 'If you want to go back down there, be my guest. I'll be waiting in the car. Anyway, I want to see what's in this.' She waved the folder she was carrying. 'This place isn't going anywhere, and we're losing light. We can come back if we need to.'

Stepan watched as she disappeared outside. The sun was starting to set, meaning that evening would arrive quickly. Natalya was right: they needed to leave. He certainly didn't want to be anywhere near the forest come nightfall. He hooked the camera strap around his neck and quickly followed. 'Wait up,' he called.

Natalya stood motionless in the waist-high grass, staring off towards the main building where the Jeep was parked. Stepan approached cautiously. He'd let her down. He should have gone down with her. He wanted to comfort her, to tell her how exploring the tunnel was the bravest thing he had ever seen.

'Natalya...' he said as he caught up with her. She didn't turn; she didn't even acknowledge him as he stood next to her. She just stared off into the distance. Stepan cursed himself again for not following her down into the tunnels. He looked at her face. Instead of anger, she wore a puzzled expression. Stepan looked across to the Jeep. He couldn't understand what she was staring at. 'What is it?' he asked.

'Over there,' she pointed. 'The long grass next to where we came in.'

Stepan followed her gaze to the gap in the fence where the huge pine trees rose up guarding the boundary of the clearing, their deep shadows made even longer by the setting sun. Below them, in front of the chain-link fence, the top of the wild rye swayed slightly, as if dancing in the wind. Stephan stood, confused for a moment before realising the problem. He couldn't feel any wind.

The movement was wrong, it was only in that very small area. Suddenly it stopped. 'Erm... Natalya... Did you see that as well?'

Natalya spoke quietly. 'Yeah, what do you think? Wind?'

The grass moved again. This time far more violently and in a defined route. Whatever was causing it was moving quickly and straight towards them.

Stepan's brain worked swiftly. The movement was still at the opposite side of the clearing. It would mean running straight towards it, but they needed to get back to the Jeep. They were already closer than whatever was coming towards them. It was a gamble, but if they were quick, they should just make it. He grabbed Natalya's hand and yanked her forwards, snapping her out of her daze.

'Not wind,' he called to her as they ran. 'Very much, not wind.'

The wild rye whipped at their legs, tangling around their ankles as if it was trying to hold them back.

The movement ahead continued to surge towards them. It was fast, much faster than they were, and closing the distance rapidly. Stepan could make out a number of low grey shapes barrelling towards them. Five or six, he couldn't be sure. They had to move faster or they weren't going to make it. He grabbed harder at Natalya's arm, putting everything he had into his legs, somehow finding some extra speed. The edge of the grass marking the start of the slabs outside of the main building came into view. They were nearly there, although he couldn't keep up this pace for much longer. His lungs burned, and a metallic copper taste started to build up in his throat. His legs were on fire. Stabbing pains shot up both his ankles as his tendons twisted against the force of his muscles. Still he didn't slow, and forcing the pain out of his mind, he leapt through the last strands of wispy grass to land on the paving slabs. The change of surface caught Natalya unaware. She stumbled forwards. Stepan felt her hand slipping, and he squeezed with all his might, hauling her back upright to regain her balance.

The grey shapes had made it to the edge of the grass too as six creatures launched themselves forwards.

The Jeep sat an equal distance between them. Without slowing, Stepan stared in horror. The lead creature had the body of a large dog, but standing roughly three feet high. Its shoulders and front legs rippled with muscle with protruding veins clearly visible under its short, black fur. Its head was covered with hairless pink flesh, with ears as simple holes in the side of its skull. Bright orange eyes shone like fire, fixed on him and Natalya.

The skin over its short muzzle pulled back tightly, revealing two rows of thin, needle-like teeth; its mouth filling with white foam as it salivated at the thought of cornering its newfound prey. It sat back, coiling itself onto powerful back legs and launched itself forwards to attack.

Stepan had reached the Jeep door. He thought he had left

it open, but now he wasn't so sure. With one hand pulling the handle and the other gripped to Natalya, he pulled one towards the other. The door flew open as Natalya found herself being flung into the passenger seat. Stepan dived in too, landing on top of her just as the lead creature collided with the open door. It recovered instantly, and recoiled for another attack.

An arm appeared from underneath Stepan, feeling for the door, fingertips stretching to make contact with the handle. Natalya reached out and caught it with her first two fingers, with just enough grip to haul it closed.

The catch caught and clicked as the full force of the lead creature slammed into the side of the Jeep. It rocked up, leaning heavily to the side before crashing back to right itself. The rest of the pack had surrounded them, preparing to do the same, coiling their powerful bodies, ready to throw themselves forwards.

Stepan couldn't see what was going on outside. He was face down across the passenger seat, frantically clawing his way across to the driver's seat. The car bucked from another attack, shaking so violently that Stepan ended up head first in the driver's foot well. He twisted to right himself, hauling himself up with the steering wheel and into his seat. The face that greeted him through the side window was hideous. Inches from his own, the creature had pulled itself up to stare down inside the car. It looked oddly humanoid until it bared its teeth. White foam spewed from its mouth, splattering onto the glass as it snapped at the air. Stepan stared in shock as the creature met his gaze, its burning eyes, so filled with hate, piercing his own.

Still focused on the creature, he felt for the keys. He knew he'd left them in the ignition. After flapping for a few seconds, his fingers grabbed the cold metal and he turned it, igniting the engine into life. The creatures looked unfazed, preparing for another attack. With both hands on the steering wheel, Stepan hit the accelerator, sending the Jeep shooting forwards. He turned sharply to point them back in the direction of the access road, and sped away.

By now, Natalya was back up and sitting in the passenger seat. She twisted round to look through the rear windscreen. White ice crystals flicked up and spiralled out behind as they thundered away, leaving two clear black streaks on the frosty tarmac.

The creatures were gone.

9

Stepan didn't slow down as he plunged the Jeep into the dark tunnel of the forest.

'Do you have any idea what just happened?' Natalya asked.

Stepan shook his head. His eyes were wide pools in a face drained of colour. He gripped the steering wheel. 'I have no idea what those things even were. They didn't look right; maybe they were diseased? I guess a forest like this is full of wild animals.'

Natalya watched Stepan's silent concentration. She spoke in a whisper, almost as if to herself. 'You think they were wild then?'

Stepan didn't reply. Natalya considered repeating her question, but the thought of what Stepan's answer might be made her reconsider.

They surged on down the narrow road and through into the first clearing. The huge radio tower loomed into view, emerging clearly through the canopy of the surrounding forest.

'Whether it was the Buzzer transmission site or not, a base this large and complex must have had serious significance. But then, if that was the case, then why was it abandoned so hastily?' Natalya asked.

Stepan would normally have talked for hours to answer such

a question, but now his eyes remained locked on the road ahead, and he remained silent.

The heavy iron gates flashed into view through the trees marking the outer perimeter of the base. They barrelled on towards them until Stepan hit the brakes hard, throwing the two occupants forwards against their seatbelts. He nodded ahead, 'You're up.'

Natalya jumped out and stared uneasily back along the tarmac. From beneath the thick needle canopy, all buildings and structures were hidden; even the great radio tower was concealed. A cold wind now blew, but the branches of the pine trees remained motionless. For a forest that should be teeming with life, there was still no sound. She approached the gates and swung the first one wide. The Jeep trundled through and stopped as she pushed them closed and hopped back into the passenger seat. For the first time since the trip began, Stepan locked the doors.

'So what did you think? Should we bring a picnic next time?' Stepan asked as the colour returned to his cheeks.

Natalya forced a smile. 'That was close, far too close. Nothing good has ever come out of that place.'

They sat in silence for a while as the evening light slowly faded into night. The Jeep thundered back onto the main road and re-joined the twinkling lights of modern civilisation.

'I think we'll have some brilliant footage. I just hope some of what I shot is usable. And of course, there's this,' Natalya said, fumbling to retrieve the old blue folder from the back seat. 'The room I found it in seemed to be an office. It looked important; you should have seen the door. It must have been armour-plated. Everything else down there was burnt to ashes.'

The cover was embossed with a large, gold-coloured crest covered in blotches of black mould. Natalya opened it up, and studied the first page as the smell of damp filled the car.

'Numbers – lists of numbers,' she said, turning the page.

'More lists.' She flicked through more pages. Each one contained four columns of decimal numbers running down the whole length of the page.

Stepan shot a quick look; he could afford no more than that in the clambering traffic. 'Is that it? What on earth is all that about?'

Natalya sat scowling at the pages. 'It could be anything. I better not have gone through all that to grab the lunch roster?' She continued to flick carelessly through the pages. 'All just lists of useless numbers.' At the last page, she paused. Here was an official looking report headed with the same crest as on the cover. In the centre of the page was the following:

KAMERA: Active
EVAC STATUS: Confirmed
CONTAINMENT SHUTDOWN: 19 September, 2010, 03.18 hrs
TEMPORARY CONTAINMENT THRESHOLD: 23 hrs
C-2 STATUS: Transport Complete
C-1 STATUS: Critical, Pending Upgrade

'Hang on, this last page is different,' Natalya said as she relayed it to Stepan. 'Does any of that make sense to you?'

Stepan drove on in silence, processing the new information. Finally he spoke, his voice slow, as if he was still deep in thought. 'The only thing is the date. That's when witnesses reported that the base was evacuated during that storm. Do you remember me telling you how it was the only time the Buzzer had ever stopped? Maybe this is something to do with the relocation?'

'It would be a coincidence if it wasn't linked, I suppose. Maybe once it's put in that context, the rest of it will start to make some more sense?' Natalya closed the final page carefully and stared out of the windscreen. Her legs were already starting to ache, and a long yawn drew its way up through her body.

The Jeep travelled through the Moscow city boundaries and on to familiar side streets. Natalya hadn't been aware of the last part of the journey at all, almost sleeping, although her eyes never closed.

Stepan pulled the car up outside Natalya's apartment block and stopped the engine. 'So... I've got a feeling you might need a hand sorting out all of the footage from today, not to mention that folder. I must warn you, I order a mean pizza.'

Natalya paused, unsure quite how to respond. She had assumed she would continue alone after this point. By the time she had thought of a response, Stepan had got out of the Jeep and she found herself looking at an empty car seat. As much as she owed him for the day, she wasn't prepared to take on a partner for the project just yet. She opened the door and jumped down to the road. 'Stepan...' she called out. 'I don't think...' She stopped in mid flow, the breath leaving her body. She had quite forgotten.

The glow of streetlights glinted off three huge dents buckled deep into the once smooth bodywork of the Jeep. Surrounding them were a number of silver gouges and puncture marks that had penetrated clean through the metal like bullet holes.

Natalya ran her fingers gently over the jagged metal, stunned into silence.

Stepan stood on the pavement waiting for her.

'Stepan, I'm so sorry. Your Jeep...'

'I think it did a lot better than we would have. I'm sure it can be repaired. If we hadn't made it back in time there wouldn't be anything left of us to put back together,' he replied with a smile.

Natalya's heart skipped a beat as the reality hit her. Her brain had blocked out the danger they'd been in. Had they taken a couple of seconds longer, they wouldn't be standing here now. Stepan's quick thinking had saved them both. She smiled back at him. 'Come on; pizza sounds great, and I've always wanted an assistant.'

She guided them up the lift and through the maze of corridors. The old building had so many design changes during its long existence that it had become a warren of hallways leading to a mixed assortment of apartments, with Natalya's being one of the smallest. The only light in the windowless hallway came from a row of dusty bare light bulbs protruding at various angles from the wall. Doors dotted both sides at random intervals leading to other apartments, all of them different and painted a variety of colours.

'Here we are,' she said, as her own red front door came into view. She wished she'd known that Stepan might come back; she would have smartened the place up.

They entered, Natalya first, firing a barrage of apologies and excuses for the chaos within. Stepan followed and in the hallway knelt down to remove his white trainers. The gesture brought Natalya a few valuable seconds. She charged into the living room grabbing piles of clothes, packets, old post – anything that she could lay her hands on – and shovelled it all behind the sofa before Stephan entered the room.

His expression didn't change. Despite the obvious differences to his own space, he felt quite at home. 'So… shall I get started then?' he said.

'Absolutely, we've got a lot to get through and work out.' Natalya opened the folder to the first page of numbers.

'Yes, that too, but let's get our priorities straight.' Stepan held out his mobile phone in Natalya's direction. 'Pepperoni OK with you?'

***

Neither Natalya nor Stepan were mathematicians. The mysterious blue folder's number matrix was a puzzle beyond both of their understanding. The final page report, however, was a lot more promising.

Natalya read aloud the results of an Internet search into Kamera and C-2.

'Kamera, meaning The Chamber. Alternatives, Laboratory 1 and Laboratory 12. Poison research laboratory of the Soviet Secret Services commissioned in 1921. C-2 was a project undertaken in the 1930s to find the perfect poison in order to counter the growing threat from chemical weapons developed by the rest of the world during World War 1'

The article described the details of the sinister project and the multitude of human experimentation involved to achieve its goal. Natalya stepped back from the monitor and dropped into her sofa. 'So, what's all that got to do with our Buzzer?'

'I have no idea,' replied Stepan. 'There's no mention of it anywhere. C-2, though, doesn't sound good. In our folder, it says "C-2 Status: Transport Complete". Do you think they were storing it at that base?'

'It certainly sounds like it. If that's C-2, then what's C-1? There's nothing about it in any of these articles? If it's anything like C-2 then being in a critical state can't be good. At NTV, we sometimes contact experts in various fields that we use for interviews. There's a history professor at Moscow University who we contact for a whole variety of projects. One of his main areas of expertise is World War II. I think it would be worth seeing if he can shed any more light on this. I'm also sure that he'll be happy for me to record an interview, which can go into the project.'

'That sounds like a good plan,' agreed Stepan. 'This is totally out of my area of expertise, but I'd love to find out what it all means.'

Natalya looked into Stepan's excited eyes. Despite the day they'd both had, he was more enthusiastic than ever. She smiled at him. 'I'm glad you're still in,' she said.

She opened her email account and typed to the professor. She told him of the project, but was deliberately vague on the details. She informed him that she had come across a document that seemed to be linked to Soviet Secret Service research in the 1930s, and wondered if he would care to take a look.

The professor's reply took only minutes to come through.

10

Natalya stood waiting outside her apartment block in the fresh morning breeze. She had arranged to meet Professor Golovin in his office at Moscow State University and Stepan had been delighted when she had invited him to come along. She stood with the black holdall of recording gear in one hand and a flower-covered document protector in the other. Hardly standard issue for Soviet Secret Service documents, but it was the only one she had.

The familiar royal-blue Jeep came into view as Stepan turned into the road fronting the apartment block. As it approached, it was obvious that the bodywork had returned to normal. With no footage of the creatures, Natalya had hoped to record the damage they'd caused. It had seemed insensitive to do it after their trip, and now, with the sight of the shiny smooth panels, she had missed her chance.

Stepan slowed the vehicle to a stop in front of her. She gave him a little wave and hopped in. 'The Jeep looks great,' she said, hoping he wouldn't detect her disappointment.

Stepan smiled. 'Luckily all the damage was cosmetic so it wasn't too big a job. I found a place with everything in stock and if you pay enough, people will work whatever hours you ask them too, even on a Sunday. Try explaining away that kind of damage to a mechanic – not easy. I did think you might like a few photos to put in the project, so before I had the work done I took a few snaps with my own camera.'

Natalya looked across at him with a sparkle. 'Stepan, you're a star.'

'I should get that in writing.' He laughed before pulling smoothly away.

The Moscow State University building was a leviathan, dwarfing everything surrounding it. The great white walls stood over twenty storeys high, forming a huge central tower that peaked with a mighty iron spire and giant star.

Professor Golovin had always been a friendly approachable character and today was no exception. After exchanging introductions and pleasantries, he welcomed Natalya and Stepan into his office with a warm smile and hearty handshake. Now in his seventies and with a head of silver hair, he wore a full white beard to match. His small half-eye reading glasses were perched halfway down his nose completing the perfect image of a stereotypical Professor of History.

It was obvious why NTV used his services. On camera, the professor's appearance alone was enough to convince anybody that he was an extremely adept historian.

The professor's office was far from plush and extremely well used. At its centre was a wooden desk dominated by an ancient-looking desktop computer. The huge CRT monitor filled half of the surface, and a large oversized keyboard the rest. An archaic system compared to the pinnacle of technology Stepan was accustomed to programming on. On one wall was a huge map of Eastern Europe studded with pins, marking various points of interest. Another was filled with two vast bookcases containing a jumbled collection of threadbare books.

'It's very kind of you to help with our project,' Natalya

began. 'We really do appreciate your time. Would you mind if I recorded some footage?'

'Not at all,' Professor Golovin replied warmly. 'I would be offended if you didn't think my responses were worth documenting; besides, I'm wearing my best regalia especially for the occasion.' He chuckled as he gestured to his crumpled shirt. 'I believe that you have an interesting document for me to cast my eye over.'

'We do,' Natalya replied as she set up her camera, 'but first I was hoping you may be able to offer us some information on a few specific areas that are troubling us.'

'I will certainly do my best. I'm ready when you are.'

Natalya squeezed the sticky tape holding the microphone, flicked the camera to record, and began with her first question.

'We have come across references to what seem to be Soviet Secret Service research projects. Do you know any information regarding Kamera, and what seems to be a project called C-2?'

Professor Golovin settled back into his chair, interlocking his fingers. 'Let me start with some background. In 1922, the Soviet Union Secret Service became aware of a threat from overseas from new foreign super weapons. The most prominent of which was poison, usually in the form of gas. I'm sure you're aware of various agents being used on the battlefields of World War I.'

Natalya nodded. It was like being back at school. The old professor obviously loved his work, revelling in any opportunity to conduct an impromptu lecture.

'In order to prevent the Soviet Union from being vulnerable, Secret Services established a poisons' research laboratory of their own known as Laboratory 1, or *Kamera*. The C-2 project you refer to was a preparation of particularly deadly properties. It was, in essence, the perfect poison. Tasteless, odourless, and impossible to detect during post-mortem. Unfortunately, this was a time in history when human rights didn't count for anything, and human experimentation was common. In order to perfect their deadly project, so-called volunteers were brought in to sample the so-called medication. It was rumoured that Pavel Sudoplatov and Nahum Eitingon, both prominent and influential leaders in Soviet Intelligence in the 1940s, would only approve poisons after extensive human testing.

'Project C-2 had a particularly devastating effect on its victims. Reports say it even caused physical deformities prior to death, which occurred merely fifteen minutes after administration. Victims appeared shorter, weaker, calm, and quiet. It certainly wasn't a screaming painful death.'

Natalya shot Stepan a questioning glance, her face paling as their eyes met. She turned back to the professor. 'And what of C-1? Was that another poison developed at Kamera?'

The professor released a long breath. 'I think it might be time for a tea break,' he said, looking back and forth between his interviewers.

'Oh, sure thing, I'll just get this,' Natalya said. She walked over to the camera and flicked the record switch to the off position.

Professor Golovin glanced towards the office door before leaning forwards. His voice was low and barely audible.

'Anything I tell you about project C-1, I would rather remain between you and me, if you don't mind. It's a kind of Lake Labynkyr Monster topic. The sort of thing that can destroy the reputation of any academic if they are heard discussing it in the media. Many a career has been discredited overnight by a paper on a Yeti or flashing lights in the sky. I, for one, do not want to be one of those unfortunates.'

Natalya spoke quietly. 'Of course not. I had no idea. I'm so grateful to you for giving up your time for this interview. The last thing I want to do is cause you any trouble.'

'Very well. Now, I must warn you, most of what I say has little factual evidence to support it. However, there are sporadic mentions of a second agent commissioned at the same time as C-2 dotted throughout history. C-1 was a project to be the opposite of C-2. Where C-2 was a poison that inhibited and destroyed humans, C-1 was a stimulant designed to enhance and strengthen. It was thought that it might be possible to boost the transmissions occurring in the human brain and so unlocking areas previously unused. It's widely known how the Soviet Union was obsessed by human enhancement projects. Their goal was to produce an army of super-soldiers, able to crush any regular human army. It is said that documented experiments even included attempts of interbreeding humans and apes, but with no reported success. Any early mention of the project C-1 stimulant reported rapid decommissioning due to there being no success. However, rumours continued to emerge that the project had indeed been successful, only not resulting in the desired outcome. The subjects exposed did show significantly increased neurone activity in previously dormant parts of the brain, but it seemed these areas had evolved to be dormant for a reason.

'Rather than the subjects displaying enhanced characteristics, they displayed signs of regression back to a far more primitive creature. It is rumoured that they reverted to an animalistic state, losing the power of reasoning, forward thinking, even speech. Not only were the C-1 victims physically stronger and larger, but also they were irrational, displaying angry and violent characteristics. Of course, with today's international laws, all such projects have been long since abandoned.'

Natalya broke eye contact with the professor, turning again to look at Stepan. She didn't need to speak. Stepan nodded in agreement. She picked up the flower-covered document protector and handed it to the professor. 'We think you should take a look at this.'

'This can't be genuine!' The professor pointed to the date

of the final report page that was draped over the oversized keyboard. 'This is September 2010. There have been no reports of new information on projects like these for decades. If this document is indeed legitimate, what we have here is very dangerous information.'

The room became silent as the occupants exchanged anxious glances, flitting from one individual to the next, all unsure of who should speak next or what to say.

'Have there ever been reports of C-1 being used?' Natalya finally asked.

The professor swallowed; his eyes were full of concern. 'This is where the rumours get even darker; where it gets even harder to establish fact from fiction. It is said that, at the stage of development it was in, C-1 should never be used. Its effects were said to be devastating, as I explained, and once unleashed, it could not be undone or deactivated. There is one rumour of C-1 being used. However, it has been flatly denied by every official ever faced with the question.

'In the 1940s, Nazi Germany swept across Europe. They had superior technology, training, and tactics. Nobody could oppose them. Domination of Europe seemed inevitable, with even the mighty Soviet Union crumbling before them. In June 1941, the Nazis were marching, unopposed, though Russia, bearing down on the city of Leningrad. If the city fell, it would mean almost certain annihilation for the Soviet Union.

'It is well documented in history that just before reaching Leningrad, the Nazi army was unexpectedly halted at the small city of Luga. It is said that a tiny collection of Russian soldiers, made up mainly of local militia, fought so fiercely and with such ferocity that they halted the advancement of the whole army for a month. This brought invaluable time to prepare and organise the opposing Soviet force, readying Leningrad for the oncoming attack. Civilians were evacuated, and fortifications and supplies were put in place. What followed was still one of the most devastating sieges in modern history, but without that extra time, it would have been a massacre.

'Ever since, the city of Luga has been known as 'Hero City'. Specifics of how this amazing feat was achieved are incredibly hard to come by. Rumours range from the cold temperature to disease. There are, however, several unofficial accounts from witnesses reporting differently. They said it was as if a madness had swept over the city, affecting Nazi and Soviet alike. Friends and comrades, driven out of their minds, abandoned their weapons and set about destroying one another with nothing more than their bare hands and teeth; tearing and literally ripping each other apart. These reports, of course, have been denied and dismissed, put down to delusions caused by combat stress of the witnesses, but it has brought about the theory that, in a last ditch effort to exist, the Soviet Union had deployed its most devastating weapon: C-1.'

Stepan stood from his seat and walked thoughtfully towards the map on the wall. It was dotted with pins, each with a coloured flag attached. 'May I?'

'Be my guest,' the professor said, removing his reading glasses.

Stepan picked out an unused pin from the side of the map. 'Do you remember me telling you about the suspected Buzzer relocation sites after the original site was evacuated? The exact locations are still unclear, but they have been triangulated to within a reasonably small area. The first is the small village of Kirsino.' He planted the first pin into the map. 'Secondly, Pskov Oblast.' He retrieved another unused pin and planted it in a location below the first. 'And then, Kolpino.' He stabbed the third pin home and stood back. 'As you can see, they form quite a large triangular area, and can you see what's in the very centre?'

Natalya peered at the map. 'Hero City, Luga.'

Stepan fixed the professor with the confident, unblinking stare of a man inspired. 'Professor, two more questions, if I may.

Firstly, do you think it is possible for this type of experimentation to be conducted today?'

'I'd have said it was highly unlikely. International law absolutely condemns any research into areas like this. It would be foolish to risk the rest of the world finding out. The consequences would be dire. If, however, the document you have put in front of me today is genuine, well, that may change my opinion somewhat.'

Stepan nodded. 'Secondly, as you've been talking about the C-1 stimulant, I have been assuming you were referring to a chemical agent?'

The Professor looked blank for a second, as if mentally recalling all of his stored knowledge on the topic. 'There is no mention, to my knowledge, of the exact form C-1 takes. It is assumed to be chemical in nature, but as I've said before, nearly all of the information on it is rumour or hearsay.'

Stepan nodded. 'Are you aware of a type of electronic warfare known as neuroweapons? Neuroweapons are designed to use electromagnetic radiation to disrupt the chemical pathways in the human brain. Could it be possible that C-1 isn't a chemical agent, but something else: long-wavelength electromagnetic radiation for example, or more commonly known as a short-wave radio signal?'

The professor shuffled in his chair, unsettled to be discussing an area outside of his comfort zone. 'I am no scientist. This project, if it even exists, is venturing into areas completely unknown. It could indeed take any form. But would they have had that sort of technology in the 1940s?'

'I'm sure you're aware of a famous Serbian inventor by the name of Nikola Tesla. Tesla's work in the early 1900s was revolutionary, and so far ahead of the age, his inventions earned him the reputation as a real-life mad scientist. His obsession with electrical energy led to a number of leaps forward including a number of radio-wave experiments in 1898 involving his infamous Tesla Coil. In the 1930s, his inventions took a darker turn. Tesla claimed to the world that he had invented a death beam called Teleforce. Although nobody ever witnessed it, he continued his claims up until his death in 1943. This may or may not have any relevance to C-1, but what it does show is that the world, at that time, was very much aware of the potential power of electromagnetic radiation.'

Natalya worked through Stepan's reasoning. 'You think the Buzzer is C-1, don't you?' she asked him.

'I think that might be a strong possibility, but I sincerely hope not. If you look at all the evidence: the new location of the transmitters, the documents you found in the old transmission base, the stories from Luga... If what we suspect has any truth, we could be digging into areas some people may wish to stay hidden. Are you sure you want to carry on with this investigation?'

Natalya gave Stepan an unflinching stare. 'Do you seriously think that we can let this drop now? It might be going off on a tangent, but we can't just stop.'

Stepan let out a long sigh. 'I guess not. In that case, I think we need to pay a visit to Leningrad Oblast, Luga City.'

11

That evening, Natalya prepared herself for the next scheduled meeting with Anderi. As well as having to convince him that she was making progress on the Lotus Flower project, it would be another evening of dodging innuendos, while carefully wording every sentence to avoid any chance of misinterpretation. It was such a frustrating waste of time after the day's research, but in order to get the time off work to investigate further, it was vital.

This time, she hurried towards the restaurant, eager to see the evening through. Stepan was back at his apartment, organising their trip to Luga, and Natalya preferred to be doing the same. When she arrived, she peered in through the large, illuminated windows to the table which they had sat at previously, but the front rows of diners and wooden screens totally blocked her view. It didn't matter; she knew Anderi would be there waiting for her.

Natalya entered the restaurant through a warm blast of heated air. Anderi sat at the same table, filling the chair. Another huge, near-empty glass of wine sloshing in his hand. Seeing Natalya, he placed it down and puffed his way up to stand as she approached. His cheeks were already flushed a deep red.

'There she is. There's my girl,' he slurred loudly through a crocodile grin.

Natalya's hand rose subconsciously to her forehead obscuring her face from any onlookers who might be wondering who this plump little man's 'girl' was. The wooden dividing screens were a welcome feature as she sunk into her seat, out of view of the rest of the room. Anderi had excelled himself once again with his choice of attire: a salmon-pink suit with a white shirt and matching pink bow tie. The colouring enhancing his crimson complexion as shimmering beads of sweet glistened on his forehead.

He leaned across the table, fixing Natalya with eager eyes. 'So how's my little blossoming flower?'

Natalya stifled a groan. 'The project's going brilliantly, thank you. I'm really making progress. In fact, I'm off tomorrow to location to shoot some footage and grab some interviews.'

'Oh, right yes, the project. How's that going as well?'

Anderi boomed a hearty laugh, totally concealing the fact that Natalya failed to share his amusement. She satisfied herself by imagining the surprise on his big round face as she produced her Buzzer project. The thought turned her lips into a dry smile.

'There you go,' Anderi beamed. 'Such a waste not to use a smile like yours. Now, how about you fill me in with what you've been up to.'

Natalya did her best, although she was a poor liar. Trying to stretch a few hours' research over four days was not easy. For once, she was grateful that he wasn't actually listening to what she was saying. He seemed satisfied, for now, but there was no way of avoiding the fact that in one week's time, he would expect a finished Lotus Flower report.

The arrival of the meal provided welcome relief from the coarseness of Anderi's conversation. He ate in a similar manner to an animal at a trough. As unpleasant as it was to watch, fortunately for Natalya, the undignified process rendered him speechless for the next fifteen minutes. She picked at her own meal. The food was excellent, but as much as she tried to appreciate what was the best meal she had eaten for some time, the grunting and slurping coming from her dining partner was impossible to ignore.

It was later than she had hoped by the time Natalya finally made her escape. Anderi had set the next review meeting for three days' time, Thursday evening. Although a day earlier than expected, Natalya had agreed. There wasn't time to argue; she still needed to prepare for tomorrow's trip. Stepan would be calling for her at 8 a.m. and she would need to be ready. It would take nine hours of driving to reach Luga.

12

Natalya sat in the passenger seat of the Jeep as Stepan navigated through the swirl of morning rush hour in Moscow to join the E105 highway out of the city and into the Russian countryside. Forests and fields replaced the high office buildings and small rural villages dotted the roadside.

'Have you been to Luga before?' Natalya asked.

'No, but I was doing a bit of research last night. Apparently, it was quite an influential city in the Soviet era, but it's been in decline ever since. It seems as if there's been very little new development in the last thirty years and its population is getting ever smaller as people move away to bigger cities.'

'It sounds lovely. Have you ever thought about being a travel agent?'

Stepan laughed. 'It does have a river running through it; that might be picturesque?'

'I'm sure it will be. It can't be all bad.'

'It'll be lovely, well worth nine hours drive anyway. By the way, can you drive?'

'Yes, I've got my licence. I'm just between cars at the moment,' Natalya replied.

'Probably very sensible in Moscow, cars generally don't move very fast anyway. Do you fancy splitting the driving? I honestly don't think I'm cut out for the whole journey without a break.'

'Yeah, no problem.'

'You'll be alright with the Jeep?'

'I should think so. When you can manoeuvre a tractor and trailer loaded with three tonnes of slurry across a ploughed field, everything seems pretty straight forward after that.'

'Really? I'm impressed. I would never have said, to look at you.'

'Hey, don't let my glamorous exterior fool you. You're looking at the 2009 runner-up of the Sverdlovsk women's horseshoe pitching contest.' Natalya laughed.

'You know, I thought I recognised you from somewhere... Mind you, I did win a college chess competition, back in the day, so I've had my share of fame too.'

'That's very impressive; I wouldn't have said you looked the sort either.'

'I know, too cool and handsome to play chess, aren't I?'

'I wouldn't say that... I meant the sort to go to college,' Natalya said with a smile.

'Oh, so that's how it is, is it?' Stepan laughed. 'And to think I went to all that trouble to book us into the finest hotel in Luga. All I get in return are insults.'

'Yep, tough break, huh?' Natalya replied laughing.

They continued on, the road ahead stretching far into the distance.

'So you're not from Moscow originally? What brought you here?' Stepan asked.

'I suppose I felt like I wanted to experience life a bit more – see the world, chase the stories. A bit of excitement.'

'Are all your family back in Sverdlovsk?'

'Yep, it's just me here. How about you? Any family?'

'I moved into the apartment I'm in now with my younger brother ten years ago. He would go out and socialise with friends, partying all night while I stayed in and focused on my career. Work hard, get a good job and the rest is easy, my parents would say.'

'Do you still live with your brother?'

'No. He moved out five years ago. He's married now, has two children and a wonderful house in the suburbs. Just goes to show how wrong some people's advice can be.'

After five hours of monotonous driving, Stepan pulled over to let Natalya take over. It had been years since she had driven a vehicle, yet, true to her word, she was quite at home behind the wheel. After his long drive, Stepan's head began to nod. He did his best to fight the overwhelming urge to fall asleep, but it wasn't long before he lost the battle.

Finally, Natalya caught sight of Luga ahead and entered its limits. Through the windscreen, raindrops fell relentlessly across the grey concrete city. Daylight was fading fast and in the dull orange glow of streetlights, pools of water sparkled through the darkness. The hotel looked like all the other buildings they had passed. It was a featureless block, identifiable only by the illuminated sign hanging over the front door.

Stepan stirred in his seat. 'Are we here?' he asked groggily.

'I guess so.'

He peered out of the window. 'Huh? Not what I was expecting, to be honest.'

'Come on, it might be lovely on the inside. I'm so tired; I don't care where I sleep tonight.'

13

Wednesday, 17 February. 9.00 a.m.

The hotel breakfast room was bustling with activity. Two of the walls were filled with long windows overlooking Luga high street, while the third offered a large well-stocked breakfast buffet. Natalya entered the room after a restless night in an unfamiliar bed. Twenty tables were arranged in a grid across the floor. Half of them where already occupied, one of them by Stepan. He was sitting at a table for two, his hair still wet from a morning shower, with a steaming pot of coffee next to his open laptop. He caught sight of Natalya in the doorway and gave her a friendly wave.

She made her way over and pulled up a chair. 'You're up bright and early. What are you looking at?' she said as she sat down.

'I'm trying to find the best place to start asking a few questions and I think it's here.' On the monitor was a website for the Luzhsky District Museum. 'I thought they might have some more information about Luga's involvement in World War II.'

Natalya hadn't really considered this far ahead. Her plan had not extended past their arrival to the city yesterday. She upended an unused cup and reached for the coffee pot. 'That's a coincidence. I was thinking exactly the same thing.'

Stepan glanced at her, with one eyebrow raised questioningly. 'Well… that's settled then. We'll head off after breakfast.'

'Absolutely, I'm sure they'll be able to point us in the right direction.'

'Yes, I think you're right… Was that really what you were thinking?'

She smiled at him. 'Of course; great minds think alike.'

'Right, yes,' Stepan replied.

Natalya rose from her seat and started towards the breakfast bar.

'Natalya…' Stepan called. 'What was the name of the museum, again?'

'Luga District Museum,' she called back.

Smiling, Stepan settled back down in his seat. 'Right you are.'

The Jeep wound its way through frosted grey paved streets surrounded by grey block buildings. The city was a sea of lifeless concrete where tufts of green plant life and trees fought hard to emerge from tiny breaks in the compacted, barren earth. Here the roads were wide, but the people were few. Luga was a city where its population rattled around in a world carved out by the Soviet Union and had been forgotten ever since.

The museum building looked no different to its neighbours, apart from the large sign hanging at its entrance. It consisted of one cavernous main hall with a cold stone floor that created a chamber of echoes intent on amplifying the inadequacy of the sparse exhibits on display. The room was deserted besides a large elderly man with short grey hair who stood with his arm wrapped protectively around a young girl.

They passed the first small exhibit of various plant life with barely a glance as they moved further into the room.

'Stepan, there's nothing here…' Natalya whispered, her voice bouncing all around her. 'It's practically deserted.'

'The website did say that there was an exhibit on the World War II campaign. Maybe if we can find that?'

'Really? You think we're going to find anything useful?'

'It's probably going to be our best chance. You got any other ideas?'

'Hello there...'

A loud, friendly voice came suddenly from behind them, making the pair both jump and spin round. A large, heavyset, middle-aged lady was crossing the room towards them, smiling. She was smartly dressed in a grey trouser suit and flat black shoes; her hair pulled back into a tight ponytail. Pinned on her jacket was an ID badge with her photograph, below which 'Museum Curator' was written in large bold letters. She approached with a confident stride as she continued talking. 'I spotted the two of you from across the hall and thought I'd offer my assistance. You seem to be looking for something specific.'

Natalya smiled back, cautious not to disclose too much information. 'We're doing research for a documentary on Luga's involvement in World War II and how it came to be awarded the status of 'Hero City'.'

The curator nodded. 'Ah... a proud moment in history indeed for Luga. A documentary, you say; that's fascinating. Are you working for any particular media group?'

'NTV,' replied Natalya.

The curator's eyebrows rose as she gave a little nod. 'It's not often we get such attention here. I'm flattered. Would you like to come through to my office? Maybe I can help you with any information you need.'

Natalya glanced hopefully at Stepan. He didn't speak, but she could see he agreed with her. 'That would be wonderful, if you could spare the time.'

The curator's shoulders dropped as she blew out a long, slow breath. 'Unfortunately, time is something I have plenty of these days.' She looked wistfully around the room, pausing to focus on the museum's only other two visitors a little way off. 'These days, this is about the normal level of attendance.'

Natalya didn't know how to respond without sounding rude or patronising, so she stayed quiet.

'Anyway, come on through,' said the curator.

They followed in the wake of the curator's cumbersome stride as she guided them through the remainder of the exhibits to the back of the museum. The office they found themselves in was no more than a windowless store cupboard. Shelving filled all the walls from floor to ceiling, piled with boxes of files and paperwork. With the smell of dust and damp, and the buzz from a fluorescent tube above, it was not surprising the curator spent her time walking out on the museum floor. She planted herself behind an empty desk, and beckoned her guests to take a seat.

Natalya continued from where she had left off. 'So, as I said, we thought our documentary would cover the dramatic last stand taken by the troops stationed at Luga in 1941, thwarting the Nazi advance and saving countless lives.'

'An excellent choice,' said the curator. 'It's an event in our history that has been grossly undervalued by the media in recent years...' She continued to describe the build-up to the battle and on through to the eventual siege of Leningrad. All the information already covered by Professor Golovin back at Moscow State University.

The pair sat patiently listening, and politely agreeing with all the points the curator made about heroism and patriotism until she slowly ran out of words.

Natalya let her finish her lecture before setting about her questions. 'I agree, it really is a fascinating event. Do you know any details about exactly how these few soldiers and militia held back this enormous and highly organised army?'

The curator answered instantly, as if reciting a well-rehearsed script. 'The city was fortified in advance with all manner of sandbags, barriers, trenches, and light artillery...'

'Is that all they had?' Natalya shot back. 'I mean, even dug in, it seems that they achieved the impossible, holding back such huge numbers for so long.'

The curator looked sceptically at her. 'How about you tell me what you've researched so far, and I'll add anything extra that I can?'

'Well...' Natalya began, and then stopped, unsure of quite how to continue.

Stepan took over the conversation. 'We have heard rumours that the situation was so grave, so desperate, that the Soviet Union was prepared to go to any lengths to save itself from total destruction. Soviet High Command was fully aware that should Leningrad fall, their part in the war was all but over. Therefore, they commissioned the use of a super weapon, so powerful that it could not be controlled; that once unleashed, could not be stopped. A game changer that was the Soviet Union's last hope, and to hell with the consequences.'

The curator sucked in a long breath. She released it slowly and slumped back into her chair. With her eyes still fixed firmly on Natalya, her expression turned into a scowl.

'You know, the lack of respect shown for the sacrifices made by the heroes in our history sickens me. The great deeds performed by our forebears, so that we can live as we do today, should be treasured by our culture. Instead, what do we get? Not only are these monumental achievements taken for granted, they're forgotten. My ancestors fought and died here in that war. They fought for you and sacrificed everything. Now all you do to repay them is to tarnish their memory with stupid conspiracy theories. People can't just accept they were brilliant, brave men defending their families and country. My great-grandfather was a hero, and do you know who cares?'

Natalya shook her head at the now crimson-faced curator, who suddenly stood, catching her thighs on the desk, making it rock violently. Her anger masked her pain as she stabbed a finger towards the doorway. 'That's how many people care. But do you know what's worse?' The curator asked slamming her hands down on the desk as pinpricks of spittle flew from her snarling mouth. 'People like you, with your slanderous opinions, who seem intent on not only poisoning his memory, but to use those heroes' sacrifice to make a quick, selfish buck.' Forming the last word sent forth another shower of spittle flying towards Natalya's stunned face.

Stepan pushed back his seat with a toe-curling screech of its feet, and placed his hand softly on Natalya's shoulder. The curator sat back down, her face shiny and red. He spoke as slowly and calmly as his adrenaline-fuelled mind would let him. 'I think this would be a good opportunity to thank you for your time, apologise for any unintended offence caused, and leave.'

The curator smirked. 'I think that's the most intelligent thing either of you have said. I wish you every failure in tarnishing the memory of our country's heroes and that you don't make a single rouble exploiting my great-grandfather's sacrifice.'

Stepan spoke quietly into Natalya's ear. 'I think we should get going now, come on.'

As they stood, the curator continued to fire another rain of insults. 'That's it, get out and stop wasting my time; you're not welcome here. You're—'

Stephan closed the door behind them as they left, cutting off the curator in mid flow.

Neither spoke a word as they left the building and returned to the safety of Stepan's car. They both sat staring out of the windscreen until Natalya turned to look at Stepan. Insider her, a strange urge to laugh was bubbling up to the surface. After the last few minutes, this was the last thing she should be feeling. A small smile formed on her lips, then broadened. Stepan grinned back. Natalya fought to maintain composure. She wasn't sure what was so funny. She tried for a while longer, swallowing hard, but it was no good. Her laughter burst forth, forcing tears to well up in her eyes. The outburst of emotion washed over her, cleansing her of the tension of the meeting. Natalya hadn't felt this good for a long time, despite her ribs starting to ache.

Hearing Natalya gave Stepan licence to laugh too. Surrendering himself, he let go, simply enjoying the moment.

'Come on, let's get back,' Stepan began as he was hit by another torrent of giggles. The Jeep lurched back on to the main road as they both continued to laugh. Through their amusement, they failed to notice the car pulling out behind that tailed them as they drove back to the hotel.

'I'll just clean myself up, then how about some lunch?' Natalya asked as Stepan manoeuvred the Jeep into the hotel car park.

'Sounds good to me. We need to come up with another plan. That last one of yours didn't get us very far.'

'My plan? The museum was all your idea.' Said Natalya.

'Oh was it now? I thought you told me you'd already thought of it before I mentioned it earlier?'

'That's right; it was my idea until it went wrong, but now it's yours.' Natalya smiled.

Stepan laughed. 'So that's how it is, is it? I understand now.'

'I'm glad we've got that straight.'

'Well, don't be long, I'll meet you back in the lobby in fifteen minutes. We can try that café over the road.' Said Stepan.

'Fifteen minutes, and this time you can leave the thinking to me.'

They left the Jeep and wandered back to the hotel. Once inside, Stepan made himself comfortable in the foyer, while Natalya scurried off to her room. She felt a mess after their stressful meeting.

Unbeknown to them both, a large figure cloaked in a dark winter coat had slipped in through the door after them, and was now following Natalya as she climbed the stairs and made her way along the corridor. He kept a discrete distance, staying a few seconds behind, watching for the doors closing slowly behind her as she passed through. When she stopped at her room, he lowered himself into his coat and hurried past her, taking note of the door number before heading back downstairs, out of the hotel and towards his car.

Over lunch, Natalya and Stepan discussed their next move.

'So then, Miss Ideas, what's the plan?' Stepan asked, through a cloud of steam rising from his polystyrene cup of coffee.

'Well… I think we might be heading in the right direction by asking people with local historical knowledge. Maybe if we can find someone that doesn't consider our project a desecration of a loved one's memory, then we might get a bit further next time. I was wondering if there were any local history societies around that might spare us some time.'

'I'm impressed. That actually sounds like a pretty good idea.'

'And that surprises you?' Asked Natalya.

'I expected nothing less. I was going to suggest visiting the local World War II memorial, to see if there was anything of interest there, but I actually like your idea more.'

Natalya grinned. 'I'm not surprised. It's probably because it's a better idea.'

'All right, fair enough. We'll call my idea Plan B,' laughed Stepan. 'I'll have a look on the Internet when we get back to the hotel and see if I can find us any local contacts.'

'Sounds good. Not bad this,' Natalya said through a mouth full of Pirozhki.

'You're right, the food here's pretty good. This afternoon's just full of surprises,' said Stepan, as Natalya pulled an expression of mocked offence.

They finished their food and made their way back to the hotel. Stepan headed to his room to begin his Internet search, while Natalya stopped off at her own room.

She opened the door and quickly threw her coat on the

bed, eager to get back to Stepan and begin researching their new ideas. Turning to leave, she noticed a small, folded piece of notepaper lying on the carpet. She picked it up and opened it. Scrawled across the centre was a mobile phone number, and underneath, the words, 'Aware of your project'. She checked the back. There was nothing more.

Perhaps the museum curator had been talking to others about their meeting. Even so, the fact that she had been tracked down disturbed her.

She rushed back to Stepan's room.

'And you're sure you didn't see anybody?' he asked, letting her in.

'Of course not, I've just been out to lunch with you. I walked into my room and there it was. What do you think? Should we ask at Reception? Maybe they saw something.'

'We could… or I could just ring the number,' Stepan said, retrieving his mobile phone. What's the worst that could happen? It could be another psycho telling us to drop the project again, in which case I'll hang up. Or it might not be. Either way, they already know where we're staying, so what do we have to lose?'

'I think we should be careful. We don't know who we're dealing with here. What sort of person introduces themselves by tracking me down and leaving a weird note? That's not normal.'

As Stepan dialled the number, Natalya stepped forwards, making a grab for the phone, but he spun away.

'What are you doing? Have you gone mad? That could be anyone's number. Hang up… now!'

Stepan had no intention of hanging up. He held the phone to his ear, and turned back around to give Natalya a wink as the call connected. 'Hello, my name is Stepan Litvin and my partner is Natalya Kovalski,' he paused before speaking again, 'We are working in association with NTV.' Another pause.

Natalya spun around in a small circle where she stood, unable to do any more than wait.

Stepan's face went blank. He lowered the phone and looked questioningly at it. 'He hung up. That wasn't exactly what I expected.'

'Then who was it then? Are you going to tell me or let me guess?'

Stepan placed the phone on the bed and sat down next to it. 'I didn't even find out his name. Basically, what you heard me say was it. He asked who we were, then who we worked for. He said if he's satisfied with my answers, he'd call back later, then he hung up. I guess he wants to know who he's dealing with too.'

'I can't believe you did that, Stepan. The note was pushed under *my* door. If he turns out to be a crazy, it'll be me he's after.'

'Then we'll swap rooms.'

'That's not the point. You didn't ask me, you just went charging in.'

'What would you have said if I had asked?'

'I'd have said we should check it out first. See if any of the staff know anything about a visitor. See if there's any CCTV of people coming in.'

'And then what? Let's say we found out that a man in a hat and coat came into the hotel and asked for this note to be delivered to your room. What would that have told us?'

Natalya paused, Stepan's logic fuelling her anger. 'Then at least we would have known he liked hats!' she snapped back.

Stepan sat in his hotel room at his laptop, staring at an empty search engine.

Natalya reclined back on the bed 'It's hard to believe that in a city apparently so proud of its history, that there aren't any local historians.'

'There must be, just not ones that put themselves on the Internet. Still, if that's the case, it's not much good for us. Maybe we should try the war memorial tomorrow after all, see if there's anything that might point us in the right direction?'

'Something to point us in any direction would be nice,' Natalya replied. Her mobile rang, and she reached for it to read the message on the screen. 'I've got to take this; it's my boss... 'Hi Anderi.'

'Hey there, my darling. It's just me checking in. I trust you're being good? Or not...'

'I'm doing very well, thank you, and making some really good progress. In fact, I conducted a very useful interview today.'

Stepan beamed at Natalya who smiled back, rolling her eyes and shaking her head.

'That's wonderful,' Anderi continued. 'I knew I was right to put my faith in you, even if those others didn't. I just thought I'd call to see if you needed any advice.'

'I think I'm OK, thanks. Maybe when I have everything together, you can tell me of anything I should have done differently?'

'Of course, I'm always willing to share my expertise to help. So, are there any questions you'd like to ask me?'

'Thank you for your concern, but I think I have everything under control at the moment.'

'That's very good. I'm sure we'll have plenty to discuss next time I see you. We make a good team me and you, don't you think?'

'Erm... Yes, I think we work well together,' Natalya stumbled.

'I think we work very well together,' Anderi enthused. 'Maybe we can work well together on our date tomorrow night. I trust you can still make it?'

'You know me, professional to the end. I'd never miss a business meeting.'

'Absolutely. Looking forward to it. I'll see you then...' Anderi finished.

Natalya dropped her phone next to her, glad that Stepan was only able to hear her side of the conversation.

'Everything OK?' Stepan asked.

'No problem. You know how some people are, they just get a bit... overenthusiastic. He's very pleased that the story is coming along well.'

'That's great, because from where I'm sitting, I'm still looking at a dead end.'

'I'm sure that there'll be something at the war memorial tomorrow. We are in "Hero City" after all.'

'I'm starting to think the heroes were in the first wave of people to leave this place,' Stepan said solemnly.

The ring of a mobile phone broke the silence once more. This time it was Stepan's, and he reached into his pocket.

'It's our mysterious letter friend,' Stepan said excitedly. He answered the call, immediately switching to loudspeaker so that Natalya could hear the conversation. The caller spoke in a slow, guarded tone, as if he was thinking very carefully about what to say.

'I hope you didn't think me rude before. I wanted to verify your details before continuing any further...'

The line went quiet for so long that Stepan was unsure whether he should be speaking. He peered at the screen, checking to see if the call had been disconnected.

'... Maybe I can help you,' the voice continued.

'That would be wonderful,' said Stepan. 'We would be very grateful if you would be prepared to listen to our questions and maybe discuss a few theories and opinions.'

'I can't guarantee I'll be able to answer all of your questions,' the voice replied slowly.

'We fully understand. If you merely listen to us discussing our project, you don't have to utter a word.

'Agreed, meet me at park Kultury i Otdykha Zarechny, at 9 a.m. tomorrow, on the bench midway along the central path.'

'OK. We appreciate your time, do you mind if I ask your...?' Stepan stopped, finding himself talking to the drone of the dial tone. 'He's gone again,' he said to Natalya, but it looks like we have ourselves a blind date first thing tomorrow.'

'Stepan, I'm worried. We have no idea who this man is, and I don't like the fact that he knows exactly who we are. Do you think we should go?'

'He seems a lot more nervous of us than we are of him. I think we should. We've got nothing else to follow up and besides, I've got you to protect me.' Stepan smiled.

'I just wish we knew who he was. You did well getting us a meeting, and I suppose we don't have anything else to follow up. I'm just saying, is all.'

Stepan turned to his laptop. 'Well, I can't do much about it now, but what I can do is get us some more information on that park he wants us to meet in.'

Natalya's mind cast back to her earlier phone call to Anderi. She was scheduled to meet him tomorrow night. It was a long drive back to Moscow but as long as she had left Luga by lunch time, she should still make it in time. That would leave plenty of time for their morning meeting.

14

Thursday, 18 February, 9.00 a.m.

The pair met early in the breakfast room. Natalya sat nervously, sipping at her steaming cup of coffee. 'I think if we just knew his name it would make me feel better, not to mention how he found us.'

Stepan sat opposite, absently twisting the end of a packet of sugar. 'If we had another way to continue the project, I wouldn't even be entertaining this. I guess sometimes you can play it safe; other times, you just have to go for it.'

Natalya smiled at him and drained her cup. Whatever developed from this odd encounter, she knew that he would be looking out for her.

Stepan finished his own coffee, and stood up. 'Well, it's as they say: fortune favours the bold.'

Natalya sighed happily. 'That's so corny,' she said, getting up from her chair. Stepan always found a way to make her feel better. She performed a mocked bow, wafting her arms theatrically at the door. 'Shall we?'

A peaceful tranquillity hung in the air at park Kultury i Otdykha Zarechny. The twisting central path wound its way through acres of undulating grassy fields and coppices of towering deciduous trees. An icy breeze played gently in the leafless branches as their soft sway sent spiralling wisps of snowy frost floating gracefully into the air.

Natalya wrapped her thick coat tighter as they slowly trudged further into the park.

'I don't think anyone has been down this way yet. Do you think he's stood us up?' she asked.

Stepan surveyed the park once more. 'I can't see anyone, but this is the right path. We should give him a few more minutes.'

Natalya let out a long, slow breath, watching the warm air mist out in front of her. 'Surely he's got to show up?'

Stepan didn't reply.

Their pace had slowed to a trudge as they reached the top of a small crest. From their vantage point, they could see across the whole of the remainder of the park to the opposite boundary. The second half of the park seemed to be as deserted as the first.

Natalya stopped, plunging her gloved hands deeper into her coat pockets. 'Now what?'

Suddenly, from behind, they heard the crunch of heavy footsteps. They turned to see a large heavyset man, over six feet tall, stomping quickly up the path towards them. He wore a grey winter coat with a hood pulled up covering most of his face, leaving just his eyes visible. They were focused straight ahead, as if he hadn't even noticed them.

Natalya took a tentative step towards the man. As he drew level, his eyes darted towards her, giving her the briefest of glances. 'Good morning,' Natalya tried with a smile.

'Follow me,' the man said, continuing to walk past.

They stayed four steps back, both struggling to match the man's long brisk strides. He led them down the other side of the crest and on to where the boundary of the park was marked out by a series of low black fences. Each fence was separated by a small gap, just wide enough to walk through to the rough dirt track beyond.

One hundred metres ahead stood the remains of an abandoned factory. Walls of small, red bricks were held together by crumbling cement. Huge collapsed sections lay as rubble on the ground, leaving a corrugated iron roof balancing precariously overhead. Its metalwork was badly corroded, riddled with rust, leaving gaping holes yawning up through to the open sky.

The man disappeared into the door-less entrance of the closest building and stood next to a pile of collapsed masonry. Natalya and Stepan followed him in; entering just as the man lowered his hood. He appeared to be in his seventies, with closely shaven grey hair. He was still imposing, but now, given his age, he appeared far less threatening than the hooded figure in the park.

He stood quietly facing them, his gaze flitting backwards and forwards between both.

Natalya adopted her most welcoming tone. 'It's a pleasure to finally meet you…' she started as she introduced them both.

The man gave a brisk nod, eager to get on with business. 'My name is Stanislav Novac. I was at the museum with my granddaughter when I overheard your… discussion. I'm not a superstitious man, but things sometimes happen for a reason. It's as if someone up there is guiding us. I don't know what brought me to that museum the other day, but after I overheard your discussion, I followed you back to your hotel. I hope you understand that due to the sensitive nature of the subject up for discussion I was not prepared to approach you without knowing who you were. That's why I left the note. I needed your names and details to run a background check before we proceeded any further.

'I have a basic awareness of the details of your project; however, I would like to learn more of your intentions before continuing. You understand that being too careful is not a concept that I am familiar with. Please start by filling me in with the level of information you have so far.'

'We started our project on a different course entirely,' Natalya began, explaining their research into the Buzzer radio broadcast. 'We discovered documents indicating a link between this short-wave radio transmission and certain experimental projects conducted in World War II that seem to have been centred in Luga. We came to the city in the hope of finding out more about these projects, particularly one we have come to know as C-1.'

Stanislav nodded knowingly at the reference. 'What do you intend to do with this information should you obtain it?'

Stepan continued the conversation. 'As I explained on the phone, we are to make a documentary. Should it be successful, I believe our contacts at NTV will prove to be invaluable in publishing our findings.'

Stanislav was satisfied that the stories were consistent. 'Maybe I can help you. I have been retired for twenty years now, but as a younger man, I was a member of the Luga City Police. My days were generally taken up with low-level crimes, shoplifting, and the odd burglary. Luga is a country town with peaceful people who look after their own. Every so often, however, there seemed to be a crime committed that was so out of character, so shockingly ferocious, that it sent the department into total disarray. These crimes were not just murders; they were unbelievable massacres. A person with no violent history would suddenly turn on friends and loved ones, and literally tear them apart. One perpetrator was actually found at the scene, having murdered their entire family with their bare hands, in the process of devouring the bodies. There were five of these crimes committed during my twelve-year service. All by seemingly unrelated people, with no motives, and no psychological problems. They were, up until their crimes, upstanding members of the community. What was even stranger was their behaviour at the crime scene. Most criminals flee. Most try to cover their tracks, but these did neither. They were all found at the scene and all the reports were the same: they seemed consumed by madness, a furious anger that literally rendered them speechless.

'Due to the ferocity of the attacks, all the perps were detained by FSB Special Services. As far as I know, none of them even made it to trial. Reports came back to the department that they had been taken to various specialised institutions where, I can only guess, they lived out the rest of their lives under heavy sedation after their apparent breakdowns. Following this, we received final standard-issue reports for each case and they were never brought up again, all evidence and documents taken by FSB agents. All members of our force were told, in no uncertain terms, that for the welfare of ourselves and our colleagues, the cases were matters of national importance, and under no circumstances should any details ever stray outside of the department.

'After intervention of the FSB, I decided to conduct some research into the history of the city and see if there was any mention of the cases before. Unsurprisingly, despite my best efforts, I found nothing until I looked way back to 1941 and the last stand of the Soviet army at Luga. That was when I came across the first rumours of an ultimate weapon being deployed; one so powerful, it was all-consuming, affecting friend and foe with an unstoppable force that transformed its victims, effectively, into monsters. These stories were few and I only found mentions on Internet conspiracy websites alongside reams of UFO encounters and such like. I know these sources have zero credibility, but the effect of the weapon they called C-1 on those men… it turned them into wild beasts. Some say they dropped their weapons and tore at each other with teeth and fingernails. Symptoms that sounded all too familiar to me.'

Natalya stood transfixed as Stanislav spoke. The accounts from history were one thing, but the prospect of this continuing to the present day made everything seem far more real.

Stepan found his voice. 'We heard C-1 was originally a

human enhancement project designed to unlock unused areas in the brain to benefit its subjects, but these areas had evolved to be suppressed for a reason and were the remnants of a far more primitive animal. In accessing them, the subject reverted to an animalistic state. Having both ancient and modern human parts of the brain competing had undesired effects.'

Stanislav nodded as Stepan spoke, also familiar with the theory.

'We are incredibly grateful for you helping us,' Stepan continued, 'but I don't understand. If the FSB have ruled it treasonous to disclose this information, why would you risk talking to us now, after all this time?'

'The links between those terrible crimes and the C-1 case had disturbed me. I thought that maybe it was a coincidence. Maybe it was the aftershocks of 1941 breaking though that affected these people. I don't know. Once I had retired, the whole thing fell out of my life, and if there have been any cases since, I haven't heard of them. However, I have recently taken on a part-time maintenance job at a government building in town. Because of my time with the police, I have been trained to notice things that most people do not – things that are sometimes too normal to be normal.

'There's a department in my building that doesn't fit in with the rest of the outfit. The staff appear to be different to the other workers. They seem more educated, more accomplished. The whole floor has its own phone system and high-speed Internet connections that are far superior to the rest of the building. Yet, the department doesn't seem to have any obvious purpose. I admit the discretion they show is perfect. The casual observer would never consider anything out of the ordinary. I have only managed to gather scraps of evidence. I have overheard conversations, caught glimpses of computer monitors before they realised I was in the room. But you wouldn't believe what I've seen: information on the current C-1 activity level, transmission broadcasting levels, even a report analysing the effects of exposure to C-1 on a subject from the city. The experiment is continuing to this very day on innocent people. I can't let them treat the civilians of Luga like lab rats. Not to mention it being against every moral, humanitarian, and international law written. I can't just stand by and let it continue.'

Natalya considered that Stanislav was a credible source. What he had said was far from the ramblings of a conspiracy theorist, but in the end, it would boil down to evidence. Careful not to offend, she thought hard for the right way to word her next question.

'I certainly don't doubt you, but do you have any solid evidence you can show us to support your theory?'

'Sorry, I do not,' replied Stanislav, detecting her uncertainty, 'but if I had, it would have made every headline around the world years ago. The people working in that department are careful not to leave anything to chance. It's subtle, but they never let a visitor to the department out of sight. All discarded information is shredded and destroyed and the main doors to the floor are secured and manned at all times. From what I can gather, it seems that department is primarily a monitoring station to log the effects of C-1 in relation to its activity levels. There appears to be a much larger complex somewhere else in the immediate area that they are in constant communication with. I would assume the main base of operations. I have lived in this city all my life, but I have no idea where it could be located. Recently activity levels at the department have peaked to a completely different level. There are more staff working there now, and new equipment seems to be delivered almost daily. I'm worried something is changing and I certainly can't imagine it would be good for any of us living here in Luga if it is.'

Stepan shuffled from foot to foot, grinding fallen masonry into dust under his trusty trainers. 'If what you're telling us is true, then this is serious. This wouldn't just be a topic for an interesting documentary, but an incident of international importance. How convinced are you of what you are claiming?'

'All my life, I have worked following up leads, discovering the truth in a web of chaos. I have had years developing my instincts, although, I admit that they are not perfect. Not every hunch turns out to be truth. This, however, is no hunch. This I have no doubts about, and it terrifies me. I am an old man, but my children, my grandchildren, my whole family, live in this city. I was born in Luga. I've lived here my whole life, and I've spent my career defending its streets. My wife's ashes are scattered in that very park. Luga is as much a part of me as my arms and legs, and I'll be dammed if I'll stand by now and let it fall to any barbaric experiments. I can't go to the authorities – they are the authority! I can't go to the media without being dismissed as a paranoid old fool. I need solid evidence and it pains me to say it, but those people in that department are better than me. I can't get a scrap of solid proof – believe me, I've tried.'

The conviction of the old man's story was impossible for Natalya and Stepan to ignore. If his theory was correct, it would be the story of the decade, and Natalya would be the breakthrough reporter to reveal it. But, if the theory was correct, it would also mean the lives of the whole city were at stake.

Stepan pulled Natalya around and leaned in towards her. 'Are you prepared to take this further?' he asked quietly.

'Erm… I'm not sure what you mean. If you're proposing to break into Stanislav's building to gather evidence, I don't think we have the necessary…qualifications to pull it off.'

'Not as such, but if there is any truth in the tale, I might be able to find it. Anyway, why would we need to break in? The days of smashing windows and black balaclavas are over. I work with some of the most sophisticated computer viruses on the planet. Even so, it could still take months to get around whatever firewalls and security they have. But if Stanislav can get us directly into the internal network from within, the security would be far less.'

Despite their whispering, Stanislav could hear every word. Behind his stony exterior, his deep-set eyes sparked a glimmer of hope. 'You mean to say you might be able to access some of the information they have on their computers?'

Stepan turned to face him. 'There's no might about it. Once I'm in, I'll be able to access all the information. Obviously, stealth is the key. I can write a program that will be totally undetectable and untraceable. Once it's been uploaded on to one system, we'll be able to access the whole network. If what you're telling us is true, it's only a matter of time before we find the material that will be useful to us.'

'Is that... legal?' Natalya asked.

Stepan hesitated before replying. 'Not exactly, but with the correct programming, it would be almost impossible to trace. Believe me; I've been working on projects for years trying to track down the source of viruses. My whole industry is in an endless, faceless war. All we can do is counter the latest viruses before the next are created. I'm afraid the only risk will be to Stanislav. If we do this, I'll need you to insert a memory stick into any terminal linked to the internal network and remove it without getting caught, and that includes security footage.'

'I can do that tomorrow,' said a wide-eyed Stanislav. 'I know the surveillance systems on the floor. I'm up there regularly for general maintenance, so they won't suspect.'

The group considered their plan. 'Meet us at our hotel bar later this evening. I assume you remember where were staying?' Asked Stepan.

Stanislav stepped forwards, grabbing one of Stepan's hands in both of his own. 'Please don't think me rude regarding my manner before we became acquainted. When you have lived a life as mine...What I mean is, thank you...' Stepan felt the old man's hands tremble, 'thank you for believing me.' He let go and stepped back. 'I won't let you down,' He gave them both a sharp nod of his head before turning and marching out of a gap in the back of the building, disappearing into the overgrown scrubland beyond.

Natalya stared at Stepan. Suddenly, he had become the renegade, and cyber freedom fighter. He was no longer the man she had come to know. This new Stepan was exciting and dangerous if he was prepared to do something like this.

The two of them started to pick their way back out of the derelict factory. Outside, the park was slowly thawing in the low rising sun. A jogger made her way around the path, forming a steaming cloud from her warm breath. From a play area, the faint shrieks of excited children blew across on the morning breeze. The sounds of a normal city awakening from its slumber. But if Stanislav's theory turned out to be true, Luga was far from a normal city. It was more like one big human testing laboratory.

***

'Right, now that's over, I'm going up to my room,' said Stepan as they arrived back in the hotel lobby. 'I might need a bit of time to work this out,' he said, as if talking about a particularly tricky crossword puzzle.

'Sounds like a good plan. How about meeting up for a room-service lunch, later on? You can show me the fruits of your labour,' said Natalya.

'Sounds good. I'll try my best to impress you.'

Back in his room, he pulled out his laptop from the bottom of the wardrobe with a flourish, placed it onto the small desk, and switched it on. It booted up instantly. His employers had not compromised on decent hardware, and Stepan was about to put it to good use.

Natalya sat on the bed in her own room, feeling redundant. She hadn't heard from Stepan and was growing hungry. Her thoughts returned to the morning's meeting with Stanislav. The thought of murdering all those people was difficult to get out of her head, and the idea that the C-1 project was still in development seemed inhumane. If it was, then it didn't seem any closer to achieving the final goal of enhancing human brain function – assuming that was still the final goal. Even if it were achieved, would the repercussions be even more terrible than the trials? Would a new sub-species of hyper-intelligent, super-strong human be born, or manufactured?

She had once read an article on ancient humans. At the time the early humans were evolving, there were at least two distinct species. Modern humans originating in Africa were fast, efficient, and intelligent, whereas the Neanderthals, further north, were short, stocky, and slow. The Neanderthals had inhabited Europe for tens of thousands of years, but they were no match for the new sub-species sweeping in from the south. In a relatively short period, the original inhabitants were extinct. Whether it was through aggression, or simply an increased ability to compete against nature, Neanderthal man was no more. If a new sub-species of human were to emerge now, then what would that mean for the rest of the human race?

Tomorrow would be crucial to the project. If Stanislav was successful and they were to uncover some hard evidence then they would be in a far stronger position.

She would need to inform the hotel manager that they would be staying another night. That shouldn't be a problem; it wasn't busy. As for her proposed meeting with Anderi this evening, she would just have to call him, and come up with an excuse. She looked at the clock. Anderi was a creature of habit. At this time, every day, he left the office for lunch to appear an hour later red faced and overly confident. If she called now he would be out. Leaving a message would be much easier than facing his questions.

She reached for the phone and dialled the number for the NTV switchboard. The automated reply gave a list of the various departments and their corresponding numbers to press. When it reached the end, it said, 'If you know the extension number you require, please type it into your keypad now.' Natalya entered the number to connect directly to Anderi's office. Carefully, she returned the phone back to her ear and held her breath.

It was ringing. She gripped the phone tightly, willing the rings to continue coming. Another ring, followed by another. The answering machine would cut in soon. One more ring. There was a click followed by a silent pause. She tilted her head back stretching out the tension in her neck as Anderi's voice answered with the familiar, chirpy message.

'Erm...Hi Anderi, it's Natalya... I'm phoning to let you know that I won't be able to make our meeting tonight. I'm... erm...well...not able to make it. I'm really sorry, I'll make it up to you. Thanks...Bye.'

Natalya hung up and exhaled. It was a terrible message and she certainly didn't mean to tell him that she'd make it up to him. Rule one with Anderi: don't say anything that could be misinterpreted. It was obvious what he'd make of her message.

Natalya looked at her watch again, it was about time to check on Stepan's progress. She'd showered, changed, and, apart from hunger pangs, now felt much better. She had redone her make-up twice – the first attempt looked as if she had put in too much effort.

She walked along the hall to his room, and knocked. Stepan opened the door, wearing the same clothes from the morning. His hair was squashed flat on one side. He had smelt better too. Despite his dishevelled appearance, his shiny, red face wore a look of triumph.

'Come in, come in. I'd like you to see this. Carry on

through.' He shut the door behind her. 'You look great by the way,' he said casually.

Natalya's face flushed, suddenly embarrassed to have found the time to have made an effort.

Stepan stood next to her, gesturing at his open laptop. 'Have a look at this.'

Lists of what appeared to be random numbers and letters streamed down the length of the monitor and seemingly beyond. There was the odd legible word, but nothing distinguishable that made any sense.

'That's…erm…great,' Natalya tried.

Caught up in the enthusiasm for his new creation, Stepan didn't notice her confusion. 'I had to write everything from scratch. At first, I thought I would access files from my work system, but I didn't want to leave any trace of a trail to follow should anything ever be discovered. Not that it will, though. The polymorphic code enables it to change its appearance to avoid all the detection software I have thrown at it, including some of my own. Essentially, it's spyware. Once on the internal network, it will enable us to have a live view of any system linked to it. On this laptop, we'll see what they see on their monitors. We can't interact, so we'll just have to be patient. It's only a matter of time before we find the evidence we need – provided it's there. Then, just to make extra sure there's no trail back to us, the program will delete itself after six hours. It will be as if it had never existed.' Stepan beamed a broad smile.

'And that's it all there? That's…brilliant.'

'Yep, all there, ready to go.'

'Very good…' she repeated, not knowing quite what else to say. Despite Stepan's explanation, the jumble of code still made no sense.

'Anyway, after doing about a month's work in a few hours, I'm famished. Let's eat before we meet our new friend again.' He thrust the room-service menu at Natalya.

'I thought you'd never ask,' she said, taking it, although she didn't need to. She'd already spent more than enough time deliberating over it to pass the time that afternoon.

15

The room that contained the hotel bar was dimly lit and tired, decorated with a floral carpet, covered in huge bare patches left after years of neglect and now hidden underneath a mosaic of impenetrable stains. The bar itself dominated one side of the room, with row upon row of bottles standing to attention behind its large wooden counter. Along the other side of the room were a number of dim alcoves, each with a round wooden table, surrounded by rickety wooden chairs.

At the bar stood a row of padded bar stools. Two men sat talking loudly as the barman tried to look busy to avoid their attention. Nobody seemed to notice as Stepan and Natalya entered the room. They made their way to the closest table and sat facing the door so that they could look out for Stanislav. Natalya selected the sturdiest seat. Its wobbling wooden legs creaked as she sat carefully to avoid a splinter sticking out from the cracked back.

'Cosy?' remarked Stepan as he surveyed the room. Apart from the three people at the bar, there was nobody else. 'He's obviously not here yet. I think we should get some drinks, just to make sure we blend in.' He shot Natalya a wry smile.

'Good idea, just to blend in,' Natalya repeated.

As Stepan made his way to the bar, Stanislav rose from

a table in the shadows at the far end of the room and slowly strode towards Natalya. She hadn't noticed him approaching from behind her as she jumped in surprise to find him suddenly standing next to her.

'Stanislav, you're here. I didn't see you when we came in.'

'I have to admit I've been here for a while. I trust you are both well and have been able to make some progress?'

Stepan returned from the bar, setting his drinks down carefully on the table. 'Stanislav, just the man. I have something very important for you.' He pulled out a small memory stick from his pocket and handed it over. Despite his best efforts in explaining the program, an expression of bewilderment washed across Stanislav's face. Stepan was undeterred.

'All you need to do is to plug that into a booted-up machine that is linked to the internal network. It will install itself in thirty seconds. After that, you can remove it. Couldn't be easier,' he finished, sitting back in his seat as if expecting a round of applause. 'As soon as you manage that, we will have six hours to gather as much information as possible before all traces of it are wiped.'

Stanislav clutched the small device as if it were life itself. 'I can't thank you enough. What you have done here may save the lives of thousands, including those of my whole family. Natalya, if I could ask one more thing of you, it would be that once the information starts to come through, please act quickly.'

'Don't you worry. If there is hard evidence, my press office will have it aired within hours,' she replied.

Stanislav nodded. 'I will leave you to your evening. Shall I meet you back here tomorrow night?'

Stepan slowly shook his head, considering. 'Come straight up to my room. If we are receiving the live information, I don't want to be far from the laptop, in case of missing anything.'

'Of course. Until tomorrow, my friends,' Stanislav said, pocketing his prize.

16

Friday, 19 February. 7.30 a.m. Federal Office for State Reserves

Anyone who knew Stanislav would have questioned the uncharacteristic spring to his step as he made his way to work the following morning. He walked quickly, with one hand plunged into the pocket of his dark-blue coverall, squeezing a small plastic rectangle as if scared it would leap out at any second. His years in the police had taught him how to avoid looking suspicious. He couldn't afford to be caught now he was so close. He would bide his time and wait for the perfect opportunity.

The Federal Office for State Reserves was a five-floor concrete slab located in the centre of the city. Its solid grey walls were dotted regularly with small windows and a single main entrance. The windows on the fourth floor each contained a closed blind, completely blocking any view in from the outside, ensuring total privacy from a snooping telescopic lens or drone camera. Stanislav felt a rush of excitement; it would take more than that to keep its secrets hidden today.

Stanislav entered the maintenance storeroom. The two fellow members of his team were already there: a man and woman, both thirty years his junior. He had very little to do with them. They would spend the whole day flirting. The fact they didn't just state their feelings for each other annoyed Stanislav.

They sat sharing a bag of crisps, whispering. He couldn't bear to watch.

Mounted upon the wall was a whiteboard listing a roster of the jobs the maintenance team was required to complete throughout the day. Stanislav sauntered over and scanned the list quickly. One job required a visit to the fourth floor: a flickering light needed replacing in one of the small back offices. Perfect. Stanislav retrieved a pen from the side of the board and marked his initials against it, as well as a number of other jobs to fill his day.

'I don't know why you're so keen,' the man said from across the room. 'The quicker we get through these jobs, the more work they'll expect us to do. We'll be run ragged.'

Stanislav ignored him as he selected a five-foot florescent tube from a pile in the corner of the room. 'I know; I'm making a rod for my own back. Still, it'll give you two some time alone together,' he said, as he picked up a step ladder and wandered out into the hallway, passing the two silent red faces of his colleagues.

He made his way up the stairs, stopping halfway to check the memory stick was still in his pocket before emerging into the fourth-floor lobby. It was a small area dominated by a large semi-circular, brushed metal desk that was manned at all times. Behind the desk, surrounded by full-length glass windows, were a pair of doors controlled by a magnetic lock which was operated by a switch located at the desk.

The middle-aged man seated at the desk, gave the briefest of fleeting glances to the struggling Stanislav with his awkward baggage. 'Room two,' he muttered coldly before pressing the button to disengage the door lock.

Stanislav propped the stepladder against the glass before pushing open the door. He then jammed it with his foot, grabbed the stepladder and struggled in through to the main office. The man at the desk didn't even look up.

The large, open-plan room was fizzing with activity. Divided into small, individual workstations with shoulder-high screening, each contained a desk and computer, manned by a diligent-looking worker. The room had no natural light, instead relying on the harsh glare of fluorescent tubes, buzzing unpleasantly overhead.

Workers hurrying about their tasks stopped to stare at the intruder in their midst before carrying on their way. Stanislav felt his pulse quicken as he fought to keep a steady pace across this lion's den. As questioning eyes fell upon him, he kept his focus straight ahead. He wasn't interested in catching glimpses of monitors anymore.

He approached the closed door of the room, hoping that with incredible luck, he would find it empty. He put down the stepladder, and thought for a moment. This would be so much easier if he could find a quiet, unused computer. Perhaps the occupier of the office had been driven so mad by the flickering tube that they had been forced to leave the room. He knocked the door and waited. It was barely a second before a voice replied: 'Enter.' Stanislav's heart sank as he pushed open the door

Inside, a suited man sat at his desk behind his computer monitor wearing an irritated expression. 'Maintenance, it's about time. It's up there.' The man gestured at the ceiling above his desk. One of the lights flickered frantically, creating a strobe effect. 'I don't know why you people don't get some better tubes; these barely last a week – totally useless.'

Stanislav said nothing. He retrieved the stepladder and placed it in front of the desk. It had been significantly longer than a week since the tube had been changed. He needed a plan to get the man out of the room. There wouldn't be a better chance than this. Placing the new fluorescent tube on the floor, he climbed slowly to the top of the ladder, buying time to think.

Tottering precariously, he reached out to remove the old

tube, twisting it awkwardly as it disengaged from its sockets. He glanced down at the man behind the desk. He had gone back to his work, paying no attention. An idea came to Stanislav, and one that might just work.

Wobbling high up by the ceiling, Stanislav gave the tube a little pull, removing it from its fixture. Gauging the distance carefully, he leant over as much as he dared and let the tube go. It tumbled through the air, twisting slightly as it fell. One end caught the side of the monitor, before the rest splintered onto the edge of the desk, sending shards of glass and phosphor powder flying across the room.

The man leapt up. 'What are you doing? You moron! Oh God, it's in my eyes!' His hands wiped frantically at his face, but this only managed to rub the stinging powder in still further.

'I'm s-sorry,' started Stanislav, his fake stammer of concern expertly convincing. 'It's my arthritis; it's worse on cold days.'

'You idiot! You total cretin! You'd better not have blinded me. How could you be so stupid? One simple task, that's all you have to do. I'll have your job for this.' He struggled his way across the floor, stubbing his toe on the ladder as he went, causing another torrent of abuse aimed in Stanislav's direction. 'I've got to go and wash it out,' he moaned, as he pulled open the door, and staggered out of his office towards the toilets.

From his perch up the ladder, Stanislav watched quietly as the pneumatic hinge eased the door back in place.

The second it shut, Stanislav sprang into action, climbing down the ladder and pulling the memory stick out of his pocket. Running around the desk, he connected it with an empty USB port on the computer. Thirty seconds, then remove, that's all it would take.

Stanislav stood staring at the computer, willing the room door to stay closed. It did. He tried counting to thirty, but in his excitement he was counting too fast. It would be better to leave it too long then remove it before the program had finished installing. Stanislav tried counting again, but much slower. After reaching thirty the device had been in place for over a minute. He pulled it out and returned it to his pocket. The computer looked the same as before. He would have checked it had worked, but he did not know how to. He needed to trust Stepan.

After fitting the new fluorescent tube and clearing up, the man had still not returned. Stanislav left the office as calmly as he could. He realised he was holding his breath. He needed to relax. He made his way across the large room using his stepladder for cover. This time, the workers were less interested in him. He reached the glass double doors and, pressing the release button, stepped out into the lobby.

Now shaking, Stanislav returned to the maintenance storeroom. The two other workers had gone. He must continue to act normally and see out the rest of the day as he did every other. Watching the clock wouldn't help.

He spent lunchtime thinking of Natalya and Stepan sitting at their laptop, pouring over the secrets that had eluded him for so long. They would phone the press office, the story would be aired on national television, and he would win.

His next job was to empty the bins on the ground and first floors, and then it would be time to go home for the day. He would head straight to the hotel after that. It would mean being early, but the wait had been long enough.

Stooping under a desk, Stanislav was met by the pungent aroma of a decaying banana. He held his breath and grabbed at the bin. Shuffling back, he bumped into something solid. Not expecting anything behind him, he crawled around on all fours to be greeted by two pairs of feet wearing shining black shoes. He looked up. Two bulky, dark-suited men with earpieces reached out their arms towards his shoulders and squeezed.

'Sir, I recommend that you come with us,' one of them said.

Stanislav's heart sank. It was a threat, not a request. These men were not security or police. Thirty years in the force had taught him how to recognise FSB agents.

Two young maintenance workers dressed in dark-blue coveralls looked on in silence out of a second floor window as their colleague was being escorted out of the building. They looked at each other with a questioning glance, neither uttering a word. The moment passed and they both reached back down, returning to work on their litter bins without any further thought.

17

Friday, 19 February, 8.30 a.m.

Usually, Natalya awoke early with impressive regularity, but not this morning. Her pounding head reminded her all too well of the night she had spent in the bar with Stepan. They'd had such a great time, but had got carried away, forgetting about the project and the importance of today. Stanislav would be putting himself at great risk to get the information they needed and now she owed him her full attention. She popped two headache tablets into her stale mouth. A shower before breakfast would make her feel better.

She got out of bed, but before she could get to the bathroom, the shrill ring of her mobile phone cut through the silence. She groaned and approached the desk where she'd left it. Flashing across the screen was the message that she'd been dreading. It was Anderi. She groaned again.

He would be furious that she had skipped on their meeting, but she knew she would have to face him, and the longer she left it, the worse it would be. She picked up the phone, and accepted the call.

Anderi's voice burst through the speaker: 'I ask you for one thing. One thing, that's all, and you let me down.'

'Anderi, I'm so sorry…' started Natalya, but her weak apology was quickly drowned out by Anderi's rage.

'And you can't even phone me in person, just leaving me a message. I've tried to look out for you, to give you a chance. I thought you were worth it. I've stuck up for you, covered for you...'

Natalya had no choice but to sit and listen. There was no lull in the onslaught, no pause for breath. As far as she could recollect, she had never done anything out of line that needed Anderi to cover for her. It would be better to let him carry on and vent his anger before trying to respond. Finally, Anderi's voice slowed, although it had lost none of its venom.

'So where are you anyway?' he asked accusingly.

'I'm so sorry. I had no intension of missing our meeting. I'm... erm... in Luga.'

'What? Luga... You better give me a very good reason, very quickly.'

'It's for my research, into the erm...' her head was spinning so much she couldn't even remember the name of the flower. 'The... erm... lotus flower?'

'What's Luga got to do with the Komarov lotus?'

Natalya was surprised that Anderi had remembered the name, considering the whole project was a farce.

'It's complicated,' was the best she could answer with. 'I'll explain everything when I see you.'

'Which will be at our usual place, tomorrow night, won't it? If you don't make it this time, you needn't bother explaining yourself. You needn't bother coming back into work either. I'm sure even you can understand that, can't you?'

The line went silent before the hum of the dial tone buzzed lightly in Natalya's ear. As much as it pained her to admit it, she was in Anderi's debt. By tomorrow night, she would have to come up with a plausible excuse and get back to Moscow to make up for everything. That, however, would mean leaving Stepan, Stanislav, the city of Luga, and possibly the last chance to ever prove herself capable of being a proper journalist.

111

She sunk back down to sit on the edge of the bed, casually running her fingers over the folds in the clean white linen. The stakes were higher now. To stay and carry on her investigations would be to sacrifice the last five years of work, to wager it all on the success of the documentary on C-1.

Out of the window, life in the city was continuing on, blissfully unaware of whatever experiments were being conducted upon it. Traffic streamed past as all manner of people sauntered by on the pavement. Old and young. Individuals and groups of friends. A young family passed, laughing loudly, pushing a stroller as a toddler scurried alongside. Natalya sighed. There was still time to let things play out a little longer.

There was no sign of Stepan in the breakfast room. Sitting alone, Natalya started with a strong coffee. The day's plan needed to run perfectly. Stanislav had to install the program, and they had to intercept the vital evidence that would put an end to the horrible C-1 experiment. She knew she ought to tell Stepan about Anderi's ultimatum, but it was embarrassing. What sort of journalist gets called back to the office in the middle of a breakthrough story? It was easy to forget that she wasn't a proper journalist. What would Stepan think of her when he found out?

There was still no sign of Stepan as Natalya finished her breakfast, so she went to his room. He answered almost instantly and let her in.

'Morning,' he said, 'didn't catch you downstairs so thought I'd make a start. What do you think?' He gestured at his open laptop. A program was running, although the majority of the screen was filled with a large black rectangle where the feed from the office would be displayed.

'Looks good. Is everything working?'

Stepan faked a shocked expression. 'Of course. When you

employ one of the best programmers in Moscow, of course things work.'

Natalya shot him a smile. 'Well, when he gets back, I'll be sure to let him know what a good job he's done.'

They had already discussed the best way to record the information. It would be a live feed, and therefore, saving the data would not be straightforward. Setting up Natalya's camera to record the laptop monitor in real time would be the simplest solution. This meant they would be able to easily pause and replay anything that presented itself.

Stepan glanced at his watch. 'And now we wait. Stanislav should be getting to work about now, so I guess we could get a live link anytime. If he's got any sense, he won't rush into it, but I can't imagine he'll be hanging around either.'

Natalya sat down on the edge of the bed and stared at the monitor. Stepan was right. Stanislav, with his cautious and paranoid mannerisms, didn't seem like the sort of man that would act recklessly. He would bide his time. Unfortunately, for her, time was now in short supply.

Stepan was sitting at the desk, swinging his legs back and forth. The time passed slowly. They considered taking shifts to watch for developments, but neither wanted to miss anything. The connection would come through, or not at all. It was the not knowing that made things worse. After Stepan had gone to such lengths in constructing the program to distance themselves from any investigation, it would have been ludicrous to have asked Stanislav to contact them with a progress update and highlight their direct involvement.

Natalya had turned her attention away from the laptop and was staring at the blank screen of the hotel television. 'Stepan?' she said quietly.

As he turned to look at her, she knew what she had to say. She would have to lay all her problems out for him. The real situation at work, Anderi's ultimatum, and the fact that

113

her assigned project was on Lotus flowers, making this whole investigation completely unofficial.

Stepan stared at her, patiently waiting, his questioning expression breaking into a warm smile.

'Erm, Stepan. I know it's a bit late now, but do think that we're doing the right thing here?'

Stepan straightened himself in his seat. 'Of course we're doing the right thing. This is what journalism is all about. I'm no expert, but finding the story, research, and investigation, uncovering the truth…we could help people. The outcome could help to save lives. We have a duty to continue. Not just for us, but for all the people of Luga. There is more at stake here than just a good story.'

Natalya nodded slowly, agreeing with every word. 'I know you're right. It's just… Well I have a lot riding on this project. If things don't go to plan, I'm not sure what I'll do.'

'If that happens, we'll leave here with our heads held high, knowing that we didn't run away when things got difficult. We'll go home. There'll be other stories, other investigations.'

'That's what I'm worried about. There may not be any other chances after this. This is my first project. It's make or break for me. This is my one and only chance.' She looked into Stepan's eyes ready to receive his judgement. His face was unchanged, smiling back at her. Silent. 'I'm so sorry. I should have told you at the beginning, but this isn't even the job I was assigned. I'm supposed to be researching flowers. I'm no journalist. I'm a runner. A glorified tea maker. This whole project came about out of sympathy from my boss, and now I've let him down. I've let you down…'

Natalya looked at the floor. She blinked her eyes hard and felt the sting of imminent tears. Stepan was there, his arm hovering behind her. She dared not look at him, taking a deep breath, working to clear her mind of emotion before she lost it entirely. She rocked back slightly as Stepan planted his free arm in the space behind her, bracing it against his weight.

'You've not let anybody down, Natalya. Certainly not me. I'm here because I want to be. Your job title makes no difference to me. As for your boss... well, the fact that you're here shows that he's put his faith in you, and I think he's right to. What you're going to give him is a story far better than flowers. Any journalist in our position would be insane not to continue. In fact, given the facts that we have so far, it should be a sackable offence not to do so. There'll be other opportunities; I can guarantee it. You're a long way from last-chance saloon yet. The difficult part is making the right choices when they come along, and that's something we are in the middle of doing right now.'

The laptop screen blinked and a view of a system's screen appeared. Stepan caught the monitor change out the corner of his vision. 'Hey, were live!' he announced.

Natalya shot up, losing her balance and toppling off the end of the bed. 'It really does work,' she said from the floor.

The black rectangle had been replaced by a selection of blue menus with general headings and a motionless cursor.

'So, this is a direct view of the computer's monitor that Stanislav installed the program onto,' Stepan explained as he carefully adjusted his seat so not to block the view of the camera recording over his shoulder. 'Stanislav must have picked a quiet spot; there isn't much happening on this system. But now we're in, we should be able to switch between other systems that are connected to the internal network.'

He started working the keyboard and pulled up a different view. 'There we go; it looks like we have some action here.'

A cursor flitted about on the screen, accessing various drop-down menus. In the background were four columns of vertical numbers, each being added to every few seconds at the top, pushing the lower figures out of view. The user was applying various filters to the data before returning to the main listings.

'Look familiar?' Stepan asked Natalya, without taking his eyes away from the monitor.

'I'm sorry, but it doesn't mean anything to me.'

'It's not the data itself, just the format. Don't you think it looks a lot like the lists we found in the front of the folder from the base? I still have no idea what it's all about though.'

Stepan changed views again to other monitors. They ranged from more of the same nondescript number lists to motionless login menus. Stepan worked tirelessly. There were a huge number of systems linked to the network. It was frustrating work. Without any point of reference, the data was meaningless, yet it could be the key evidence they were searching for. Maybe when Stanislav looked at the footage with them later, he would have some ideas.

Stepan flicked to view a different system, ready to be greeted by more data lists, but this one was different. 'Natalya, look here. This looks like a report. Are we getting it on camera?'

She checked. 'Yes, we're still recording.'

Stepan sat up closer to his laptop and began reading out aloud. 'Progress report summary…'

Suddenly, the text disappeared, the view replaced by the black rectangle from earlier.

'What the…?' Stepan furiously worked the keyboard. 'We've lost connection. They've cut us off! How did they…?' He turned to face Natalya.

'They cut us off? I thought they wouldn't be able to detect us.'

'There's no way they could have known, surely. The program was perfect…'

Natalya stared back at the blank space with wide eyes. 'And you're absolutely sure it was them that cut us off?'

Stepan returned to the laptop with another frenzy of activity. Natalya had never seen Stepan so engrossed. The speed he was moving at was mesmerising. His fingers flew across the keyboard in a blur, accessing and inputting information before Natalya had even a chance to register it was there. The whole time he worked, his head shook ominously. As quickly as he started, his hands stopped, and he turned away from the laptop. 'Absolutely positive. It's definitely them. Finding the program is one thing, but tracking its source is quite another.' He didn't sound confident. Moments ago, the program was impossible to find. A look of doubt filled his pale face.

'What do you think happened?' asked Natalya. 'Do you think they caught Stanislav installing it?'

'That could explain how they knew it was there, but I tested it with all the detection software I had, and it avoided it all.'

'But Stanislav seemed so careful. Surely, he'd be too clever to get caught. I mean, he worked for the police all his life, so he would know a few tricks. Do you think we should try to call him?' Asked Natalya.

'No way. Let's say they have caught him; they'll have taken his phone. If we call him, they'll know exactly who we are, and where we are, in no time. They'll arrest us straight away. If he hasn't been caught, then we can only assume he will try to meet us here this evening as we arranged. All we can do is to make sure we're here if he turns up.'

'And if he doesn't show up?'

'Let's worry about one thing at a time. It may not come to that. The first thing we need to do is work out what was happening on that computer before the signal cut out. Can you find that last view we had on camera?'

They huddled over the small LCD viewing screen on the back of the camera as Natalya pulled up a paused image of the last few seconds of the transmission. The print was small, but readable:

Progress Report Summary – pre-upgrade
C-1 exposure levels beyond critical...
Current population of ground-zero resisting effects...
Transmission signal to be increased to maximum current capacity...
Imminent total effect inevitable...
Probability of effectiveness at increased levels: 99.9%...
Signal transmission strength increase scheduled for noon, February 20...

The colour drained from Natalya's face. 'That's tomorrow.'

Stepan rubbed his hands over his face. 'This looks bad. If these people are already getting a dose of C-1 that they class as beyond critical, and then they boost the signal, they have no chance. There's only a 0.01 per cent chance it will fail. Tomorrow, we'll be looking at a city of super-soldiers. That or mindless, murdering animals.'

'What on earth do we do now?' Natalya asked.

Stepan looked stunned. He was out of his depth. 'I say we stick to the original plan. Call NTV. Tell them everything. Get this story aired. The more people that know about it, the better, and the safer it will be for us. It'll cause mass panic, but they'll be forced to stop the transmission upgrade.'

Stepan shot back over to his laptop ready for the go-ahead.

'OK,' Natalya agreed. 'I don't think we have a choice. This has to be stopped, and I don't see any other way.'

Natalya knew that Anderi was already furious about skipping their last meeting. Now, a short while after he had put the phone down on her, she would have to call him to say that she would also miss the next one and had gone completely off task. She would be lucky if he heard her out, let alone took the story seriously, but this was the only course of action. The timeframe was too short, and there was no alternative.

Natalya dialled the NTV number on her mobile. It briefly rang before the automated switchboard cut in. She entered Anderi's extension number, willing it to be answered. For once, she actually needed to speak to him. The phone continued to ring. It would be impossible to leave a message about this; she needed him to answer. There was a click and the sound of Anderi's voice, but this time, it wasn't a recording.

'Natalya... I have to admit I didn't expect to hear from you before tomorrow. I trust you are still able to make our date?'

'Hi, Anderi. This is really important. I have something big and I need you to listen really carefully... Please,' she added, remembering who she was talking to.

'Err... OK then. Go on, I'm ready.'

'I've been making steady progress on the Lotus Flower project. But I've, erm, extended the project,' Natalya began.

'You've done what? Extended it? What are you on about? I was very clear on what I wanted you to cover. That and the importance of our progress meetings. You've gone and disregarded both, haven't you? Is it that difficult to follow simple instructions?'

'I'm really sorry I've had to tell you like this, but I think you're going to be really impressed with what I've got. I've been researching another story—'

'Another story...? Look, Natalya, your task was simple. Follow my instructions and produce my article. We were going to go far, you and me. I trusted you, allowed you time away from the office. Where are you? Luga? That's nothing to do with my project, is it? You've completely disrespected everything I've said.'

'I've still been working,' Natalya tried, 'but just not necessarily on the one project. Please listen and give me a minute to explain...'

She clumsily recounted her story from the beginning as Anderi quietly listened.

'The reason I'm putting this to you now, and in this way, is because of the last part of the progress report. They are upgrading the signal strength tomorrow, with 99.9% chance of it working. Whatever effect the Buzzer is going to have on these people, it's going to happen, and it's going to be tomorrow.'

The line was quiet for a while. 'What on earth are you going on about, Natalya? You're talking rubbish.'

'I'm not, Anderi. Please understand, I've done a lot of research into this. I know it's going to be big.'

'I honestly don't care, Natalya, if you've researched the greatest story ever published. It's not the one that you were instructed to cover. You're not a journalist, and you never will be. Not on my watch. In fact, I'm standing you up tomorrow night, that's if you were ever considering showing up to our meeting. Don't bother now, and don't bother coming back into work again either. Do you hear? You've let me down, Natalya.'

'I'm so sorry, Anderi, really, so sorry. I'm going to email you everything I have on the story I was telling you about. Please read it. I understand why you're sacking me.'

'You're still not listening, Natalya. I said I don't care...'

Natalya's temperature rose as she began to pace small circles around the floor. Anderi had a right to be angry, but he wasn't listening; he couldn't see the bigger picture. 'Look, please try to see past the fact that I didn't follow your instructions exactly. This is a huge story; people's lives are at stake. In fact, the welfare of the world. Please try to see.'

'You didn't follow my instructions exactly... you didn't follow them at all! You did whatever you felt like and played me for an idiot. You lied to me...'

'Anderi, for once, please try to see past your massive over-inflated ego and listen to what I'm saying. Read the email; run the story. We are running out of time...'

With that, the line went dead. Natalya fell onto the bed, still holding the phone to her ear.

Stepan got up and went to her. 'Now, I know I could only hear half that conversation, but I'm guessing that it didn't go to plan.'

Natalya, shaking, dropped the phone. 'I know that I was wrong to go off task, but I thought he would be able to see past that. Could we still send him the email with our research? Maybe once he's cooled down he might look.'

'Absolutely. I'll send it now. Do you think he listened to anything you were telling him?'

'I doubt it. Maybe I shouldn't have lost my temper with him. Maybe I could have talked him round.'

'You mean round the "massive over-inflated ego" bit?' Stepan smiled. 'From what I could hear, he deserved it. I'll send him everything we have. Surely he won't be able to resist the temptation to read it for long. Then he'll see what a fantastic job you've done.'

Natalya let out a long sigh and fell back on to the bed. Not only had Anderi rejected her story, now she didn't even have her old job to go back to. 'So what do we do next? Or is that it?'

Stepan sat on the bed next to her. 'I really don't know.'

Without NTV, and with so little time, they were powerless to stop the upgrading of the C-1 experiment. So many people going about their lives in the city all unaware of the danger. Those people didn't deserve this. Neither did the rest of the world, for that matter. Once the word was out that Russia had succeeded in its experiment, other nations would respond, wars would be started. This was so much bigger than just the city of Luga. Natalya rolled onto her side to look at Stepan. 'We can't let this just happen. If we could just buy a bit of time, just another day. Time enough to get the story out some other way.'

Stepan didn't respond.

Finally, Natalya stood up. 'I guess it's time to check out then; admit defeat.'

'We can't do that,' Stepan said. 'We can't just run away, knowing we are on the brink of this humanitarian disaster.'

'What more can we do?'

'You said it yourself: try to buy time so that we can find a way to publish the story.'

'Easier said than done. Just how do you think we should go about doing that?' Natalya snapped.

'Well...' Stepan considered, 'we need to stop the transmission, so maybe we could go for the source.'

Natalya threw him a dubious stare. 'And how do you think we could do that? We can't break into a secure government facility, and even if we did, then what?'

'We don't necessarily have to break in...' Stepan's brain churned through the problem. 'This is a long shot, one in a million...' He stood up, and next to Natalya. 'There are three transmitter locations. Two are in highly populated areas, so I'm assuming they will have excellent security facilities, secure communication pathways, and so on. The other, though, is in the wilderness near the village of Kirsino, about two and a half hours' drive from here. There, communications would be trickier, usually involving satellite links and cabling – a lot more vulnerable. If I could gain access to the network there, I have some very nasty programs on my system at work that could create just enough havoc to create a short delay to the transmission upgrade. It's not straightforward though. Even if we get into a position to gain access, it won't be like before when we could bypass the main security. This time we'll have to break through it.'

Natalya felt a tiny glimmer of hope. 'Really? You really think you could do that?'

'I have no idea until I get to see what level of security they have. I don't have time to write another new program so I'll have to download one from my system at work and modify it. There will also be a much higher chance of it being traced back to us. Are you willing to take the risk?'

'I honestly don't think we have a choice, do you?' She smiled. 'Anyway, given that I no longer have a job, I think a hike in the countryside would be lovely.'

'In that case, I'll find us a virus. If we leave soon, we can make it to Kirsino, upload the virus, and make it back here by nightfall. Then, hopefully, we will find Stanislav waiting for us in the bar.'

18

With Stepan at the wheel, they sped along the highway. It would be incredibly tough to find the transmission site in the thick woodland surrounding Kirsino, and they would need daylight to find it. The surrounding open fields turned into sparse forestland that became ever denser the further they travelled. Soon the trees were totally engulfing the road as it carved its relentless pathway through the ancient landscape. The multi-lane carriageway gave way to a single tarmac road, which itself was replaced by a loose surface track. The roads getting steadily worse as the Jeep became closer to its destination.

Stepan tried again, for a second time, to explain about the virus he had in store for the transmission site. 'It's a direct action virus. Much more aggressive then the last one. Once installed, the program will replicate itself exponentially, clogging up their entire system in seconds and leaving it unable to process even the simplest of tasks. They won't even be able to open Solitaire, let alone perform a signal upgrade. That, though, is the easy bit. We have to find the transmission site first.'

'So, where do you think we should start? I know you said that the area of this base has been triangulated to be in the vicinity of the village, but do you have any ideas on how to actually find it?'

Stepan thought about it. 'Erm, not exactly.'

'I know we could just hope to stumble upon it, but the old base wasn't exactly conspicuous, and I can't imagine that they would let their security levels slip when designing this one.'

Stepan inhaled a long deep breath. 'I have studied satellite photos of the whole area on the Internet, as have a lot of other people that have an interest in the Buzzer. Nobody has been able to find any signs of the new base—'

'What do you mean?' Natalya interrupted. 'We've come all this way and wasted all this time and the base probably isn't even here?'

'No, I'm not saying that. I've done my research; don't worry. There is definitely a signal being broadcast out of this area. Of that, there's no doubt. It's just not obvious from where.'

'Well that's encouraging. People have sat for days, studying piles of research and come up with nothing. We have a few hours and...' Natalya glanced at her phone to confirm her suspicions. 'No Wi-Fi signal.'

Stepan coughed a nervous laugh. 'That's about the crux of it, yeah.'

'Surely there must be a theory about what's going on? You've seen all the information; what do you think?'

'The most common theory is that the satellite photos have been manipulated in some way to hide it. That would explain how a complex as large as the one at Povarovo could be hidden, but I don't know. It doesn't sit right with me... I erm...'

'So do you have any theories that do sit right with you?' Natalya asked quickly.

There was a long pause from Stepan before he replied. 'No,' he said simply.

Natalya slumped back into her seat with a weary sigh. This was Anderi's fault. He had everything they needed to blow this story out the water, and expose it to the world. Only he chose not to.

Silence filled the Jeep as they journeyed on. Natalya scanned the surrounding area, peering into the passing trees, hoping to luck upon a clue that might help them. Finally, she spoke. 'I guess we'll have to try to find this place the old fashioned way.'

'Which is...?' Stepan asked.

'To find the nearest bar, make a few friends, and question a few well-oiled locals.'

Stepan let out a short laugh. 'You know, that's not a bad idea.'

'I know,' Natalya replied flatly.

The track had brought them out at a high point overlooking the clearing of Kirsino village. From their vantage point at the top of the crest, the village looked like a model. Quiet and picturesque, an idealistic rural community, nestling in a beautiful grassy glade scattered liberally with early wild flowers. Simple grey stone buildings stood next to a huge disused open-pit quarry that was filled with water. It created a tranquil glistening mirror that shimmered in the afternoon sunlight. They travelled down the hillside into the clearing.

'This all looks very pretty, Stepan, but where is everyone?' asked Natalya.

'It has been a while since I looked it up, but there should be thirty-nine people registered as living here.'

'And how many people do you think live here now?'

Stepan parked the Jeep up next to the water's edge and studied the buildings. 'Not many. Maybe we should go and investigate?'

'There must be someone around. You don't think it's been abandoned, do you?'

'I've no idea. Abandoned or evacuated? We should check it out.'

They approached the village on foot. There were signs of people everywhere: washing hanging out to dry on lines, well-kept vegetable gardens, but not a soul to been seen. The village was a ghost town. An eerie silence filled the air as they approached the first houses. The windows were all covered by thick curtains, blocking any signs of life.

Stepan crouched down at the side of the track. 'Look here, fresh footprints.'

'So where is everyone? I don't like this place, Stepan, it's creeping me out. As for finding a drunken bar around the next corner, I think we'll have about as much chance of finding a big red Buzzer destruct button.'

Stepan stifled a laugh. 'I really don't know, but I think you're right. There must be people here, but where?'

'It might look deserted, but I feel as if we're being watched.'

'You're right; perhaps they're shy and saw us coming,' he joked.

Only the sounds of their footsteps broke the peace as they continued to walk past the houses. Within the next few hours, the light would start to fade and with it, the chances of successfully finding the transmission site.

The layout of the village had little order, but the track they turned on to now was larger and more used. It stretched two hundred metres in a straight line, only wide enough for one vehicle, but dotted either side by low, single-storey houses.

Suddenly, Natalya froze. Instinctively, she reached out to grab Stepan, but with her gaze straight ahead, she clutched only at the air. At the opposite end of the track, stood a motionless, lone figure. The woman stood staring straight back at them, her loosely wrapped shawl blowing casually in the light breeze. Steadily, she began to turn away.

'Hello... Excuse me...' Natalya called, her voice ripping through the silence.

There was no reply. Slowly the woman began walking towards a gap between the houses next to the road.

Natalya called again. 'Excuse me...'

Still there was no response.

Natalya took another step forwards. She didn't want to give chase, but she couldn't let the only other person in the village just walk off. She took a few more steps, quicker this time, and called out again. 'Hello, please talk to us, we need your help.'

The woman was about to disappear between the buildings when Natalya broke out into a run. Her movements loud and cumbersome on the loose surface. Stepan had joined her, crashing along on the track next to her. The woman moved so gracefully in comparison. The folds of fabric rippling behind, dancing with motion. Without even so much as a sideways glance, she stepped between the houses and out of view.

Natalya and Stepan were only moments away from the gap. Natalya slowed her pace, cautious of what she would find. She reached the point where the woman had disappeared and stopped. Stepan drew level with her. The building's grey walls created a sheltered alleyway. Sparse clumps of grass sprouted up through the hard dirt, but otherwise, it was empty.

Natalya crouched down, breathing hard as she spoke. 'I think this is going to be harder than we first thought.'

'It seems so. I really don't know what we should do.'

'Why won't anyone talk to us?'

'At least we know there are people here. We've got to keep trying.'

'You're not with them, are you?' said a woman's harsh voice from behind.

Natalya and Stepan spun round and stumbled backwards. The woman had been close enough to reach out and touch them. Slowly, she raised her hand and lowered the shawl obstructing her face. She appeared to be of a similar age to Natalya. Strands of long brown hair fell forwards over her stern expression as she fixed them with staring brown eyes. 'You're not with them are you?' she asked again. 'I heard you talking.'

Stepan threw a quick glance at Natalya before shaking his head. 'I'm not sure who you mean, but it's just the two of us, I promise.'

The woman's face continued to scowl. 'You shouldn't be out here, not tonight. What are you doing here?'

Something in the woman's expression stopped Stepan from asking her outright if she knew where the base was. 'We're... erm... just travelling through,' he began, having to think on his toes. 'We had some car trouble.' He pointed vaguely in the direction of the Jeep. 'We saw the village and hoped we could find some help.'

'That's not going to happen tonight. I suggest you move on quickly and try the next village.'

'Normally, I would take your advice, but with the Jeep the way it is, I don't think that's an option,' Stepan replied.

Natalya stepped forwards, her eyes pleading. 'We're just so frightened in case we can't make it to the next town, and we end up stranded in the forest.'

The woman studied her for a moment, before turning back to Stepan. 'Well, you can't be out here, not tonight.'

'We don't want to be out here either,' Stepan said. 'Is there anybody nearby that could help us?'

'No. I don't think you understand: it's a curfew night.'

'A curfew night?' Stepan repeated.

'I've already said too much. You need leave this place now.'

Stepan thought for a moment, and then turned to Natalya. 'If we can't find any help, I'll have to call for a breakdown service. Out here, it will take them hours to get to us, but I don't think we have a choice—'

'No!' interrupted the woman. 'You can't wait out here, and don't call anyone else.'

'Well... if you have any other ideas...' Stepan said.

The woman looked back and forth suspiciously between the two, but said nothing.

'Please help us,' Natalya sniffed, her eyes somehow beginning to water.

'Well, if you can't leave, you need to get inside. You'll have to come with me. We can't do anything tonight. You can sort your car out tomorrow.'

'You're so kind. Thank you so much,' Natalya sniffed. 'We don't mean to cause you any trouble.'

'Just keep quiet and come with me.' The woman turned round and marched towards a group of houses.

Stepan raised an eyebrow as Natalya wiped her eyes on her sleeve. 'Nice touch,' he whispered.

'Thanks, but do you think we're doing the right thing? What about Stanislav? If he didn't get caught earlier, he'll be coming to meet us in our hotel tonight. Unless we leave now, there's no chance we'll make it back in time.'

'If he could see us now, what do you think he'd say if he knew we'd passed on this chance?' asked Stepan.

'I think he'd tell us to do what we could to stop C-1.'

'Me too. In fact, I'm positive that's what he would say. We can't leave now.'

'I know. I just wish we could get a message to him somehow, to let him know we haven't bailed out on him.'

'He'll know soon enough. After all this is over, we'll track him down and explain. He would want us to see this through—'

'Well, are you coming or not?' The woman had stopped to shout at them.

Natalya hooked her arm through Stepan's and shot him a smile. 'OK then, let's see this through.' They jogged to catch up.

The woman spoke again as she heard them approach from behind. 'This is my house, here. You need to come in right away; we've already been out far too long.'

The house was one of a pair, with a red roof and surrounded by a low brown picket fence. Its windows were all obscured by thick curtains. The woman strode up a short path and opened an old wooden door covered in peeling green paint.

'We can talk when you're inside, just please be quick,' she said, ushering them in with a sweep of her arm.

Natalya and Stepan entered straight into a living room, and removed their coats. The front door was closed with a bang behind them. Inside, the house was dark, the only light coming from a flickering oil lamp placed on a small wooden table. The woman pushed past and stood in the centre of the room, on a brown, threadbare carpet.

'Well, come in and sit down,' she said, pointing at an old floral sofa.

'I don't mean to pry,' Stepan began cautiously, as he lowered himself into the seat, 'but you mentioned this was a curfew night?'

'It doesn't happen very often, but yes. We don't ask any questions. All we know is that there's a government facility in the forest. We follow their curfews and, in return, they don't bother us. We don't go looking for trouble.' She settled down into an old, brown, wingback armchair. 'Anyway, I don't even know your names...'

'I'm Stepan,' Stepan began, 'and this is Natalya.'

'Well, it's nice to meet you both. I'm Maryana and I'm sorry for earlier. These nights are stressful for everyone in the village. When I saw you wondering around out there, I panicked. Nobody goes outside until the trucks come through. After that, it's back to normal.'

'Trucks?' asked Natalya reaching down to squeeze Stepan's hand.

'Yes, a convoy. Every time there's a curfew, they come through during the night.' Maryana studied her new guests. 'Have you two been together long?'

'No,' replied Stepan and Natalya simultaneously. They looked at each other and smiled. 'What I mean is... we're friends,' explained Stepan.

Maryana smiled. 'Right... Well, I was about to brew some tea, before I spotted the two of you running around out there. Can I offer you a drink?'

'That would be lovely,' replied Natalya, as Maryana disappeared into an adjacent room.

Stepan moved close to Natalya. 'Those trucks are our ticket to finding that transmission base,' he said in a quiet voice.

'I know,' whispered Natalya.

'We need to be ready to leave as soon as there's any sign of them.'

'Yeah, but I'll feel bad running out on her. She's taken us into her home.'

'She'll thank us when she realises what we're doing.'

'I guess so.'

'Here we are,' Maryana announced as she came back through the door. She carried a tray loaded with a steaming pot and three cups. 'I'm afraid I don't have much food to offer; I wasn't expecting guests, but I can offer you some *shchi* to warm you up.'

'That sounds wonderful,' said Natalya. 'With the day we've had, I'd quite forgotten how hungry I am.'

Maryana smiled. 'Stay where you are and I'll put that right.' She headed back out of the room.

Natalya whispered to Stepan, 'Can't we tell her the truth? She's being really nice.'

Stepan shook his head. 'We can't risk it. And it's not fair to get her mixed up in all of this.'

'So you've had a long day?' Maryana called through to her guests. 'Where are you heading?'

Natalya looked at Stepan. 'Over to you then…' she whispered, poking him in the side.

Stepan's concocted story seemed to satisfy Maryana's curiosity as they all talked casually into the night. The food had been good and the house was surprisingly cosy.

Natalya stifled a yawn. She had listened quietly as Maryana described her life in the village. A lifestyle that seemed all too similar to that of her own childhood. It wasn't long before her eyelids started to feel heavy.

All the while, Stepan listened out for any sign of the trucks. As he had recounted the story of living with his brother, Maryana seemed to grow visibly uncomfortable at the mention of family. Stepan quickly changed the subject, eager not to upset their host.

Natalya blinked slowly, moaning a huge yawn as her brain finally started to slow down. A tranquil wave of calm relaxation relieved the tension from her body. Her eyelids growing even heavier, even more relaxed...

19

Saturday, 20 February, 6.00 a.m.

Natalya awoke suddenly as Stepan shook her arm. 'Natalya,' he whispered. 'They're here, wake up!'

'I'm here, I'm awake,' Natalya said, rubbing her eyes. She looked around the room. Maryana was slumped in her armchair, snoring lightly.

'They just came out of nowhere,' continued Stepan. 'I was starting to think they weren't coming.' He pulled at Natalya's arm. 'Come on, we need to go now, before we lose them.'

Natalya pulled herself upright. Stepan was right: the sound of engines from outside was unmistakable.

He had already reached the door and was carefully manoeuvring the latch as quietly as he could manage. He gestured for Natalya go outside.

She took a quick glance at Maryana, who still slept soundly. 'Thank you,' she whispered, before grabbing her coat. She bundled it on before plunging out into the icy air.

Travelling along the main track through the village was a convoy of four large, canvas-backed military trucks. They surged along, floodlighting the way ahead with rows of high-powered headlamps.

Stepan was ahead, sprinting through the darkness towards where they had left the Jeep. Stumbling out into the cold, Natalya took chase, her legs still heavy, as if refusing to be woken fully from their peaceful sleep. She could see that the trucks were already leaving the village as their tail lights quickly disappeared.

Stepan reached the Jeep and quickly jumped into the driver's seat. 'Now, where do you think a convoy of four mysterious, unmarked trucks could be heading at this time of the morning?' he asked Natalya when she had caught up with him.

Natalya caught the glint in Stepan's eyes. 'I think we should find out, don't you?'

Stepan started the engine in one fluid motion. 'I do indeed,' he replied.

Stepan turned on the Jeep's sidelights and leapt the vehicle forwards onto the track. The main headlights would stand out a mile in the pre-dawn darkness and the less they were noticed, the better. It was hard work trying to avoid the potholes during the daylight but now it was almost impossible. Stepan cursed as a front wheel slammed into a chasm in the road surface. He battled with the steering wheel, trying desperately to keep the vehicle on course. The red tail lights ahead were becoming even more distant.

Bouncing along, they skirted around the outside of the village and then off into the dense forest. Visibility was poor as the surrounding trees absorbed the last of the moonlight, plunging them into inky darkness. From the tiny amount of light emitted from the Jeep's sidelights, Stepan could make out huge tree roots, spoil heaps, and fallen trees, all perilously close to the edge of the track. One small mistake in his steering could totally wreck the Jeep.

He finally caught up to the convoy, but kept his distance until the brake lights of the trailing truck indicated that they were slowing down. Stepan followed suit and turned off his lights. The trucks came to a halt about a hundred metres ahead of them, but they were difficult to make out in the darkness. Stepan stopped the Jeep. To one side of the last truck, were four silhouettes, backlit by a security light fixed on a post at the side of the road. The figures were gathered together, moving casually as if talking. One of them lifted up an arm to their head. Were they on the phone? Natalya checked her own mobile, surprised. 'Stepan. I've got a full signal, and it looks as if one of them up there has taken a call. What'd you think they're doing?'

He grunted an uncertain response. 'These surely have to be our guys. I can't imagine this is a popular commuting route. If we are close to the base, then it makes sense that they have set up mobile communication links.'

'If we are close to the base, then I can't see it anywhere. What you think we should do?'

'It's out there somewhere. Only, I doubt that we are going to be able to just follow these trucks in.'

'What you mean? So how do we get in?'

'I mean they're going to have security, aren't they? We're not going to be able to just tag along at the end of the convoy and drive right through.'

'I guess so. So what do we do?'

'I think we'll have to split up.'

'How's that going to help? That is not a good idea, Stepan. I thought we were doing this together.'

'I can't think of any other way. I'm going to go up there.' He pointed towards the trucks. 'I'm going to climb in the back of one with my laptop and hide until it's inside the base. Then I'll try to upload our virus. You are going to take the Jeep and get back to the hotel. As you've got your phone, make sure you tell as many people as you can about our story. It needs to be headline news around the world. There's a good chance I'll be caught, and if I am, with the story out and what we've done to stop it becoming common knowledge, they'll have to release me.'

'Stepan, there's no way I'm leaving you here, it's too risky. What if they don't let you go? What if something goes wrong? No, I'm coming with you.'

'And then what? Think about it. If we don't get into the transmission base then we're helpless to stop C-1. If we both go, and get caught, even if the virus works, it's only a matter of time before they try again. Then nobody will know what's going on. Nobody will know we're here. There'll be no one to bail us out.'

'I guess so.'

'I know so. Even if I do this, the chances of uploading the virus in time are slim, but it's all we've got.'

Stepan took Natalya's hand. It trembled slightly as her eyes glistened through the darkness.

'Will I see you again?' she asked softly.

'Of course you will. Once the world knows what's going on here, we'll be heroes. And they won't be able to hold the hero of Hero City prisoner for very long, will they?'

'I suppose not. Just promise me you'll be careful.'

'Don't worry, I've got this.' Stepan gave Natalya a reassuring smile as he picked up his laptop from the back seat. He unzipped his coat and tucked the computer inside before pulling the zip back up. 'The lengths I have to go to, to impress a pretty girl,' he said.

Natalya didn't have time to reply. Stepan was outside the Jeep. He shut the door as quietly as possible. Natalya leaned forwards, putting her hands on the dashboard, and peered into the darkness. She watched Stepan scurry off before he disappeared.

Stepan fixed on the trucks ahead of him as he crept along the edge of the track. The engines had been left running, drowning out the sound of his footsteps. The four drivers had still been mingling around the other side of the last truck, but he was still too far away to make out what they were saying. If he was careful, they wouldn't notice him. He decided to head for the lead truck, as it was the furthest from the group. He edged closer, making sure for as long as he could, that he could still see all four. He couldn't risk one of them wandering away and chancing across him. As he drew level with the last truck, he could make out their voices, over the drum of the engines.

'Once we were waiting here for an hour,' one man said. 'Well, they had better not keep us that long, or we'll drop everything off here. They can carry it the rest of the way themselves, for all I care.'

'I'd love to see that,' another replied.

Stepan moved quickly forwards. His footsteps on the grassy verge were silent, but he couldn't afford a trip or the snap of a fallen branch to give him away. He glanced back down the road to where Natalya waited in the Jeep. Both were invisible in the darkness. So long as she waited until the trucks moved on, she should be fine.

Stepan moved up to the lead truck. The canvas cargo area was secured by belt straps held tightly in position by large buckles about half a metre apart. He reached up and gave one a wiggle. On the side were two buttons. He pressed them firmly, and the belt slipped through. The gap it had left would be big enough for him to get through. He wasted no time as he reached up and hauled himself up, over, and inside. He turned to reach back through the gap, fixing the belt back as tightly as it would go.

Pulling a mini torch out of his coat pocket, he discretely shone it around the cargo area. In the middle stood a square wooden crate, about two metres in size. Stepan peered through the gaps between the panels. Inside, stood a smooth cylindrical shape, covered around the outside by large metal cooling fins. At the top were four connection points for high-energy cables. Stepan had seen similar equipment before, but nothing on this scale. This was an enormous transformer. The sort of component necessary when dealing with high-powered equipment. No doubt connected to the extra power required for the C-1 upgrade.

Suddenly, he heard the clunk of the cab door as it opened and then closed. After a moment, the truck surged forwards. Stepan spun around, thrown backwards by the sudden movement. He grabbed the side of the crate to steady himself. A short while later, the truck slowed again before making a sudden sharp turn. It was travelling much slower, and the surface of the road was considerably rougher. Stepan sat down, wedging his back up against the side of the crate as he countered the nauseous sway of the truck.

The convoy had left the main dirt road, turning down a tiny forest path, no more than a line of cleared foliage through the trees. Huge protruding tree roots and rocks restricted progress to a slow crawl as the four trucks stalked on down the path deeper into the trees.

From the light of the lead vehicle, a small concrete guardhouse came into view. The way ahead was barred by a huge sliding gate in a chain-link fence that stretched off into the forest and out of sight. The convoy halted as a guard approached the first truck with a rifle casually slung over his shoulder.

Stepan sat motionless, holding his breath, pleading for the truck to start moving again. There were voices outside but through the thick canvas sides of the truck he could only guess at what they were saying. There was nowhere to hide should the cargo area be inspected. He could do nothing but sit and wait.

20

Saturday, 20 February 6.30 a.m.

Directly beneath Stepan, the Kirsino Subterranean Base Commander, General Valentin, sat back in his comfortable chair. At the age of fifty-nine, he ought to have been coming to the end of his distinguished career, but after a lifetime in the army, he had proved to have an exceptional talent and efficiency. He was a man of small stature with a bald head and thick tortoiseshell plastic-rimmed glasses. In civilian society he would be easily overlooked. There was a loud knock at the door before his second in command, Captain Malinov, entered the room.

'The convoy has arrived, sir. They are requesting access at the main gate.'

'It's about time. This upgrade will be difficult enough without them being late,' he snarled back. 'Do all the papers check out?'

'Yes sir, everything is in order.'

'Then get them inside. We've lost enough time as is it.'

Captain Malinov lifted his two-way radio and gave the order to let the convoy proceed.

General Valentin usually felt stressed. The critical nature of his ongoing mission meant coping with pressure was a normal occurrence, but on occasions such as these, the tension was at boiling point.

'You know, the day I was offered this command,' he began, 'they told me to never judge or condemn the actions of our forefathers. That no matter how bad things became, their unmeasurable loyalty to the motherland is the reason we are still speaking Russian today. I disregarded that advice on the first day, and not a day has gone by since where I haven't cursed those fools for unleashing C-1 onto the world.'

'Had C-1 not been deployed at that time, we wouldn't have a country to defend, sir,' replied the captain. 'Surely that was worth the risk? Without it, the Nazis would have marched straight though to Leningrad, and 1941 would have been the year to mark the fall of Russia. There would be no last stand at Luga, no Hero City. The C-1 mission was a success, and the Nazis defeated.'

'And if it hadn't worked, and Russia had fallen, do you think that would have been worse than what C-1 brought to the world? Those men were playing with forces far beyond their control. Those areas of the primitive human brain had been suppressed through tens of thousands of years of evolution, they were not meant to be reopened. The modern human brain was quickly overpowered. All reasoning, forward thinking, and even speech, were lost. It was a crime against nature. You know I'm not a religious man, Captain, but C-1 is playing God. Nobody should have that power, and nobody should be subjected to its effects whoever they are, be them Nazi or Russian civilians in the wrong place at the wrong time.'

'It's true; there would have been collateral damage,' Malinov replied. 'All humans caught within the half a kilometre radius would have been affected, including the civilians and militia stationed in the city of Luga. But in return for their ultimate sacrifice, once all records of the C-1 project had been erased from history, they were awarded credit for the success of the operation.'

'A comfort to them now, I'm sure. I understand what was

at stake, Captain, but C-1 simply wasn't ready. There was no off switch. To create a device containing a piezoelectric crystal capable of producing a transmission with a five-hundred metre range that was powered by the Earth's own magnetic field... it has an unlimited power source... Could they not see what might happen, and what they were leaving for the next generation to clear up? They had no fail-safe. Even when they were working on its development, they needed a counter-wave signal like our Buzzer throughout the whole of the Kamera laboratory to protect the scientists from its effects – they knew the dangers. You say it was a success, but look at us now.'

Captain Malinov considered this. 'They effectively made an off switch. Suspending C-1 over a shaft tunnelled one kilometre down into the earth, and rigging explosive charges to detonate after a month to drop C-1 down into the depths of the earth. Collapsing the shaft around it should have sealed it away forever...'

'Only it didn't, did it, Captain? It may have taken forty years, but the effects of such a devastating weapon could not be so easily tamed. The Luga authorities dismissed the first cases as random violence and insanity in the 1980s. But after a sequence of such horrific massacres within the city's normally peaceful community, it was soon obvious they were out of their depth.'

'There was no way the C-1 development team could have predicted the device would have reacted in the way it did after it was sealed. The geology under Luga is unique. They could not have predicted that those elements in the bedrock would mimic the properties of the crystal and amplify the signal...'

'No, but it did. Soon, the people of Luga were to suffer the effects of C-1 again. Not only had a devastating weapon been unleashed without proper testing, but also the signal was being amplified exponentially. It's been over thirty years since those first cases, when the range of C-1 breached the one kilometre radius to emerge from its tomb. It's still gaining power even now, the signal becoming ever stronger. Our Buzzer counter-wave transmission is the only thing holding back the storm…What's the size of the area that would be affected by C-1 current levels according to our latest estimates?'

'Over a one thousand kilometre radius, sir. Half of Eastern Europe, including Moscow.'

'And do you have any idea how many people live in half of Eastern Europe?'

'An estimated fifty million, sir.'

'Fifty million people relying on us to get this right. We're on borrowed time, and the Buzzer is always one step behind. We simply can't keep up with the increasing power of C-1. Soon, the counter-wave will fall short. We have already amplified our own signal to longer tones, relocated the device closer to the source; even boosted its effects with two surrounding relay stations. But even with our upgrades, this is too big to keep as a national secret anymore. I am in command of the only defence against a weapon buried one kilometre under Luga that would turn any human within one thousand kilometres into a mindless, crazed, killing machine, and I'm running out of time. We need the rest of the world on our side.'

Malinov gave a long sigh. 'Maybe you're right, sir, but what about the global reaction when they find out the secret that Russia had been hiding for decades? And then who would rally the world together afterwards, once they know we're on the brink of the biggest humanitarian disaster the world had ever seen – and have been since 1941?'

'It's only a matter of time before the world discovers what we are doing here, anyway. Even amateur radio enthusiasts can hear our broadcast if they tune to the correct frequency. It won't be long before they discover its true purpose. It's almost as if they don't want us to achieve C-1 shutdown. C-1 is getting too powerful. We are protecting whole countries who have no idea how much danger they're in. Estonia, Lithuania, Latvia – even as far as Poland and Sweden – Stockholm and everything in between. Every human, young and old within range, devastated without prejudice… May I remind you, that this all started in 1921, with the C-1 project originally intended to increase human performance… I'll tell you one thing: the level of human performance required to clear up the mess they have left us in now is above anything I've ever known. At least on that part they were successful.'

'And it is our duty to continue to protect those countries, sir. May I remind you that we need this upgrade operational in the next twenty-four hours.'

'You're right, Captain. Once again, we are to place another plaster over a wound capable of consuming so many. Are we prepared to commence?'

'Absolutely, sir. The automated relay stations at both Pskov and Kolpino have both been prepared to receive the amplified signal, and we are ready to install the new components here as soon as they are unloaded. Everything is awaiting your command.'

'Right, well let's set about buying ourselves a few more months and get this upgrade online.'

***

Natalya sat huddled in the Jeep, surrounded by the deep dark of the night. Stepan had sacrificed himself and she had done nothing to stop him. She needed to get a grip, she needed to do her job and break the story to save him, not to mention the city of Luga.

The convoy still waited ahead, but there was no time to waste. Moving her seat back as far as it would go, she slid down into the foot well, taking her mobile phone with her.

The email that Stepan had prepared earlier and sent to Anderi containing all the information and evidence of their project would still be available. If Anderi and NTV weren't interested in the story, then she would need to find someone that was. She worked quickly to forward the email to every media contact she had in her address book. When that was completed, she continued to look up the contact details of other press offices. Newspapers, television, national and international. Natalya sent the email to them all.

A rumble from outside caused her to pause and take a glance outside. The trucks were moving off. Stepan was heading into the lion's den and it was down to her to help him out. She returned to her phone; the more contacts she made, the better. In the scramble to report a big story, the media world would move quickly to be the first to break the news.

21

Finally, the voices stopped and Stepan heard the sound of footsteps retreating. The truck made a slow surge forwards and Stepan breathed deeply. He pulled his laptop in front of him and booted it up.

The gates retracted and the convoy began to file through the gap into the forest beyond. In the beam from the trucks headlamps, thick tree trunks cast long shadows down the path and across to a large, shining metal structure ahead.

The building resembled a giant hanger that had been sunk into the ground, leaving only the top two metres of its domed roof visible. The surrounding pine trees had been left undisturbed so that they continued right up to its edge. Their large, needled branches spanned out overhead forming a thick natural roof. The path led straight to the building, dipping down into the ground, where a bright light from inside shone out through two huge open doors.

Stepan felt a roll in his stomach as the truck followed the decline of the path. Through tiny gaps at the base of the canvas sides, shafts of bright light shone through into the cargo area. The sounds of bustling activity came from all around as the sound of the trucks engine went from a dull thrumming to a loud, echoing roar. He tried his laptop, searching for available networks. The computer scanned for a few seconds before one secure local area network popped into view.

'OK, let see what we've got,' he breathed, as he attempted to connect.

The laptop whirred before displaying an elaborate gold crest on a light blue background. It was the same arrangement that was on the front of the folder they had retrieved from the base at Povarovo. In the centre of the screen was a black box with four white spaces, the first filled by a blinking cursor.

Stepan thought for a moment. It was a four-digit access code. That seemed simple enough, however he was more than aware of the ten-thousand possible combinations there could be. Stepan began a frenzy of activity on the laptop's number pad, starting with the standard obvious arrangements. Each attempt he entered was blocked, clearing the figures and offering another chance to re-enter the pass code. Stepan cast his mind back to the four-digit numbers relevant to the project. The frequency of transmission: 4625; the years that the coded voice messages were broadcast: 1997, 2002, 2006; the date the transmission site was moved: 5910. He tried them, but all were incorrect.

He sat back, knowing he was on borrowed time. They would be monitoring the network and it wouldn't be long before they realised that the unidentified IP address of his laptop was trying to gain access. He thought hard, recalling any figures relevant to when C-1 was first deployed. The year 1941. Stepan tried it – no good. He wiped away beads of sweat off the palms of his hands. More specifically, the date, 29 June 1941. It was the wrong number of figures, but he tried various combinations anyway, all with no luck.

His pulse was accelerating as tinnitus filled his ears with a disorientating rush of sound. He was starting to panic. The activity outside was getting more intense; it wouldn't be long before they started searching the trucks. He needed to crack this code and yet his mind was refusing to think logically.

His hands were shaking. Taking a deep breath, he cleared his thoughts. He thought of Natalya. She would still be in the woods. She was relying on him to get this right. Stanislav, too, back in Luga. In fact, unknowingly to them, the whole population of the city was depending on him. He needed to be more systematic. He thought back to the coded messages that had been broadcast from the Buzzer over the years, but it was impossible to remember any of the specific details in the broadcasts. He could only recall the very first message from this new transmission site. It had been the strange music, 'The Dance of the Little Swans' from *Swan Lake*. This had assumed to be a random choice of content to test the new transmission equipment. Nobody had even come up with a theory as to why that particular song had been chosen.

Stepan retrieved his mobile phone from his pocket. If Natalya's phone had coverage earlier due to the base's boosted communication links, then his should do too. Its little screen shone back at him with a full signal. With trembling fingers, he typed the name into the search engine. The results appeared instantly. '… A famous dance from Tchaikovsky's ballet, *Swan Lake*. Created to imitate the way cygnets huddle and move together. From the ballet's second act, fourth movement of No. 13.' Stepan read the last sentence again. He typed the numbers 2,4,1,3 onto the laptop.

The screen burst into life, filling with icons and menus, all layered over the large golden crest. He released a huge sigh and began working on the laptop with amazing speed. His mind focused only on uploading the virus.

Shouts echoed from outside. Even through the canvas, it was easy to hear what they were saying.

'The trucks… The signal is coming from the trucks. Search them all. Get those sides open, now!'

Stepan entered the final command to begin the upload. A small blue bar raced along the monitor as the percentage counter shot up to show progress. From outside the truck, a frenzy of activity began, as the canvas covering was being worked loose on both sides. He was surrounded; there would be no escape. He glanced back at the laptop. The blue bar had disappeared, to be replaced by a short message, 'Installation Complete'.

He only had seconds, but that was time enough to access one more program. A program always installed on his company's laptops as a last resort should a system ever fall victim to cyberattack. It was designed to wipe everything clean, to destroy all contents down to the last morsel of coding. Stepan ran it now. The laptop monitor flickered for a second and went blank.

The cargo area filled with light as both sides of the canvas were simultaneously flung aside. Three men stood either side of Stepan, with rifles trained directly at his head. Slowly, Stepan rose to his feet and raised his hands.

A voice screamed at him to freeze. From either side, a man leapt into the cargo area and pulled his legs out from under him. Stepan slammed face down onto the floor of the truck, hitting his head hard. A well-placed knee in the back prevented any movement as a third man jumped into the truck and frisked him violently.

Stepan didn't struggle. He lay perfectly still, not daring to give the men an excuse to use their weapons. His arms were drawn behind his back and a sharp plastic cable tie, drawn mercilessly tight, locked his hands together.

＊

Deep underground, on the main computer servers of the Kirsino subterranean military base's internal network, ran a small program, completely disguised as a harmless, inanimate fragment of coding. As its installation completed, the program activated. It replicated once, and then the two programs replicated again to make four. It took less than a second for the exponential growth to complete its task. Every connected device within the base promptly stuttered and froze. All the processes governed by the overwhelmed system crashed. From that moment, the Buzzer's relentless broadcast fell silent.

22

Natalya placed her mobile phone down by her side. She had spread the story as wide as she could, and now it was time to move. Once the military found out they had been sabotaged, she ought to be as far from here as possible. Natalya slid over into the driver's seat, pulled the Jeep round and headed back out of the forest. Although Stepan had told her to drive back to the hotel, she decided to stop at Kirsino village first. After everything that Maryann had done for them both, Natalya needed to tell the woman the truth. It was the least she could do.

Driving as carefully, but as quickly, as she could, Natalya's thoughts returned to Anderi. This was all his fault, and if Stepan had been caught, that was all Anderi's fault too. All she had wanted was some recognition for her work. If he had given her that promotion, she would still be at home now. If only he had just aired the story…

A tune came quietly from her mobile phone. It was an incoming call. Without taking her eyes off the road, she grabbed it quickly. 'Hello?'

A familiar voice replied. 'Hi hun…'

'Anderi! I'm so glad you called.' Natalya was shocked at how genuinely she meant it. 'I really need your help.'

'Well, my dear, it seems as if you have made quite a name for yourself this morning, informing every competitor imaginable every last detail of our story. What on earth do you think you're doing?'

'Anderi, I'm in big trouble here. I have a whole city of people moments away from mass mutilation that could lead to goodness knows what sort of international crisis. I tried to tell you. I contacted you before, but you weren't interested. I had to take matters into my own hands.'

'Of course I was interested. I just needed a little more time to come to terms with the information.'

'You weren't, Anderi. You told me you didn't care, and, as I remember, you sacked me.'

'Not at all. I think this is all a big misunderstanding. I've called to congratulate you on your fantastic work, and as you are *my* journalist, we need to come up with a plan to work together to cover the story.'

'That's rubbish and you know it, but at this moment, I don't care. Air the story. If I can help you, I will.'

'That's my girl. I'm on my way into the office now to work on our coverage. This is going to be everywhere. Leave it to me.'

'Thank you, Anderi. I know you're only doing this for your own career prospects, but I do really mean that. Thank you…' A short burst of interference crackled on the line, but Natalya choose to ignore it. 'I'll keep you informed with any new developments as they unfold.'

There was no reply from Anderi, although the line remained connected. There came another buzz of static, and then another sound. Not interference. More like the sound of bubble wrap being twisted, straining and creaking as its air bubbles popped slowly the tighter it was wound.

The phone's silence was finally broken, not by Anderi, but by the screech of car tyres. The screaming rubber on tarmac seemed to last an impossibly long time, building ever louder until finally it ended with a sickening crunch.

'Anderi? Are – are you OK?' Natalya's voice trembled as her face flushed with heat. There was no answer. 'Anderi, are you still there? Is everything all right?' She heard only silence, as she steered the Jeep with one hand and tried to focus on the road ahead.

A soft panic began building inside her, starting low in her stomach and aching outwards, filling more of her body the longer the silence lasted. Then the earpiece burst into noise, erupting with blood-curdling chaos. Every follicle on Natalya's body tingled as the sound gathered into the crazed scream of a wild beast as if being gutted alive.

She threw the phone down onto the passenger seat, but the inhumane screeching continued, lasting longer than any breath ever could. With a trembling hand, she reached over and disconnected the call.

Her chest muscles tightened, squeezing all the air out of her lungs. As she gasped for breath, the blood drained from her head, and the world started to spin wildly. Breaking sharply, she threw open the door of the Jeep and sucked in the cool morning air. The spiralling world gradually started to steady. She took another large gasp, but her insides clenched like a taut fist, sending her sprawling forwards out the vehicle, gagging and choking. The remaining contents of her stomach emptying out on to the ground.

Still trembling, and with the rancid taste of acid in her mouth, she attempted to focus her thoughts. Something was very wrong in Moscow, but what? She climbed back into the Jeep, leaving the door open, in the hope that more fresh morning air would help to clear her head, and picked up her mobile phone from the passenger seat. A scrolling line of text across the display read: 'No signal'. She turned it off, then back on again, but it rebooted to display the same message.

It didn't make any sense. Whatever had happened to Anderi, Natalya still had a job to do, and Stepan would need her help. She would continue on to the village at Kirsino, out of this wretched forest and back to civilisation. Gathering herself together, she closed the door and drove along the remainder of the track until it ran uphill towards the crest where she and Stepan had first overlooked the pretty village of Kirsino.

23

Kirsino transmission base was a centre of flawless clinical efficiency. Only the very brightest and most loyal had the privilege of working in the vast subterranean complex, and General Valentin expected the very best out of every one of them. The control room was its nerve centre. Glaring white walls surrounded five banks of computers, each home to an operator entrusted with tasks of monitoring, maintenance, and research.

At this moment, all activity in the room lay dormant. The usual drone of conversation silent, replaced only by the hum of dozens of computer cooling fans. The operators remained at their posts, staring helplessly at collections of blue error messages that had accumulated one after another in quick succession, until every system had simultaneously crashed.

With the countermeasure down, they should have succumbed to the effects of C-1 instantly, yet every occupant of the room remained unchanged. Nobody moved. The finest scientists Russia had to offer sat terrified that the smallest action may destroy the delicate balance and plunge them all into the abyss forever.

In an instant, the silence was shattered. The double entrance doors flew open and smashed into the walls as a furious General

155

Valentin hurtled through, closely followed by Captain Malinov. Every occupant of the room held their breath as their snarling, pink-faced leader marched his way to the front of the room to make his address.

'As it is obvious to you all, we have been the subject of a terrorist attack.' Nobody spoke as the general paused for breath. 'All of our primary systems have been compromised. All communications and processes, including transmission of the counter-wave, have terminated. We have total and catastrophic shutdown.'

Murmurs swept across the room as questions rippled through the operators. Finally, a voice spoke up from the crowd. 'How is it that we are all still here? Have we been nullifying and working to combat a weapon that has been a dud all along?'

General Valentin's face flushed further at the interruption. He had never been addressed in such a manor in his whole career, and certainly not from one under his own command. He looked out at the terrified group, scanning the faces to identity who would dare to speak so out of turn. Their frozen expressions gave no one away.

Valentin decided to continue. 'Upon construction of this base, the engineers equipped it with a fail-safe mechanism should such a catastrophic system failure arise. A system with just enough power to secure the base and immediate area. In 1931, the original Kamera laboratory conducting C-1 development allowed scientists to work on the project unaffected, by transmitting a counter-wave similar to the one that we do today throughout the compound. In 1938, this original counter-wave generator was decommissioned. It was removed and replaced by a more sophisticated mechanism and has lay dormant, in storage, until the construction of this base.

'It was decided to recommission this relic by moving it here to act as a fail-safe device. The instant our main transmission failed, it initialised to a totally independent secondary system.

But we are far from in the clear. The device was lashed together in 1931, meaning it is still lashed together, but it *is* the only thing keeping our minds our own, comrades.

'As it stands, every human mind within a one thousand kilometre radius of Luga has been exposed to the full effect of C-1. Our fail-safe is protecting us. It is emanating from this base at its centre, covering our whole complex and the immediate surrounding woodland. If we set foot outside its invisible boundary, we will also be affected, our minds lost to C-1. There is no cure. While operational, the device will keep us secure, but once a person has been exposed, it will not correct the damage done.

'In short, we are cut off. Isolated in a five-kilometre island with no communication or links to the outside world. Between safety and us will be hundreds of kilometres of hostile territory filled with people who have been exposed to the full force of the unrestricted C-1 transmission. Their condition after exposure… well, shall we say, is unknown.'

Valentin turned to his second in command. 'Get them to fix what they can. I need a status report and damage assessment on my desk within the hour. In the meantime, get that terrorist into the interview room. Now!'

24

The first light of dawn began to creep steadily over the horizon, bathing the landscape in its welcoming orange glow. The mighty pine trees of the rolling forest shimmered as frost-covered pine needles sparkled in the low morning sun.

Natalya slowed the Jeep to a halt as she reached the summit. The road ahead began to fall away, swooping down into the grassy glade of Kirsino village. Although still a kilometre away, from her vantage point she could see out over the whole extent of the village. Its houses looked tiny, all joined together by the dull lines of dirt tracks.

This time, however, the village looked very different. There were people everywhere, a churning little community bustling around the buildings. Maryana would be down there too. There was no doubt she would be angry about her guests' deception, but once she understood what they were really doing, then maybe she would help. Natalya started to move the Jeep forwards, but something made her look back at the scene, and she stopped. The people's movements... something looked off, but it wasn't clear exactly what. From this distance, it was hard to see real detail, but the villagers were moving oddly. They seemed hunched over and lumbering. Maybe it was a trick of the light, but the people were out of proportion. For a start, they were much too tall.

Natalya continued to stare silently down on the village, unaware that the limit of the safe zone created by the subterranean base's fail-safe device fizzed like an invisible barrier only a couple of metres ahead of the front of the Jeep. Unbeknown to her, any human who stepped outside of its range would immediately succumb to the full effects of C-1.

She recalled that there had been rumours of C-1 causing physical alterations to its victims, but if Stepan's plan to stop it had failed and the upgrade had taken place, how was it affecting people here in Kirsino? Not to mention what was happening in Moscow. Natalya looked down at her hands on the steering wheel. Why was it not affecting her? She looked up and watched the villagers continue to lumber slowly between the buildings. Whatever had happened, the evidence in front of her was unmistakable. In addition to the bodily changes, it had also been reported that those affected would be filled with uncontrollable aggression and range. Natalya couldn't risk confrontation. She couldn't risk going into the village. Stepan might need her help, and he was now in the only place where she may find answers. She would have to go back.

She reversed the Jeep and turned around. The rising noise of the engine caught in the wind and drifted down to the village below.

One of the creatures stopped its aimless rambling, and turned its head in the direction of the sound. It stood nearly nine feet tall with huge arms that rolled with swollen muscles. With its back unable to support the extra upper body weight, it hunched over, planting its massive fists in the ground ahead to act as stabilisers. Its skull had twisted as it had enlarged, caving in on one side, and paralysing the muscles. The result had caused its face to slide downwards, leaving the right eye drooping and the lid falling permanently closed. Its lower lip had fallen away, exposing a jaw where a row of huge twisted teeth protruded out like yellow tusks.

It had noticed something at the top of the hill, the flash of early morning sunlight reflecting off a moving vehicle. It only lasted for a second, and then was gone. The creature took a few steps forwards, but the glinting light didn't return. It waited, and then turned its head to look at the other creatures milling around the buildings. None of them seemed to have noticed it. It turned back to the crest making a low grunt, then suddenly began bounding forwards, using its huge arms as well as its legs to haul itself forwards at speed like a great ape.

In no time, the creature arrived at the summit of the hill, but the source of the reflection was nowhere to be seen. It sat and sniffed at the air. It smelt differently; it smelt... dirty. The creature hadn't noticed it before. Hauling itself back to its feet, it began circling. The smell was centred in the area but a vapour led off down the other side of the hill. The creature took one last look back towards the village. The others hadn't reacted to it leaving. Turning back, it took another sniff to confirm the direction and bounded off to follow the trail.

Natalya drove back through the forest as fast as the road conditions would allow her. She had done what she had needed to and Anderi had confirmed that the media had received her story and were taking it seriously. The C-1 experiment would be common knowledge, and her and Stepan's part in stopping it would make them famous. The base would be aware of the media attention by now. She would walk right up there and demand to speak to Stepan before they made things worse for themselves. Maybe then, she could find out what was happening with the rest of Russia.

The journey to the base seemed shorter in daylight. When she reached the place where they'd stopped earlier, a thought came to her. What if Stepan hadn't been caught? Perhaps he was wondering around in the forest, right now, trying to find a way out. If she drove right up to the base, any guards would probably arrest her and take the Jeep. But if Stepan was still out here, he would be stranded. It was a long shot, but she couldn't take the risk. She looked around, and carefully moved the vehicle off the forest road, driving a few metres towards a cluster of smaller trees. Here the cover from their branches reached lower. She parked the Jeep behind them, and arranged a collection of fallen branches to conceal it further. If Stepan was in the area, there might be a chance that he would come across it.

Leaving the doors unlocked and the keys in the ignition, Natalya made her way down the narrow path following the same route the trucks had earlier. She continued until her way was blocked by a high sliding gate with coils of razor wire wrapped tightly across its top. A tall chain-link fence continued on both sides as far as the eye could see through the trees. To one side of the gate, stood a small grey guardhouse, with a tiny barred window, and open metal door. Beyond the gate, stood the base entrance. It was similar to the outbuilding at the Povarovo base, but much larger. It looked like an aircraft hangar that had been partially sunk into the earth, with its huge double doors firmly closed.

Natalya took a deep breath and strode towards the guardhouse, but there was no sign of any activity. 'Hello there,' she called, waiting for a response. 'Hello… is there anybody there?' she called again as she approached.

There was still no reply. She peered inside. The guardhouse resembled a small office. A desk was pushed against the wall under the window, while on the other side stood a water cooler and an empty weapons rack. She entered slowly, but it was obvious that the room was empty. On the desk sat a control panel containing two buttons. No doubt to manoeuvre the gate. She pressed both of them, but there was no response from either.

A few seconds later, the silence of the forest was broken by a series of loud crashes coming from the direction of the forest road. Natalya poked her head out of the door, the sound was getting louder. Through the shadows of the forest canopy, a large, lumbering figure approached. It moved quickly, propelling itself forwards by swinging its enormous arms and then running a few steps. It then brought its arms back to repeat the process. Natalya stared in disbelief at the huge creature and without hesitation, ducked back into the guardhouse, pulling the door closed behind her. A large bar on the back of the door served as the lock, and she slid it smoothly across. Dropping to the floor she scrambled under the desk, drawing her legs up tightly, squeezing into the cramped space.

Outside the guardhouse, heavy footsteps crunched closer, then ceased. Natalya froze. She could sense the creature looking in for her through the window. She would be out of view, so long as she stayed where she was, but that thing had seen her close the door. It knew she was inside. She held her breath while she listened.

The silence seemed to last forever before she heard the creature moving again. She let out a breath; perhaps it was moving away. Suddenly the guardhouse door shook as it took a heavy hit. Dents buckled inwards just above the sliding bolt, as the creature pounded its fists against the door. Natalya winced at the sound of creaking metal, but the door held firm.

Huddled underneath the safety of her desk, there was nothing she could do, but wait it out. She would hide until the creature hopefully got bored and moved on.

25

Stepan found himself locked in a holding cell about three metres square. His possessions had been confiscated, but at least his bonds had been cut. The glare of the fluorescent light off the white walls dazzled his eyes to the point of being painful. He sat on a low shelf-bench, and stared out through a railing of iron bars. On the opposite side of the corridor was another cell, identical to his. Inside, huddled in the corner of the room was a figure, his head bowed low. Adjacent to both cells was an office. Two guards sat inside, behind a thick glass window next to a doorway providing the only way in and out.

'Hey,' hissed Stepan to the figure opposite. He didn't respond. 'Hello? You OK in there?'

The figure raised his head slowly from his knees and fixed Stepan with a puzzled stare. 'Stepan?' he replied.

'Yes… How do you…? Stanislav? Is that you?'

The old man stretched his legs straight, continuing to stare blankly at Stepan.

'Stanislav, what are you doing here?'

'They caught me. I managed to install the program, but it must have been discovered and traced back to me before I had a chance to leave. After they arrested me, they brought me here.

Listen, do you know what's going on? This is really important; we've got things very, very wrong—'

'Don't worry,' Stepan interrupted with a smile. 'Everything will be OK. We did it. We found the evidence of C-1 that you were looking for. There was a huge upgrade scheduled for today. We had to stop it, so we came here, and I uploaded a virus, which has crashed everything. No upgrade, no more Buzzer. Everything stopped. They'll fix it eventually, but Natalya's out there now breaking the story to the world. This whole thing will already be global news, and once they know what we've done, how we stopped it, we'll be heroes. We'll be out in no time.'

Stanislav didn't move his body, but his face filled with a look of horror.

'Stanislav, did you hear me? I said, we did it. The Buzzer – C-1 – it's over.'

Stanislav stared with wide eyes. 'Is there any way to stop what you've done? We need to stop it. We've got it wrong…'

'Stop it? No, it's already activated. It's done. What do you mean, 'We've got it wrong'?'

'For years, I thought the Buzzer was C-1, but it wasn't. The Buzzer was the only thing keeping us safe from C-1. Stop that and it's the end of us all. Why didn't I see it before? They told me everything. It all makes sense now. Why did I interfere? I even had a stupid website to tell as many people as I could, to try to bring the Buzzer down. Doomsday Conspiracy, I called it. Well, it's doomsday, all right, and I'm the cause.'

'Stanislav, I don't follow. What are you saying?'

'I'm saying that we're the bad guys. All that time I had to figure it out and I didn't – not even when a reporter from Moscow offered to research and publish the whole story. It couldn't have been easier. All they wanted was an interview from me. I was already visiting the city at the time and had one more night before returning home. It was as if it was meant to be. Everything was set – the time, the place. They would have researched the project and discovered the truth way before all of this happened. But, after all that, do you know what I did? Nothing. I didn't even show up for the meeting. I'm a paranoid old fool.'

A loud slam sounded from across the room as the two guards burst out of the office and strode over to Stepan's cell.

'Stand up, now, and put your hands on the wall!' one barked.

Stepan did as he was told, but turned his head to look at Stanislav. He had drawn his knees up to his chest and turned to face the wall.

'Don't worry, it'll all be OK,' Stepan called out. 'Everything went to plan. Just hang on and we'll be out of here in no time.'

One of the guards entered his cell and punched him hard in the stomach.

'Did I tell you to talk?' the guard shouted. 'You don't do anything in here unless I tell you to. Hands behind your back.'

Stepan's hands were once again bound tightly together behind him. The guards pushed him forwards roughly as Stanislav began rocking back and forth on his cell floor.

'We've done something terrible today,' Stanislav called, as Stepan was taken past his cell. 'What we've done is unforgivable. We've got it so wrong. Everything we know has gone.'

The guards hauled Stepan into a maze of barren corridors. He stumbled along, his head swimming as he tried to make sense of Stanislav's words. Every so often, a shove on the shoulder forced him to change direction around the many twists and turns until they arrived at a small room. It was a similar size to his cell, dimly lit, and with solid, windowless, walls.

In the centre of the room, General Valentin and Captain Malinov sat behind an otherwise empty table. Stepan was forced to sit in a chair opposite them.

'Let's start with your name?' Malinov spat, as if trying to rid himself of a bad taste.

'Stepan Litvin.'

'And with which organisation are you associated?'

'Organisation? I'm not with any organisation?'

The captain's face contorted into a sly smile. 'You expect me to believe you're a freelance terrorist?'

Stepan recoiled. 'I'm not the terrorist here. What you people are doing to innocent civilians… You're the terrorists.'

Malinov shot the general a fleeing glance before continuing. 'The damage your actions have caused is immeasurable. I can only assume that you intended to take your own life. That, however, is where you have failed. That failure leads us all to this point. Your responses now decide where we go from here. I suggest you think very carefully about what you are about to say—'

'Hang on just a minute…' Stepan interrupted, leaning forwards as far as his bonds would allow. 'I caused immeasurable damage? Your project here is sickening, not to mention against every international law written. When this gets out, and it will, there will be serious repercussions.'

The captain paused. It felt as if they were having two different conversations. He tried again, his voice firm and level. 'Are you aware of the damage your actions have caused?'

Stepan squirmed in frustration. 'Damage to you maybe.'

'To me? I'm one of the only people you haven't damaged. We have estimated fifty million people have succumbed to the result of your actions.'

Stepan felt a surge of light-headedness. Grey patches appeared in his vision. 'What do you mean "fifty million people"?'

Malinov turned to Valentin. The old general's expression had remained unchanged from the beginning. Without speaking, he simply nodded his head. The captain turned back to face Stepan. 'You really don't know, do you?'

Stepan's face paled.

'Congratulations, Stepan Litvin,' Captain Malinov began. 'You have just conducted the largest act of terrorism the world has ever known…'

26

Stepan's feet skimmed the floor as he was dragged back along the corridors. He could only recollect fragments of what the captain had explained to him about the devastation that had followed his disruption of the Buzzer, but it was clear: his actions had unleashed the effects of C-1 on the world. He was the most wanted terrorist in the world.

After his ties had been removed, a rough shove propelled him forwards into his cell. Behind him, he heard the door slide shut with a hefty *clunk,* followed by the sound of the lock turning. Underneath the dazzling glare, he rubbed at his wrists before dropping his head into his hands. In trying to save a city, he had shut down the only protection from the weapon he was trying to destroy. 'Only it isn't just a city,' Stepan whispered to himself. 'It's fifty million people.'

There would be no international media knocking on the door of the base. No hordes of people demanding to see the hero who had saved them to be released. Nobody was coming. His story would be untold. And what of Natalya? There was no way she could have made it. He closed his eyes, and saw her face. She would have been exposed to the full force of the C-1 transmission. What would it have done to her? He felt tears well up in his eyes. Maybe the most merciful outcome would be for it to have killed her.

'Oh, Stanislav, what have we done…?' Stepan turned round and looked across the corridor. The cell was empty. He ran to the bars, and waved through them in order to attract the attention of the guards, who had disappeared back into their office. 'Hey!' he called out. 'Hey! You in there! Where's the guy in the other cell?'

One of the men looked up, then, with a sly smile, sauntered over to the door and opened it. 'Which guy you mean?' he mocked.

'You know who I mean. The old guy in the cell over there.'

'Oh, your friend, was he?'

'What you mean, "was he"?'

The guard laughed. 'Well, when a terrorist responsible for killing millions of innocent people tells me he wants to rid the world of his disgusting existence, who am I to stop him? Maybe I even gave him a little push, so to speak… Let me know if you want to join him, won't you? There's another bag in here with your name on it. Oh, by the way, he left you this.'

The guard pulled a crumpled ball of paper out of his pocket, and dropped it at Stepan's feet. 'If you need a pen and paper, let me know, won't you?' he called out on the way back to his office.

Stepan picked up the note as if it was a coiled viper. Carefully, he flattened the page against the wall of his cell, turned around to lean against it, and started to read.

These are my last words. For what my apologies to the world are now worth, I offer my utmost. No amount of regret can ever undo the atrocities that I have set in motion, but let it be known, I shall spend eternity in repent, forever seeking forgiveness for my actions. The only thing left for me is to rid the world of my burden for I can ask no redemption for my crimes. Please let it be known, my actions were not brought about through malice, but simply the misguided, paranoia of a foolish old man.

Stanislav Novac

Stepan's heart beat quickly as a wave of emotion caused his legs to turn to jelly. He slid to the cold stone floor, where he sat alone with his thoughts. He was just as responsible as Stanislav, if not more. He placed the note on the floor next to him. Tears welled up as he dropped his head in his hands. Maybe what Stanislav had done was the only right course of action. Maybe he too owed the world a similar debt.

***

Captain Malinov stood in General Valentin's office and lowered the clipboard containing the status report he had just recounted to his commanding officer.

'So basically, that's it, sir. We are in full lockdown. Everyone from the surface level has been brought in below ground, and all external doors have been secured. No one in or out.'

'That's good. And the condition of our operating systems?'

'Everything processed by the central server is gone. The counter-wave itself, but also, research and development, transmission monitoring, all communications, surface surveillance, and security—'

'OK, Captain, I get the idea, thank you. And we have everyone working towards rebooting the main server?'

'Around the clock, sir.'

'The likelihood of success is?'

'Virtually nil, sir. The hardware has been heavily corrupted. Without a complete replacement, it's almost an impossible task.'

'And the primary signal generator? What's the chance of getting that back online?'

Malinov didn't answer. His expression told the general all he needed to know.

'So what *do* we have to work with, Captain?'

'Our basic backup systems are functioning normally. They run on a totally separate system. We have power, including air ventilation to all areas. Even the backup signal generator... well, it's running as smoothly as you would expect. We are monitoring fluctuations in its output. It won't last forever, but currently, it's holding.'

'And food and water supplies?' asked Valentin.

'Critically low on both – a couple of days at a push.'

'So, with communications down, there is no way of contacting the outside world. Even if we could, any rescue attempt would have to travel one thousand kilometres through the affected zone, instantly turning any human who stepped within range, and we've next to no supplies. Captain, I'm open to suggestions.'

'I think, that is in my opinion, we should continue to work on rebooting our operating systems at the very least, so that we can make contact outside the affected zone.'

General Valentin considered this. 'Then what would we do? Let's say we are successful and establish communications. Then what?'

'I don't know, sir.'

The general shuffled in his seat, and forced himself upright. 'I'm not saying it's a bad idea, but I think we should be focusing on the bigger problem – we need to get out of here, and I think I have a plan...'

27

8.00 a.m. One hour after C-1 activation

Valentin began to pace his office. With the base crippled and supplies at critically low levels, to linger any longer would certainly be fatal. Without even so much as a working camera topside, there was no telling what they would be facing once they passed outside the main doors, but there was simply no other options. He stopped and turned to Malinov.

'The vital piece of equipment keeping us all currently of our own minds is the original Kamera backup signal generator. Despite its fragility, we would have to take it with us – it must be possible to transfer it on to a portable generator. This would create a safe-zone bubble which could move with us, allowing us to travel out of the thousand-kilometre range of the C-1 transmission at Luga. The safe zone would prevent the base personnel succumbing to the effects of C-1, but it will do nothing to those outside who had already been exposed. This plan may be our only route out, but how much of Russia is there left to go back to?'

Malinov looked thoughtful. 'Have we reached the stage where by taking such a risk is a viable option, sir?'

'This is not a decision that I have taken lightly, I can assure you, Captain. Despite our own personal needs, our team is the world's best chance of developing a method of permanent shutdown for C-1. With the current status of our facility, we are not working to our highest level of efficiency. We are no closer to establishing a solution to our primary objective; therefore the logical progression is to relocate in order to continue our research.'

Malinov remained silent.

'Do you not agree, Captain?'

'No, I mean, of course I do, sir, absolutely.' Another silence hung in the room.

'Is there something bothering you, Captain? Do you have an opinion to share? I welcome your input; that is why you are here. You may speak freely.'

Malinov ground his foot into the carpet, shifting his eye contact. 'You know, sir, that I have always held you in the highest regard...'

'Are you going to get to your point?'

'Absolutely, sir. I do have certain... information that may be useful to our mission. Information that is considered classified.'

'What information? Why have I not been informed of this until now?'

Captain Malinov broke out into a light sweat. 'I have information on a method of permanent shutdown to C-1.'

General Valentin was famous throughout the Russian military for his cold, calm, ruthless efficiency. Most would say robotic. At this moment, he was as far from his usual persona than he had ever been. Red heat surged up his neck, flushing his cheeks a bright red.

'What? There is a method of permanent shutdown, and I wasn't informed? You better start talking, Captain, and it better be good, else you'll find yourself outside, fending for yourself against whatever's out there.'

'Please, sir, you must understand, I was acting under orders...'

'Whose orders? On whose authority were you acting to jeopardise my mission?'

'My orders came directly from the President himself... I'm only telling you now because... Well, because Russia, as we know it, may soon cease to exist.'

'You need to think very carefully about what you say next, Captain. It will be extremely important to the duration of your stay with us. Tell me what you know.'

Captain Malinov took a breath. He needed to steady his nerve. He needed to be thinking clearly. 'Absolutely. I understand. As you are well aware, the effects of C-1 should never have reached this magnitude. The device was buried in 1941 and that should have resulted in its termination. It was only due to the unexpected interaction with the unique geology under Luga that led to its amplification over the subsequent decades. That led to the formation of our project in 1982 to mask its effects—'

'So far you have told me nothing new,' interrupted Valentin. 'I am well aware of our own history.'

'Well... After the... success of the C-1 device at Luga, the Soviet Union wasn't prepared to turn its back on such an effective weapon. Research continued into its development and perfection. My orders were to report all progress of our project here to help in that development.'

'So your orders were to betray us. To betray me. To be a mole for this development project. You've played me for a fool and look where it's left us...'

'In order to develop the project beyond C-1, other similar devices were created. These prototypes were only small, having the range of only a few metres. After all the necessary data had been gathered from them, they were disposed of, underground, in the Arctic wasteland of Northern Siberia. It seems the geology there didn't have the same repercussions as Luga. The prototype transmissions remained restricted to their original range. Many of the devices have been hidden for decades, deep under the ice, out of range and safe. Occasionally, over the years, an Arctic explorer may venture too close and succumb to the transmissions, but cases are very rare. On these few, unfortunate, occasions the only repercussions have been a flurry of reported Yeti encounters before those affected eventually perished from the cold.'

'There are more devices? How many more?'

'I don't have access to an exact number, but... dozens.'

'And how does this help our situation? From all that you've told me, our current position seems far worse.'

'Last year, a bizarre, natural occurrence had been discovered. The region in question, the Yamal Peninsula, was subjected to a meteor strike. Upon impact, a short, but highly intense and extremely powerful energy pulse was emitted. It was the effects of that pulse that drew the attention of the world's media to "The End of the World". Suddenly, dozens of mysterious craters and sinkholes all opened up together, all over the peninsula. Some nearly one hundred metres wide and just as deep. They were perfect circles, with perfectly vertical walls, falling down into the ice. What they weren't aware of was that each one corresponded to the location of a disposal site of one of our devices. The media flocked to the site of these strange new craters. Hundreds of reporters, all eager to come up with their own theories for the event. The development project was in a state of panic. Should investigators venture too close and succumb to the effects of the devices, it wouldn't be long before the world reacted to Russia's "research".

'The media arrived. Reporters even climbed down into the craters and then... nothing. Not a single person had been affected, at any of the sites. The devices were deactivated. The energy pulse emitted from the meteor seemed to have the perfect properties that we have been searching for to initiate permanent shutdown. In doing so, it must have disrupted the ground above causing the craters to appear. Using data from the area, we were able to pinpoint the impact site and the exact properties of the energy pulse emitted. We had found the recipe that leads to C-1 deactivation.'

'And you have that perfect recipe, Captain?'

'Yes, sir.'

'With you now, in this base?'

'Yes, sir.'

'You're a fool, Captain, a damn fool.'

'Please sir, understand that I was acting under orders.'

Valentin stared directly into the eyes of his once most trusted colleague. 'I don't care about your orders. Now that the C-1 transmission has been activated, there is no way we can create the energy pulse required to disable it.'

'Well, sir, there may be a way...' Captain Malinov began.

'There's a way!' Valentin shouted. 'You mean to say that we could have put a stop to this whole thing before this catastrophe happened?'

'They needed to keep C-1 active in order to study it. Our counter-wave transmitter had it under control. I was assured that if it ever escalated to a level that we could no longer cope with then they wouldn't hesitate to shut it down.'

'Oh, that's very reassuring. And do you not think it's reached that level yet, Captain, or shall we leave it a few more years to see how things pan out? May I ask how we can create the energy pulse, or is that still classified?'

'In the 1980s, the Soviet Union considered itself on the verge of finding the solution to shutting down the C-1 device. It was clear that a large burst of energy would be required. Therefore, in preparation, a project capable of creating such a pulse was commissioned. This was a particle accelerator. It was to be constructed in a small village south of Moscow, Protvino. Construction began, including three, twenty-six kilometre circular tunnels. It would be like nothing the world had ever seen. Even by today's standards, it has only recently been matched at CERN. Unfortunately, the construction of such a revolutionary machine was hard to keep secret. Information on its designs were leaked, and the eyes of the global scientific community were soon fixed on Russia's new development.

'Of course, the true purpose of the accelerator was far too dangerous to risk being discovered. Officially, the project was abandoned mid-construction, due to lack of funding. Its door sealed shut and any further access denied forever more. But in reality, the entire project was moved north to a second, secret location. There it was completed, deep underneath acres of evergreen forest, totally hidden from view and there it waits.'

'So we've been able to end this whole thing since 1980!' Valentin yelled.

'No, sir. Although the energy pulse theory was correct, the construction of the accelerator was vastly premature. It has only been in the last few years that we have known the exact specifications of the energy pulse that we would require the machine to create to shut down the C-1 transmission.'

'You've known for years. This is ridiculous. Do you know if this machine even still works after so long?'

'I have no information on the machine's current state.'

'Well, where is it? We need to find out.'

'It was moved to Povarovo, sir, before you took over command. It's underneath our old transmission base.'

Valentin slammed his hands down on his desk. 'I think you need to be leaving now, Captain, before I do something I regret. Do everything you can to get us on the road as soon as possible.'

Malinov didn't argue as he saluted, then quickly turned and left the room.

Valentin had always considered his emotional detachment from life to be his strength. Where others were hampered by compassion or pity, Valentin applied logic. It had got him to where he was now. But as hard as he tried, he couldn't detach himself from the ruthless betrayal he had just experienced.

He had worked alongside Captain Malinov for twenty years and for all of that time he had been deceiving him. He cursed himself for being oblivious for so long. He had lost a dear comrade, but he had gained a plan. It was time to revisit his old command.

28

12.00 noon. Five hours after C-1 activation

A motley collection of supplies and equipment had been gathered in the main entrance area, in preparation for the evacuation to Povarovo. It looked more like a collection of desperate refugees than a convoy worthy of the Russian army.

One of the four large trucks that had delivered the equipment for the final counter-wave upgrade had been converted into a mobile transmitter and power unit to maintain the protective bubble around them as they travelled. The other three would act as transport for the base personnel, and were now laden with the remainder of the rations.

It would be a tight fit, but there would be enough room to fit all twenty-one of the scientists, researchers, computer programmers, and maintenance workers on board, as well as the security team. The guards would be the convoy's only protection once they left the base. Each one was armed with a rifle, although it had been a long time since any of them had fired a weapon in a conflict. The heavy, cumbersome weapons would be better suited to hunting game than any military application.

Valentin had turned down shouldering one of the rifles himself. His Makarov semi-automatic pistol would be all he needed should it come to that. The truth was, nobody knew what would happen once they set foot out of the doors. If the stories were true, then the aggression of the Affected may well cause them to destroy each other, leaving nothing but a clear path all the way to Povarovo.

They would follow a seven-hundred-kilometre route south and to the east, carefully avoiding the concentrated population centres. At a steady pace, they hoped to make it to the base in nine hours. It would mean travelling some of the way in the dark, but the plan was sound. The alternative: to linger and starve underground.

Valentin was confident he had made the right choice. They would face the journey with strength and courage. He approached the first of the trucks. The heavy drumming of a diesel generator grew louder the closer he became. The whole of one side of the cargo area had been removed allowing adequate air circulation around the machine as it churned out the vital power needed to keep the transmitter functioning.

The transmitter itself – a solid black device, not much larger than a shoebox – had been placed to the rear, linked to the generator by a multitude of coloured cabling as if it were on a life-support machine. As it was silent, there was no way to tell if it was active, besides the obvious repercussions. It had no switches or dials. Not even a comforting power light. It had never been designed to be used after so long and certainly not to be mobile. The theory was logical. So long as it continued to function, the safe-zone bubble would continue to exist, with the transmitter at its epicentre.

Valentin was distracted by the squeak from the wheel of a trolley and turned to see a pile of wooden creates being pushed slowly towards him by a young man in a blue laboratory uniform. He noticed General Valentin and stopped instantly, raising his hand in a smart solute. The general returned the gesture.

'At ease, soldier. What's your name?'

'Coombs, sir,' he replied, his eyes wide. He had never spoken directly to the general before; personnel of his rank simply didn't.

'S-sir... They s-say there are monsters out there. They s-say we won't survive the journey.' He had heard the rumours going around the base. He knew his stammer was worse when he was nervous, but this was his chance to ask the general directly. He wouldn't get another

'Maybe that's true,' Valentin replied. 'I can't deny that venturing outside of those doors may be the last thing that any of us ever do. There is a good chance that, whatever we choose to do, we will soon meet our end. I can't guarantee safety. But what I can do, is offer a choice. If it comes to it, would you rather be down here, cowering in the shadows, having it creep up on you, lingering, slowly? Or would you rather be out there, standing proud and tall, meeting it head on?'

The young man's face tightened into a determined smile. 'I'm with you, sir.'

The general nodded; there was courage in the man's eyes. 'Coombs, have you ever fired a weapon? Have you ever seen combat?'

'No, sir.'

'Then let's hope that's still the case after the day's through.'

'We'll be OK, sir. We'll find a way.'

Valentin raised his hand in a brisk salute. 'We will indeed. Carry on soldier.'

Coombs smiled, returning the gesture.

At 2.00 p.m., Valentin had given the order for all personnel to assemble in the main entrance. He hadn't elaborated further, however it was obvious that the evacuation was imminent.

Stepan had remained in his cell, isolated and unaware, when the two guards appeared and unlocked the door. They entered inside and grabbed him roughly by the shoulders.

'Come on; we're going on a little trip. Hope you're ready for it,' one announced.

Stepan didn't respond. His legs felt unsteady as they hauled him to his feet. The guard that had spoken produced a long cable tie; the other pulled his arms forwards and with a zipping sound locked his wrists tightly together once again.

The corridors twisted ahead of him as the guards bundled him along. His head span wildly as he tried to find his footing, but his chaperones were not prepared to slow down. Stepan didn't have time to consider what was happening. It took all his effort to stay upright. Finally, they arrived at an opening and Stepan was pushed through into a cavernous space beyond.

He was standing at the main entrance to the building. Huge, metal girders arched their way over the domed roof before diving down vertically into the solid, concrete floor. People swarmed everywhere in front of him, carrying all manner of items, each looking as busy as the last.

Parked in the centre were four familiar trucks. It seemed like a lifetime ago since he was following them in the Jeep with Natalya sitting next to him. He had tried to save her; he thought he was protecting her. Emptiness built up inside him, growing stronger as he focused on the memory. He didn't fight it. He didn't want to. He deserved every ounce of the horrible, hollow feeling it gave him.

A sharp shove in the back snapped Stepan back to the moment as he was moved forwards through the bustle of people. They all gave them a wide berth, most choosing to ignore him. Stepan caught the eye of a lady scurrying past holding a tablet computer. She was a similar age to Natalya, but her hair was a little longer. In Stepan's confused brain, she looked very similar. Their eyes locked briefly, and Stepan smiled. The lady scowled back, her eyes filled with anger before returning to her business, her eyebrows arched in disgust.

They stopped next to the last truck of the convoy. The canvas sides had been partially rolled up, revealing wooden benches secured along the length of the cargo area.

One of the guards grunted at Stepan. 'You can get in there and come with us, or stay here. The general says he's not prepared to execute prisoners, but if you choose to stay here, well, that's your choice.'

'What d'you mean "stay here"? Are you letting me go?' Stepan replied.

The guard laughed. 'Yeah, if you like. You'll be free as a bird until we're out of range, then the full force of C-1 will get ya. You see, we've got a backup system, and it's coming with us.'

'Oh, right. I suppose I'm getting in then.'

'Probably your best option,' the guard said, pushing Stepan up the ramp into the back of the truck. 'But if you change your mind, that's fine by us.'

Stepan sat quietly as the guards climbed in and sat either side of him. Others began to clamber aboard, all looking upon him as the terrorist he had now become. He averted his eyes to the floor. He couldn't bear to meet their stares. They were right to hate him – he hated himself.

Valentin stood watching the final preparations as the last of the security personnel assembled in a protective formation at the front of the convoy. Despite all being bundled into Russian Army all-weather protective clothing, they were as far from a Russian Army regiment as you could get. Everything was set. The equipment and supplies were organised. His mission objectives were clear. Drive the convoy to the abandoned base at Povarovo. Activate the particle accelerator to produce an energy pulse, which, in theory, would deactivate the C-1 device under Luga.

He had fought many enemies, some of which he had very limited intelligence on, but nothing like this. If there were any humans left in the affected zone, how much human would be left in them? Everyone knew the stories, but they were from over sixty years ago and Valentin didn't entertain rumours.

All activity ceased as the general stood next to his security team. Captain Malinov was standing on the opposite side. Valentin had avoided him as much as possible since his betrayal. However, due to maintaining effective command throughout the mission, they would be forced to travel together in cab of the lead truck.

Everybody was silent, the only sound being the quiet thrumming of the diesel generator powering the counter-wave transmitter. The general was not a man suited to passionate speeches. He gave a simple nod of approval, and gestured for the main entrance doors to open.

With a screech of grinding metal, the mechanism reluctantly scraped into life. A thin streak of light opened up between the huge doors as the afternoon sunlight crept in through the narrow gap, getting brighter the wider the opening became. Soon, the trees of the surrounding forest gradually came into view. Nobody moved; nobody spoke. The silence was as unnatural as the new world they had prepared themselves to be greeted by. The doors reached their fully opened position with a final *clang* that echoed out into the forest.

Valentin walked to the opening. In one hand, he held a pair of small field glasses. The other firmly gripped the handle of his unfastened Makarov pistol. Looking out, beyond the main gate and perimeter fence, he noticed a movement at the edge of the forest. He looked through his field glasses to search for it, but whatever it was had gone. A deer perhaps? The convoy behind him were becoming restless. Valentin turned around to face his men and with one last silent nod, he raised up his arm and a roar of diesel engines spluttered into life.

A shadowy form crouched low amongst trees, the other side of the perimeter fence. Steadily, it started to rise, like the slow unfurling petals of a flower. It continued to grow larger. It wasn't moving forwards, just expanding as it continued to stand upright. At eight feet tall, it had still not reached its full height.

General Valentin had taken a deep breath, preparing to give the order to move out, when one of his guards shouted, 'Sir! Look!'

He spun round, reaching for the grip of his Makarov. The figure looked vaguely humanoid but was much taller than any person he had ever seen.

The huge creature stood, staring straight back at them for a moment before slowly beginning to move. Using its huge arms, it swung itself forwards towards the gate in a great lumbering stride. It landed heavily, and then paused, as if waiting for a response.

Valentin could only stand and watch, fascinated by the sight before him. So, this was one of the Affected.

A splintering crack reverberated a little way to Valentin's right. The sound spread like a shock wave out of the hangar, rolling into the land beyond, echoing off the surrounding hillside. The massive figure went limp, crumpling to the floor as if it were a puppet whose strings had been cut.

Valentin spun in the direction of the sound to see a young, trembling man still staring down the sights of a freshly discharged rife. Normally he would have screamed at him so hard, his throat would have been raw. He felt the anger boiling inside, building steadily until he was bursting at the seams. How dare the man fire without an order! Forcing the swell of emotion back down deep within himself, he maintained his focus on the young man. He hadn't moved. Valentin could see all the other guards staring at him, waiting for his response with terrified eyes, their courage hanging by a thread. He felt his pulse steadying. Very slowly, he began walking towards the quivering man. He was still braced in his firing position. Even when Valentin stood next to him, he didn't move.

The general placed one hand on the stock of his rifle, pushing it down, gripping it tightly. The other hand he rested gently on the man's shoulder. Leaning towards him, he spoke in a voice that only he could hear. 'Stand down, soldier. It happens to us all.' That was a lie. Normally, that kind of ill-disciplined behaviour would lead to a court martial and instant discharge, but not today. The young guard nodded silently, relinquishing his rifle.

Threading his arm through the long strap, Valentin swung the weapon across his back and began marching back towards the convoy. 'Kirsino transmission station security, assume your positions aboard the convoy... It's time to move out,' he yelled.

The convoy started to crawl out of the hangar. The first encounter with the Affected had not gone as expected. The stories indicated the subjects would experience an increase in body mass. This seemed true; the enormous form was certainly formidable. Its mental state, however, was not what had been expected. Stories suggested they would be consumed by rage, ferociously violent, devoid of all reasoning. This specimen had been none of those things. More confused, curious even. It had made no aggressive gestures towards them.

Captain Malinov sat in silence in the driving position with General Valentin next to him. Every whisper of wind through the trees sent his head spinning around, attempting to identify what may have caused the movement, only to stare aimlessly into the depths of the forest. The perimeter fence and gate lay just ahead, the final barrier between the safety of the base and the new world beyond. The security gates were closed, blocking their way, they had no way to open then, but to a truck of this size and weight... breaking through the fence would be no more than a minor inconvenience.

'Evacuation of the base has been successful, sir. Encounters with hostiles have been minimal,' began Captain Malinov.

'Is that what it seemed like to you? A hostile? Because from where I was standing, we shot first.'

'Sir, it made a clear advancement on our position...'

'An advancement? There's a three-metre high fence between us. How can that be an advancement?'

'You saw the size of that creature, sir. That fence would have been useless if it had wanted to get through. There was no way of knowing the Affected's next action. It could have been catastrophic.'

'Exactly, there was no way of knowing. To assume hostility was foolhardy. How human was that Affected, Captain? How far gone?'

The Captain drove forwards, unable to reply.

Valentin continued. 'Were they approaching to attack, or to seek our help? We know nothing, and until we do, we have no enemy here. Do you understand?'

'Yes sir.'

'If I wish for you to give me another report, then I'll ask you. For now, just concentrate on getting us out of here.'

29

The creature had tried to break down the guardhouse door on several occasions that morning, each time to no avail.

During the silence that followed an attack, Natalya had crawled out from her hiding place under the desk, and taken a drink from the water cooler. Then she'd chance a peek out of the window. After each attempt, the lumbering form had retreated to the treeline. It seemed content to wait out its siege. For the rest of the time, Natalya had stayed hidden, even managing to doze a little before another round of pummelling greeted her ears, but the attacks had become less ferocious, and less frequent as the hours ticked by. It was as if the creature was gradually forgetting about her.

Having just crept out for another plastic cup of stale water, Natalya took the opportunity to stand for a while, as far from the window as possible so as not to be seen. Being hunched up under the desk for so long had made her joints ache. Once again, she switched on her mobile phone. She had turned it off to save battery power, making sure it was set to mute to avoid it making any noises that might attract the unwanted attentions of her stalker. There was still no signal, but the time read 2.30 p.m. She'd now been stuck in here for at least six hours. Given that she had hidden the Jeep not that far away, she had thought, several times, about making a run for it, but decided that trying to slip past the creature wasn't worth the risk. After seeing the speed at which it had moved, there was no chance of outrunning it for long if it took chase. Besides, Stepan could be out there somewhere. At least, in here, she was relatively safe. She considered sending him a quick text message, even though it wouldn't actually reach him yet. Wherever he was, he might eventually receive it. If she told him about the Jeep, and where she was, and warn him about the creature, perhaps he could get her out.

She checked the status of the battery – there was just enough charge – and set about composing a note. She hadn't been typing for long when she was interrupted by a mechanical grinding noise coming from outside. Her heart quickened. It sounded as if the hangar doors were opening. She quickly finished her message, pressed the Send button in the vain hope that it might, waited a few seconds, and then switched off the phone. She looked out of the window, just in time to see the creature lumbering along the edge of the forest towards the base before it disappeared from view. For a moment, Natalya wondered if it might continue its barrage on the guardhouse door, but nothing happened. It must have been more interested in what was happening outside. But if someone was coming out of the base, maybe Stepan would be with them. This could be her chance.

The grinding sound stopped with a *clunk* as the base doors fully opened, followed by the sound of diesel engines starting up. She needed to get out of the guardhouse; get their attention. She stepped to the door and slowly tried to slide back the bar that had kept her safe from the beast outside, but it wouldn't budge. The upper part of the metal door had buckled inwards a bit more each time it had been beaten, and although the rest of it seemed intact, the damage caused by the creature's pounding had distorted the locking mechanism. She pulled hard at the bar that held the lock in place. Nothing happened. She tried it several times, and although it rattled back and forth, she couldn't get it to slide open. Then there was the sound of a gunshot.

For a few minutes, nothing seemed to happen outside. All she could hear was the hum of engines in the background. Then, there came shouting. It was hard to make out what was being said, until the voice barked, 'It's time to move out!'

'No!' Natalya called, shaking the sliding bar on the back of the guardhouse door as violently as she could.

Moments later, a loud clattering noise sounded from outside, as if the chain-link fence had simply been driven through. She looked out of the window just in time to see the first truck trundle past, heading off along the track towards the forest road. She watched as three more trucks passed by, the people tipping perilously as they passed over the rough surface of the forest floor. Natalya studied them closely.

Stepan had been on the last truck. Although facing away from her, there was no mistaking him. She turned back to the door. Pulling the sliding bolt was not going to work, but there was no way she was going to be trapped inside this guardhouse for any longer. It seemed that the creature had been shot, but was it dead? In any event, she had to get out of here.

Natalya was tired, scared, and hungry, but with all the strength she could muster, she kicked at the door before trying to open it again. Two, three, four times, and on the fifth time, just as she thought her legs would give out, she slid the bar open. She burst through the door, and with only a glance at the creature that now lay a few feet from the broken fence, sprinted as fast as her aching joints would allow her, back towards the Jeep. She would catch up with the convoy, find Stepan, and then get some answers.

30

General Valentin instructed Captain Malinov to pull the truck over to stop at the crest of the hill overlooking the village of Kirsino. The general had always tried to work with the villagers' best interest in mind. The curfew he had imposed was to protect them, although quite how effective it had been was yet to be seen. He stared down into the valley. Six huge figures stood barring their path.

Valentin climbed down from the truck and walked around in front of the halted convoy. He ordered all security personnel to disembark and form a front line ahead of the vehicles.

'I need six volunteers,' he said.

As the people moved forwards, he studied them quickly. Captain Malinov was one of them. As much as he hated to admit it, he may need him now. He was the best shot he had by some margin.

The general started forwards steadily down the hill. 'On me. Keep your weapons lowered; we don't want to provoke an aggressive response. These people are Russian civilians, they are not our enemy.'

As the group strode forwards, the line of Affected didn't react. This time there could be no mistakes. They could not afford another incident. These people were the families he was trying to protect.

A low moan emanated from the group so loud that it reverberated off the surrounding landscape like the sound of an air raid siren. Valentin stopped his advance. The sound chilled his bones; it was not the sound that a human could make.

The line of figures ahead started to amble towards the general and his volunteers. He turned to look across at his men, and could see the fear in their eyes. 'Steady men, hold your ground,' he instructed.

The Affected were gathering speed, closing the gap between them. They were just fifty metres away.

'Ready arms!' called the general.

The men raised the barrels of their rifles as the sound of the Affected's huge footsteps thumped up the slope towards them. Many were over eight feet tall, their arms swollen to massive proportions like those of a mountain gorilla. Huge ripples of muscle rolled over the surface of their flesh. The extra upper body weight caused their bodies to stoop forwards. Had they stood fully upright, they would have been even taller.

Valentin looked down the sights of his own rifle, picking out a figure. Its skull had enlarged, increasing massively in size, but in doing so had distorted and twisted. Its mouth had slipped around its face, almost sideways, but its eyes were focused straight back at him. Orange pools of fire burning brightly. Valentin had seen eyes like these before. He knew them well – eyes that could not be reasoned with.

The general's decision had been made. 'Fire…!' he yelled.

Small eruptions tore across the bodies of the approaching creatures, impacting on them with the sound of pebbles falling onto wet sand. Only one fell. The rest didn't flinch. Huge open wounds appeared all over their bodies, pouring out blood, yet they continued moving as if oblivious.

They were only twenty metres away and still closing.

'Again...' shouted Valentin, 'Head shots only...' He lined up his rifle to target another, slowly releasing a deep breath. 'Fire...!'

Another salvo of explosions opened up across the charging line of creatures. This time, the shots were more effective. The line of Affected fell in unison, slamming into the ground as their momentum continued to slide them forwards, mere metres from the line of rifles.

Through the chaos, one creature remained, still on its feet, barrelling forwards at full speed. It was too late for the man in its path. For a split second, his face held an expression of disbelief, before the terminal impact. The full bulk of the creature smashed mercilessly into the man's helpless body, launching it into the air as if hit by a freight train. His lifeless form arched through the air, still clutching his weapon as he disappeared from view.

The creature turned, releasing another low roar, turning its arms out wide to flex its enormous muscle. The blood pouring from a hole in its shoulder did nothing to hinder its movements.

Valentin stood ten metres away, his emotions numb, his conscious brain shut down. Now, he acted on the instincts of an old warrior. In a single motion, he dropped his rifle, unfastened his Makarov pistol from its holster, and strode forwards. The creature's attention was diverted from him as it prepared another attack. Five metres... two metres... Still the creature didn't turn. The general raised his pistol high, far higher than any head shot should be.

Too late the creature realised the danger approaching and turned its massive body towards Valentin. The general didn't hesitate. At this range, he couldn't miss. At this range, it was an execution.

The weapon discharged, the kick of the recoil absorbed in the general's powerful hand. The creature's massive head bucked on impact as the bullet tore out of the opposite side and the huge body cascaded into a lifeless lump at Valentin's feet. He didn't flinch. He moved forwards to stand over the fallen mass and discharged another round into the enormous, distorted skull.

The fallen bodies of the other Affected lay all around. None of them showed any signs of life. They had communicated with each other, worked together to coordinate the attack. It was not the action of mindless animals as the stories suggested. Suddenly, a scream from behind ripped through the moment of silence. A sound of shrill, mindless panic. Very definitely human. Valentin's blood ran cold. The sound had come from the waiting convoy.

He didn't look to see if the others were following. Gripping his Makarov firmly, he tore back up the slope towards the sounds. 'On me! The convoy! Everyone here, on me!' There came more screams. A panicked cacophony that rolled down the hill towards him.

Most of the volunteers were forty years younger than Valentin, but there was plenty of running left in the old generals' legs. The others, weighed down by their rifles, struggled to keep up as he led the charge. He ran, cursing himself for trusting the stories he had heard about the Affected being mindless animals. He had severely underestimated the threat and now his men were paying the price.

Stepan sat motionless on the bench in the cargo area of the truck. His guards had left when the general had called for volunteers. The others around him were shuffling nervously, exchanging frightened glances. It was obvious that something was wrong. Everyone had heard the Affected's roar, and the sound of gunshots from up ahead. With the canvas partially drawn up, they were exposed and vulnerable. No one dared to speak.

One lady, sitting on the bench opposite Stepan, turned around to get a better view of the situation outside. Another burst of shooting erupted, this time far louder, coming from within the convoy. The truck lurched backwards as it was hit by a heavy impact, knocking everyone off the benches and throwing the lady backwards to the floor.

Stepan crouched down as those around him staggered to their feet. Swift cracks of gunfire echoed from all around as a huge crash sounded in the direction of the next truck along. It was followed by a blood-curdling scream. The people with him panicked. They clambered over the sides of the vehicle, running aimlessly in all directions. Stepan stayed put. He couldn't easily escape, his hands were still bound, and even if he could, logic dictated that he'd be better off staying out of view. He shuffled closer to the cab end of the cargo area and squeezed himself underneath one of the benches.

Another shriek sounded nearby, cut short by a sickening crunch. Suddenly the massive form of one of the Affected lurched backwards into view beside the truck. More shots filled the air as the huge beast reeled, taking shot after shot to the body, and yet still managing to stand. Its body was a mess of pulverised flesh as blood poured from dozens of deep gunshot wounds. It grabbed the side of the truck in an effort to keep itself upright. Stepan curled up as tightly as he could. If the creature so much as glanced inside, he wouldn't stand a chance. With a grunt, the beast steadied itself and charged back towards its attackers.

A fresh salvo of gunfire opened up, causing the *twang* of a ricocheting bullet as it bounced off the cab of the truck. If Stepan was going to survive, he needed to get out and take cover, and now. The closest shelter would be underneath the vehicle. He shuffled out from the corner, and climbed up on to the bench where he had originally been sitting. He peered outside, the sleepy village of Kirsino spread out below him. Yesterday these monsters had been people, happily living out their lives here. Good people, like Maryana. The thought turned his stomach. Slowly he swung himself over the edge of the truck, and lowered himself down to the ground.

He dropped onto his knees, then onto his front, and began to crawl, command-style, between the wheels of the truck. The road surface scraped into his wrists and knees as he scrambled, but it was all he could do to keep out of sight. Even if his hands weren't strapped together, he had never fired a weapon in his life. He wouldn't know where to start to fight back.

Wriggling frantically, he squirmed beneath the vehicle. The smell of diesel overpowered his senses, causing his head to swim. Rolling onto his back, he shuffled round so that he could position himself parallel with the underside of the truck and using his bound hands, pull himself into a more central position. Suddenly, a vice-like pressure closed around his left ankle. Moving his head to look, a sense of doom washed over him. The biggest hand he had ever seen was wrapped firmly around his foot.

There was little Stepan could do as the creature began to pull. His body scraped along the ground as it turned towards the other side of the truck. It wanted him out, and no amount of holding on would have stopped it. He reached out for the front wheel as he went past. His fingers managed to reach the tyre, but merely scraped along the rubber as he continued to move past. The creature gave his leg one final yank, hauling him clean out onto the road. Stepan felt the pressure leave his ankle, but it was too late to do anything now. He lay there helpless, forced to look upon the final face he would ever see.

The thing standing over him was enormous. Its head had distorted into being almost flat on one side, pushing its nose downwards to be on the same level as its huge, protruding jaw. The hideous result gave its head the appearance of being made from wax that had then been melted by a hot flame. Its eyes fixed on Stepan, as he winced. His whole body clenched, waiting for the final blow.

From his right came the screeching of tyres. There was a thud of impact, a blur of dark blue as a fast-moving vehicle skidded past, and a loud squelch of flesh against metal. Stepan pulled himself up into a seated position and stared in disbelief. The wheels had missed his feet by inches but it was his Jeep. Whoever was driving it had slammed the monstrous beast into the next truck.

Slowly, the vehicle limped backwards as steam hissed up from what was left of the bonnet. The body of the creature fell to the ground, its huge bulk collapsing into a lifeless heap. For a few seconds, nothing happened, until the driver's door opened.

Stepan looked in amazement as a small female figure clambered out and rushed towards him. 'Natalya? Is that…? How did you…? I thought you were…' he spluttered as Natalya helped him to stand up.

She hugged him tightly. 'It's good to see you too, Stepan.'

'I can't believe it! You're OK…' Stepan's voice broke, his vision misting behind tears.

'I'm fine, but what about you?' Natalya asked, nodding towards his bound hands.

'This? Oh, it's nothing. I'm fine now. They just held me in a cell until the base evacuated.'

'Well, we have a lot to tell each other, but at the moment I counted three more of those creatures out there,' she said.

31

Valentin had made it back to the convoy to find a slaughter. The Affected had taken them by surprise. The remaining security personnel had only managed a few shots before being totally overpowered. The general had managed to take down as many of the creatures as he could, but the priority was the signal generator. If that was destroyed, then it would be the end of them all. He battled through to find the crucial truck intact, but totally unguarded.

He stood alone, back pressed against the side of the cargo area. Three Affected were lumbering towards him. Slowing his breathing, he raised his Makarov, aimed for the head, and squeezed the trigger. Instantly, the first beast fell, dropping to the ground as the general aimed at the second. It was coming at him fast. He fired the second shot. The next creature came crashing down. The third was nearly upon him. It was smaller, both in height and bulk than the others, not much taller than Valentin, but still with the muscle mass similar to an adult brown bear. If it reached him, he wouldn't stand a chance.

He only had seconds to react. The general paused as the realisation hit him, this must have been a child. He dropped his arm. The Affected was still coming at him, its arms waving wildly as it let out a piercing roar. Whatever this thing may once have been, it wasn't anymore. But he had wasted valuable seconds, and the creature was a stride away. Once again, Valentine took aim and squeezed the trigger. It responded with a hollow click as the housing slid back to reveal an empty chamber.

Natalya easily tracked down the three remaining Affected, the sound of their heavy movements was unmistakable. They had now converged on the old man that Natalya had identified as the leader.

A discarded rifle lay on the ground, a couple of metres away. Natalya sprinted across and picked it up. Stepan stayed with her.

'What are you doing?' he said. 'Don't mess with that.'

Natalya ignored him, sliding the bolt back as a spent round shot out of the side of the chamber.

'Do you know what you're doing?' He asked.

Natalya still didn't reply. She looked to see another round available in the magazine as she slid the bolt back into position. 'Come on,' she called as she ran towards the one remaining Affected. The man had taken down two, but he wasn't going to get the third in time. She crouched down on one knee, levelling the barrel.

Stepan crouched next to her. 'Are you actually going to fire that?' he hissed.

Natalya continued staring down the sights.

'Natalya… don't. You could hit him…'

'Shh! Just one minute. I'm OK. Let me concentrate.'

'Please don't kill yourself, Natalya.'

'I'm not going to kill myself, just be quiet.'

'Be careful, just…'

The rifle discharged with a crack that left Stepan's ears ringing. They both watched as the creature fell, crashing into the ground at General Valentin's feet. 'No different from shooting rabbits,' Natalya said, smiling.

Valentin instinctively looked up to see where the shot had come from.

'That was incredible...' Stepan began as Natalya rose to her feet.

General Valentin had picked his way around the fallen body and was striding towards them.

'Yeah, thanks, and with no help from you,' Natalya said in a raised voice. 'I thought you military were supposed to be fearless? Don't be shy to step in next time.'

Stepan looked blankly at Natalya's cold stare.

'That man is not military,' the uniformed man began, 'but I am. I am General Valentin.' He offered his hand to Natalya. 'To whom do I owe my life?'

'I'm Natalya.'

'I'm very grateful for your services, Natalya, but may I ask how I managed to be so lucky to have you here at the right place at the right time, and...?' He left the sentence unfinished.

Natalya swallowed and glanced quickly at Stepan. 'Erm... I live here,' she said, gesturing at the village, 'but I saw you were in trouble and thought I'd help.'

General Valentin studied the young lady standing before him with some suspicion. She didn't wear the clothing of a Kirsino resident, although she could handle a gun like a farmer. 'Well...' he considered. 'I'm very glad that you did. We need to check for survivors. Come with me.' He turned and walked away.

'Well, are you going to help or just stand there?' she asked Stepan. 'Who is he anyway?' she called after the general.

'He's the cause of all of this,' he called back, as he crouched down next to the remains of a young man whose neck had been broken.

Natalya caught Stepan's eye and shot him a tiny smile. 'I'm sorry,' she whispered. 'I thought it might be better, for now, if he didn't think we were together. But you do need to tell me what on earth's been going on.'

32

General Valentin scanned the bodies lying around him in vain. He needed to find Malinov. If he was alive then there was still hope to put an end to all of this. Small human forms lay twisted and broken into horrible contortions amongst huge bloody mounds of motionless muscle. They would check them all, but the chances of finding survivors were not promising.

The body of his second in command lay on its side in the dust of the road, heavy and numb as Valentin rolled him onto his back. There were no signs of a fatal injury. He placed two fingers on his neck. The pulse he felt was strong.

'I need some help over here,' he called out.

Natalya was still reeling in shock from Stepan's explanation of the last twenty-four hours. Tears had filled her eyes as he told her about Stanislav, but there was no time to dwell on it for now. She had to stay strong, and act detached.

'Is he alive?' she called to the general, as she ran over to him.

'Yes. This man holds the key to putting a stop to all of this. We need to get him over to that truck as gently as possible.'

'There's a way to stop it?' Natalya asked.

'In theory, yes. There's another base… It was where we were heading.'

'What's the plan? Where are you going?'

'I'm afraid that's classified. I don't know how much of Russia is left, but until I do, I can't share any further information.'

'You know, I would be far more likely to offer you my help if you tell me what we're dealing with.'

'Young lady, I am grateful for your help so far, but you are not in a position to barter, believe me.'

Natalya scowled at him. 'Well, if you say this guy's important, let's get him up.'

Stepan, still with his hands bound, could only stand and watch as the two struggled with the dead weight of the captain, manoeuvring him into the truck containing the transmitter. Valentin had climbed aboard and crouched down next to Malinov, checking him for any concealed wounds. There didn't seem to be any, but he must have taken a serious blow to the head to render him unconscious. He covered the man with an all-weather survival coat. Malinov would come around in due course, but for now, there was no time to wait. They needed to get to Povarovo.

Climbing down from the truck, Valentin checked his empty Markov pistol and loaded his final clip. On the ground were two rifles. He picked them up and threw them aboard. 'We need all the ammunition, and supplies from the trucks, that we can get,' he said, addressing Natalya. He looked at Stepan with renewed concern. 'Not you. You stay here.'

'I'd be a lot more help if I wasn't tied up,' said Stepan, holding his arms out in front of him.

The general looked at him in disgust. 'How did you survive, and all these good people not?'

'Maybe the world is giving me a chance to right my wrongs?'

'You could live a hundred lifetimes and still not have enough time to do that,' Valentin spat.

'I know that, but I want to do what I can to help end this.'

'I should leave you here. Leave you to suffer the same fate as these innocent people.'

'I understand. It's what I deserve. But you need all the help you can get right now, and perhaps there are still lives out there that we can save.'

General Valentin sighed and retrieved a combat knife from his belt. 'If you cross me, I will not hesitate to shoot you where you stand.' He reluctantly began to cut Stepan's bonds. 'Do I make myself clear?'

'Yes, perfectly,' nodded Stepan. 'I know I can't ask you to trust me, but I promise that won't be an issue.'

***

General Valentin drove the truck steadily as they continued their journey south-east. In the passenger seat, Natalya and Stepan sat squashed together in silence, staring intensely out of the windscreen. The sun had set, and now they travelled in the last light of the day. Captain Malinov still lay unconscious in the cargo area, next to the portable transmitter and amongst the supplies that they had managed to bring on board.

Without looking at Stepan, Natalya dropped her hand to her side to squeeze Stepan's tightly. 'Do you think he's OK back there, your captain?' she addressed the general.

'He'll be fine. He's suffered worse,' replied Valentin.

'I should go back there and sit with him. Just to make sure. He'll be confused when he wakes up.'

'You're staying here,' ordered the general. 'You saved my life, but with all due respect, I don't know who you are. I'm not about to leave you alone with the only man able to stop all of this. You have not told me how you came to be at Kirsino village; I accept that, and I owe you as much not to force it out of you, but we have some way to go before we can start trusting one another.'

'I'm from the village...' Natalya began.

'That's a lie and we both know it. Unfortunately, I need your help as much as you need mine, right now, so for our mutual benefit, we need to work together. That includes our reformed terrorist.'

Stepan thought it best to keep quiet.

'How long have we got before we become affected like the others?' Natalya asked.

'We will be unaffected as long as that generator back there holds out. We have enough fuel to keep it going, but that is not the issue... It's old... which means were working to a clock that could stop at any moment.'

'Right. And how long do we need?'

'At least another seven hours for our journey, anything else, I'm not sure.'

'And you think the generator will last that long?'

Valentin sighed. 'Given it's a relic of a bygone age, I'm surprised it's lasted this long.'

Their route avoided the main populated centres as much as possible to reduce the chances of further contact with the Affected, but some were unavoidable. Ahead, a small town came into view – a collection of lifeless buildings frozen in time. The roads were filled with the twisted metal carcasses of vehicles destroyed or abandoned. Traffic lights repeated their endless cycle without anyone to direct, but the empty wind. The only movement came from a twisting spiral of smoke that rose from the smouldering ruins of a nearby building. Valentin picked his path carefully through the destruction. They could not afford a delay, or risk damage to the truck.

'I can't believe a whole town has been reduced to this,' said Natalya.

'A whole town destroyed in an instant,' Valentin replied. 'And there'll be many more like this all over Eastern Europe. The overall death toll will be catastrophic.'

'The death toll... fifty million?'

'Yes, that was our most recent estimate... Have you two been talking?'

'Yes, Stepan has filled me in on the basics.'

'I'm glad you two seemed to be getting on so well.'

Natalya paused as Valentin turned the truck onto an empty road.

'You know what's strange...' she began.

'Would you like me to give you a list?' Valentin replied.

'Well... if the death toll is so high, where are the bodies?'

Valentin did not reply straight away. She was right: the Affected were supposed to be aggressive. The population of the town should have been littering the streets. 'Just keep a look out. We can't risk any more confrontations. Clearly, there's no way to second-guess these creatures; we have no idea how they think. We need to stick to the plan. That's the only way through this.'

They passed through the town without incident, and most of the buildings were behind them when a dark grey shadow appeared to spread across the road ahead. It was the remains of an overturned coach. Huge gashes had been ripped in the side and roof causing triangular shards of metal to twist outwards as the vehicle was torn apart from within. It lay empty, except for the outline of a small human figure sitting in the driver's seat still gripping the steering wheel, his quick death sparing him any horrific transformation.

In the back of the truck, Captain Malinov came to. He managed to sit himself up and find a position wedged next to the churning generator. His head was still spinning from what he assumed must have been a heavy blow, but he could feel no other injuries. He remembered the ambush to the convoy. He remembered the panic. The rifles were slow and the Affected had already caused much destruction. He had tried to rally the men, but it was too late... that was the last recollection he'd had. Now, he was in a moving truck, and alongside the counter-wave transmitter, so presumably, they were still heading towards Povarovo, but there was no easy way to check. The canvas cover was fully down, but only strapped in a couple of places. This left the loose parts flapping. He had plenty of air, but not enough of an opening to see outside. There was no choice but to sit and wait.

***

General Valentin had grown visibly wearier as the darkness had deepened into the night. He was hungry and struggling with fatigue, their progress slowing with each hour that passed.

'I can drive,' offered Natalya, as the truck weaved off course once more.

Valentin snorted a laugh. 'That's not happening,' he replied.

'I can handle the vehicle and I can keep us moving while you have a few hours to recover.'

'This mission is my responsibility. I can rest when it's over.'

'Have you seen the way you've been driving the last few hours? You're tired, general. After everything that's happened, you need a break.'

'You'd have me trust you with the only machine keeping us safe, and the life of the only man who can stop this? Listen to what you're saying and ask me again if you think it makes sense.'

Natalya sat in silence for a moment. 'You're going to get us all killed. If you fall asleep at that wheel, that's the end of everything. It's not just our lives that are at stake here.'

Valentin continued staring straight ahead. His vision was smearing over, his body screamed at him to rest. Carefully, he pulled the truck off the road and on to soft grass.

'We rest here. We are in the middle of nowhere, so should be safe. I have seen no Affected moving about since it got dark, so I must assume they too need their sleep, but we need to keep vigilant. You two stay where you are, I'm going to check on Malinov.'

Fumbling for the keys, the general pulled them from the

ignition. They were plunged into darkness as he lowered himself from the cab. The journey had caused his legs to cramp as he felt his way to the back of the truck. He opened up the access ramp, and drawing a torch from his pocket, he swung its light across the cargo area before noticing Malinov sitting up and blinking back at him.

'Captain Malinov, how nice of you to join us. Are you lucid?' asked Valentin, as he climbed up into the vehicle.

'Yes, sir... I believe so. Just a knock to the head. I think you need to bring me up to speed on our situation.'

'There's no time for details, but we were ambushed by the Affected as we travelled through Kirsino village. The convoy was destroyed, but as you can see, our portable generator is still operational for now and we have a few supplies. Our current location is about three hours outside of Povarovo. I... I'm afraid we are the only survivors. That is you and I, the terrorist, and a young woman named Natalya, who claims she is from the village.'

Malinov remained silent for a moment, letting the general's news sink in. All their people, gone. It did not bear thinking about. 'Who's Natalya?' he queried.

'She saved my life in the ambush, but other than that her details are unknown. She has lied about her background, so I can only assume she has something to hide. However, based on her actions during the attack, she appears to be currently working with us. I have not disclosed the details of our mission to either.'

'Yes, sir. And our current situation?'

'I've been driving for too long, and I would rather not linger, but I need rest, and we all need some refreshment. After which, do you think you can take us the rest of the way?'

'Absolutely, sir,' replied Malinov rising to his feet. The cargo area of the truck spun wildly as he staggered and grabbed the side of the generator to steady himself.

Valentin looked on. 'In your own time, Captain.'

General Valentin awoke sharply to Captain Malinov's voice.

'Sir. I'm sorry to wake you, but I think we should start to head off. We want to arrive at the base as soon as possible in daylight.'

Valentin wiped his brow on his sleeve as he worked himself upright in the driver's seat. He checked his watch. It was just after 3.00 a.m., he had been sleeping for five hours. Looking across the cab, he noticed that both Stepan and Natalya had gone.

'Where are our guests?' he asked with curiosity.

'In the back,' indicated Malinov. 'I agreed that they could try to get some rest, in exchange for keeping an eye on the cargo—'

'Did you think that wise, Captain?'

'Given the circumstances, I didn't think that they were likely to try anything untoward. Besides, there's not a lot of room up here, and they were beginning to smell...'

Valentin chuckled. He couldn't remember the last time something had amused him to the point of laughing. 'Very well. Are you ready to drive?'

'Yes, sir.'

'Then bring Natalya back here. She may be useful. The other one can stay in the back – for now.'

The sun rose over the frost-covered pastures of surrounding farmland. With Malinov at the wheel, they surged along the road as it coursed its way over the rolling landscape leading them through the hills, eventually to the top of a high crest that overlooked a vast shimmering lake below.

On the surrounding grassland, a huge group of Affected lumbered slowly around the water. The group was hundreds strong. All of them huge, but varying in height and build. Malinov pulled the truck to a stop. The group was half a kilometre away, and had not yet noticed the truck at its elevated position.

The creatures moved slowly at the water's edge. Some steadily trudging, others using their huge arms to help swing themselves forwards, their movements careful and considerate to the slower members as they crouched to drink. Occasional low moans caught in the breeze and wafted back to the truck.

'Welcome to the human race,' said Valentin.

'That's fascinating,' Malinov whispered. 'The stories, all the reports, they indicated they'd be filled with anger and hate. Instead, they've grouped together in harmony, and that sound... they're communicating.'

'What are they all doing out here?' asked Natalya.

'It has been said that the Affected will have impairment of the modern human brain,' Valentin replied. 'If they have regressed, then they are now relying more on instincts. Food, water, shelter, they are the basic needs for any animal. I suppose they have no need to stay in towns anymore.'

'Do you think we can get around them?' asked Natalya.

'Wild animals won't attack unless they see us as food or a threat,' Malinov said. 'Let's hope they don't see us as either.'

He moved the truck forwards steadily. The road would take them no closer than two hundred metres to the edge of the group. As they approached, the sound of the engine caught their attention. The Affected swung their huge bulks from the water to face them, their heads turning to track the vehicle as it went past. Some of the larger members of the group stepped forwards, gently moving smaller ones behind them as the group closed ranks. Their contorted features and burning orange eyes locked on to the truck. They held their ground, but none of the creatures made any sign of aggression. Hundreds of monsters stood motionless and silent; any of them capable of overturning the truck with one swing of their huge arms.

Inside the cab, the occupants met the creatures' stares in silence. Even as the truck reached the closest point to the group, the Affected still did not move.

The truck continued slowly along the road, but now the distance between the two species increased. The front line of enormous bodies stood shoulder to shoulder, forming an impenetrable barrier, turned to track the vehicle as it sped away into the countryside.

'I guess you were right,' Natalya said.

'I told you, we weren't food or a threat,' Malinov replied.

'Is that what the reports have said?'

'Just basic animal behaviour. Aggression takes up resources and risks injury. Animals will only use it out of necessity. If we need any further proof that these creatures are no longer human, then that was it.'

33

Sunday 21 February. 9.00 a.m.

As the truck neared the end of its journey, a quick stop was made to bring Stepan out from the cargo area. He was allowed to sit back in the cab with the others, but with Malinov still driving, Valentin took up a lot of space on the remaining seat, meaning that Natalya was almost sitting on Stepan's lap.

The rolling countryside passed them by until a village appeared on the horizon. 'D'you think we should get off this road? You're going to take us straight through the centre of those buildings,' asked Stepan.

'I think you should stop giving me orders, terrorist,' barked General Valentin. 'If you don't want to end up in the back again, I suggest that you stop talking.'

'Hang on a minute,' Natalya interrupted. 'He's right. We need to avoid direct contact with the Affected. Taking us straight into a village is asking for trouble.'

'I totally agree with you. But if we are to stop this, then that's where we need to go,' Valentin replied.

'Is this where the base is?' Natalya asked.

'Indeed. This is where my captain informs me he can put a stop to all of this.'

On the fringe of a vast evergreen forest, they entered the

forgotten village. Curtains fluttered nonchalantly through broken windows of barren rooms. Doors creaked in the morning breeze. The buildings stood abandoned, waiting patiently for their occupants to return. The village stood as it had done for an age, only now without a soul. They had arrived at the forgotten village of Lozhki.

Out of sight of the general, Stepan reached round for Natalya's hand, squeezing it tightly. He lent towards her and whispered so quietly, he wasn't sure if she had even heard him, 'We're heading back to Povarovo.'

The truck surged through the empty streets until reaching the familiar dirt track that marked the beginning of the access road to the abandoned base.

Ahead, the base's main gates loomed into view. Malinov didn't slow the truck; he knew they would be unlocked, but there was the sensitive cargo to consider. He drove on, forcing the gate's iron bars to buckle and give way. They scraped along the ground with a sickening screech, slowly grinding their way back across the frosty tarmac as the truck roared through.

In front of the main building, Malinov brought the vehicle to a halt and the four occupants jumped out. Natalya shivered, and not just because it was cold.

Valentin crunched around to the cargo area and pulled out two rifles. Making sure his Makarov was fully loaded and he had spare ammunition, he walked to the front of the truck.

'It's time for you to deliver on your claim, Captain. Time to end this devastation. This is what it comes down to... The traitor...' He handed a rifle to Malinov. 'The mysterious woman...' He handed the second rifle to Natalya. 'And the terrorist... I suggest you find something to defend yourself with.' He turned back to the captain. 'And I suggest you waste no time in taking matters from here.'

The captain took a second to process the situation. 'Right, sir. The machine we need is underneath us. The control room can only be accessed through the basement in the main building. Unfortunately it has been sealed shut to preserve its contents.'

'And you have the ability to unseal it?' asked Valentin.

'Maybe, sir. I need to take a look...'

'We don't have time for "maybe", Captain.'

'No, sir, of course not. I shall need to see what I'm dealing with to work this out. I don't suppose you transferred the metal cutting torch to our truck, did you?'

'Captain, had you disclosed the details of your plan, then I would have brought all the essential equipment required. Unfortunately, as commanding officer, I seem to be the last to know a lot of things at the moment.'

'Of course; it won't be a problem, but let me check the cargo truck for anything that may help.'

Malinov returned shortly with a small filled backpack.

'Are you ready?' asked Valentin.

'Absolutely. Come on,' lied Malinov as he strode towards the entrance of the main building, the rifle slung over his shoulder.

Heaving the main doors wide, they entered into the dust-filled debris of the lobby. Two disintegrating pillars of cracked plaster stood tall through the warped metal framework of a false ceiling. With the metal bowed and broken, many of the white ceiling panels had fallen, leaving dark holes like missing teeth, through to the space above. Piles of fallen white plaster lay on the dark tiled floor, where black and green stains of mould and lichen crept across every surface.

Malinov led the group through to the top of a staircase that descended down into total darkness. 'Down there is a straight passageway. At the end is a sealed metal door. That's how we get into the control room.'

Stepan moved forwards to peer down into the gloom, but Valentin grabbed him by the shoulder.

'You're not going anywhere. If you think that I am going to let the terrorist who caused this anywhere near the only machine capable of ending it, you have another thing coming. You and I will stay here.'

Stepan thought about objecting, but stayed silent. He knew his argument would only serve to waste time.

'I'll go with the captain,' offered Natalya. 'There doesn't need to be two of us up here with him.'

'I don't need anybody down there with me, either.' Malinov replied. 'It might be dangerous.'

'Dangerous? Isn't that all the more reason not to go alone? If this is our one chance, and you're the one person who can stop this, then you'll need some backup.' Natalya didn't look back as she began to walk down the steps. 'Come on, Captain, you're wasting time.'

Malinov quickly caught up with her. 'If you're coming, you'll need this,' he said, handing her a torch.

The two of them descended slowly, with Malinov leading the way into the damp, stale air. At the foot of the steps, the flat concrete walls of a tunnel continued straight and uninterrupted into the darkness. As they progressed further, the smooth walls began to glisten with moisture. Puddles of water gathered at their feet until they were steadily splashing through a constant shallow pool.

'So what's with this door we have to open?' Natalya asked.

'It's not much further now but it will be a problem. Upon completion of the machine, the door was welded shut until the time was right.'

'Welded shut? So how do we get through it?'

'Honestly, I have no idea. It's solid plate steel. Even with a controlled explosion, I'm not convinced it would be enough to get through it, and then we can't risk damage to the machine or a cave in. I really...'

Malinov froze. His beam of torch light streaked out ahead

of him through an empty doorway and into a darkened room beyond.

'Is that it? Is that the control room?' asked Natalya.

'Yes,' came the flat reply.

'So, where's this door you're so worried about?'

Malinov tipped his torch beam down to the floor of the passageway. Where the steel doors should have been, a pile of wet, thick, twisted metal now lay to one side. Across its surface, Malinov could make out long scratches and puncture marks. Any hinges had been sheared off. The other half of the door was nowhere to be seen.

The captain approached cautiously. Caught on the broken shards of sharpen metal were clumps of short matted fur.

Natalya walked up next to him. 'Well that's the door problem solved.'

'I'm afraid,' began Malinov, as calmly as he could 'that we may have just discovered another problem. Natalya, I need you to go back to the surface now. Tell the general that I have accessed the control room and that he should leave now. Ready your rifle.'

Natalya considered this. As much as she wanted to turn around and run, she was part of this bigger picture now, and needed to right her part of what she had helped, unwittingly, to go wrong.

'No, I'm not leaving you down here alone. Come on, you're wasting time again.' With that, she stepped forwards over the remains of the steel door, to shine her torch into the room beyond.

'Please listen, Natalya. Do not go in there,' pleaded Captain Malinov.

34

Natalya's swinging torchlight played across a row of four large CRT monitors with bulbous glass screens. Black office chairs stood before them standing on a floor of grey carpet tiles. Beyond them, and filling the far wall, was an array of glass cabinets. Inside each one, ancient circuit boards were attached to enormous wheels of tightly wound analogue tape. To the left of the room, on the far side, was another open doorway that led into another tunnel. The door itself was undamaged, opened inwards into the room. A large square window was set into the wall next to it.

Natalya gingerly stepped forwards. 'It's like a time capsule in here. Everything still looks new, but it's got to be forty years old.'

Malinov stood next to her, his rifle raised. Not that he could see much in the darkness. 'Keep your voice down,' he whispered.

'There's no one here, Captain,' Natalya confirmed as she shone her torch around.

The captain lowered his weapon and reached for his torch, focusing its beam of light on the open entrance. He walked over and pushed the door closed. 'Not even a lock,' he muttered. 'You don't understand what sort of danger we're in being here.'

Natalya swallowed. 'You're worried about the dog things, aren't you?'

Malinov spun to face her. 'How do you know about those? Who *are* you?'

'I'm no one. Just a journalist, actually. Well, not even that. But I've been here before. I've seen them.'

'And you got away?' Malinov was incredulous.

'Barely.'

'But how?'

'It's a long story, and I would rather not have to do it again, so if you don't mind doing whatever it is you have to do, I'd like to be getting out of here sooner rather than later.'

Malinov moved to the main breaker switch on the wall behind him, and switched it on. One by one, six bare bulbs above them produced a dim flicker, slowly spluttering into life. At the far side of the room, one burst with a loud *pop* sending a shower of powdered glass sparkling from the empty metal fitting.

Inside the cabinets, the wheels of tape started to spin rapidly back and forth, as the antique monitors flickered with a dull green glow. Text scrolled across their screens for the first time in nearly half a century as the room awoke from its long hibernation.

Everything seemed to be in working order as Malinov pulled up a chair in front of one of the computer terminals.

'These machines are ancient,' he said, fixing his eyes on the display. 'I've never come across an operating system like this.'

'Do you think you'll be able to understand it?' Natalya asked.

'It's not complicated, just old. It shouldn't be a problem. From what I can see, all the systems seem to be operational.'

'How long will it take?'

'Not long, I just need too...' Malinov's voice trailed off as he continued to work.

The background noises from the old computers filled the room. The whir of the tape wheels, the hum of cooling fans, the rhythmical tapping of the keyboard as the captain worked.

He began pressing the keys faster the more familiar he

became with the systems, although still nothing like the speed Stepan had reached on his laptop.

Malinov leant back in his chair, nodding his head in satisfaction at his work. 'I'm making progress. I'm through to entering the specifics.'

A splintering crack echoed from the closed door, quickly followed by another from the window next to it. The view through was obscured by the inky darkness of the tunnel beyond, but it was obvious what had caused the sound. Pushed against the glass was a hideous, familiar face. The dog-like creature's humanoid skull, its jaws filled with multiple rows of long needle-sharp teeth, looked like it was smiling through a muzzle of white foam. Another hollow bang rang out from behind the door, but the first creature hadn't moved. There was more than one.

'Err... Captain, are you seeing this?' Natalya spluttered.

Malinov didn't flinch. 'I need another minute. I am so close, but you need to go now. Run!'

'You need to come too. There's no time for heroics. You might be the only one who knows how to stop this, but we both need to get out.'

Another thump came from behind the door. The face behind the window had vanished.

'Natalya, there's no lock on that door, but it will hold them for a little longer. I have to finish this. Please go; I'll be fine. I have my rifle.'

'That's not going to happen and you know it...'

Suddenly, the captain rose from his chair. 'Right, OK. Let's go. Take this,' he handed her the backpack. 'You lead the way.'

'Are you done?'

'Yes, finished. All done.'

'In that case, let's go.'

Natalya hoisted both the bag and the rifle over her shoulder, and using the torch to guide her, shot a quick glance towards the other doorway as she went back into the tunnel. The door was still holding the creatures, and the captain was right behind her. There was only one tunnel, only one direction to run. She took flight, her feet splashing heavily in the shallow water. Deep lungfuls of stale air fuelled her muscles as she ran. Even as a burning sensation built up in her thigh muscles, she didn't slow. She kept on running, concentrating only on the sound of her footsteps splashing in the water. She kept her rhythm – her footsteps, her rhythm. Only hers…

At the foot of the steps back to the surface, Natalya stopped and turned to look behind her. The captain wasn't there.

***

Malinov had kept behind Natalya for the first few steps before deciding to turn around. She was one brave lady, but he didn't need her help to programme the energy pulse. There was no need for them both to be down here. He watched her thunder away from him into the darkness, and then made his way back towards the control room. He needed to finish what he had started.

The creatures where still contained, but the door holding them was shaking violently. Before sitting back in front of the computer terminal, he took the rifle off his shoulder, disengaged the safety catch, and laid it gently across his lap. He had to work fast. The energy pulse would need to be perfect – there would only be one chance.

A flash of movement from behind the window caught his eye as the bashing from behind the door stopped. He took a quick glance, but there was no time to be distracted. The keys glistened as the captain's fingers transferred nervous sweat onto their white surface. But the silence coming from behind the door gnawed at Malinov's instincts. At least with the noise, it was obvious where the creatures were, and what they were doing. He could only afford another quick look. The door handle was moving, ever so slowly downwards, before it flicked back to its original position. The creatures were working out how to open it.

Pure force wasn't going to work, but a simple turn of the handle was a different matter. Malinov only had seconds. Just at the moment the door swung open, he hit the last key, completing the final sequence of commands, sending the precious information through to the sleeping machine. All was set; the pulse was inevitable.

To his side, the creatures' clawed feet scraped across the carpet. They weren't capable of mercy. They had been designed for one purpose only: to kill on sight.

Malinov carefully pushed back his chair and, remaining seated, slowly turned to face his nemesis. He had observed the projects created by the Predator Weapon Programme many times over his years stationed at the base. Always behind bars, or in the exercise pits, but there was nothing to separate them anymore. He should have destroyed them when they abandoned the base, but he had designed them, grown them, and raised them. They were not pets, certainly not his children, but in a moment of weakness, and for the first time in his life, he had disobeyed a direct order.

There were three of them in the room with him. The lead creature being the pack alpha. It circled around him only two metres away. Its heckles raised, bearing its hideous mass of needled teeth. Its orange eyes fixed on Malinov's, staring deep into his soul. The captain didn't stand or run. He maintained eye contact with the creature's unflinching stare, while moving his hands to rest on the rifle in his lap. He knew the animal would be able to sense his fear, but he did his best not to let it show.

'I know you can understand me,' Malinov spoke slowly. 'You remember who I am, don't you? I spared your life once. I spared your pack.'

The alpha stared back, its snarl unchanged. White froth dripped from between the horrid gaps in its rancid teeth. The other two creatures had circled around too, blocking the exit back to the surface. There was no escape for the captain that way. Slowly, he stood from the chair. 'I ask nothing of you, but to repay what you owe me. Let me leave and consider you debt repaid.'

The alpha leapt up on the desk, next to where Malinov had just been working, sending a computer monitor crashing to the floor. It landed with a splintering crack as the glass screen smashed into a shower of glistening razor-sharp shards. As the creature bore down on him, it was close enough to smell the stench of its rotten breath.

Malinov instinctively raised his rifle to target the creature's head. His lips trembled as he tried to maintain his calm. 'Repay your debt and we can both leave. If I die, I'm taking you with me.'

The alpha bowed its head, its jaw moving as its lips twitched awkwardly making rapid clicking noises with its teeth. It did not attack. Somewhere, inside its genetically modified brain, it knew its extraordinary existence was about to come to an end.

Is it possible? Malinov thought with wonder, *that the creature was trying to communicate with him?* He concentrated harder on the creature's mouth, trying to make sense of the effort it seemed to be making.

Out of the captain's view, three more creatures had emerged from the open door behind him, and had begun to silently stalk closer. The alpha continued to focus Malinov's attention, its mouth still jerking clumsily.

'What are you trying to say?' the captain asked, before realisation hit him.

Captain Malinov wasn't able to register what happened as he fired his rifle. He didn't see the bullet pass through the head of the alpha, killing it instantly. He felt no pain, as the five remaining members of the pack pounced on him, their combined force bringing his body to the floor and killing him in one fatal blow. As his rifle clattered across the floor, the pack stood over him, their open jaws salivating at the prospect of their latest meal.

35

After lying dormant for forty years, the particle accelerator burst into life. Nothing about it visibly changed, but around its twenty-six kilometre rings, superconducting magnets surged. Two high-energy particle beams fired simultaneously in opposite directions in two separate tunnels. Directed by the powerful magnetic fields, each beam accelerated to the verge of light speed before being redirected into each other's paths to intersect. The result was a collision of monumental power. An invisible energy pulse burst forth, sweeping across the surrounding land.

Almost instantaneously, it reached Luga, penetrating easily into the deep bedrock and finding its target. The earth beneath the city shook. Rocks splintered and cracked. With a mighty rumble, the whole city began to sink slowly down into the earth. The tired grey block buildings crumbled as if they were made of playing cards. As they collapsed into piles of rubble, they released clouds of dust, which ballooned into the air. Black ribbons of roadways flexed and twisted as the ground beneath them gave way. For a moment they resisted, the tarmac stretching like a strip of toffee before finally splitting and crashing down into the earth with the rest of the city. The Federal Office of State Reserves, with its secret C-1 monitoring station that had protected the city for so long, reduced to nothing more than a powerless pile of circling debris.

Huge vertical walls of rock penetrated ever deeper into the earth, marking the limit of the city's descent, as homes, parks, and the possessions that represented the lives of so many plunged out of existence.

Too late, the Affected trapped within realised the danger they were in. Running in all directions, they lurched clumsily through the wreckage, the sound of their low moans lost under the roar of the sinking city. There was nowhere to go. Many lay, crushed, under falling debris; others made it to the few open areas away from the tumbling buildings.

Huddled together in the dust-covered grassland of park Kultury i Otdykha Zarechny stood an ever-increasing group of creatures. Instinctively, they had tried to escape the collapsing city. With their huge bodies powerless to stop the overwhelming forces at work around them, they could only stare helplessly up towards the sky as the ground below them fell away.

This was no sinkhole in Siberia. A perfect circle, three kilometres wide had just descended out of existence, taking the whole city with it. The Luga River meandered along its usual sluggish course until encountering the edge of a vast cliff where it plummeted straight down in a mass of foam and spray into the darkness of the chasm below. The water fell relentlessly, painstakingly dooming the last remaining life and ruined city to be lost forever under what would soon become one of the deepest lakes in the world.

Still buried, far underneath the wreckage of the city, after nearly eighty years of incessant screaming, the C-1 transmitter finally lay quietly, never to shout again.

36

Natalya shone her torch back along the tunnel. The captain was nowhere to be seen. He had lied to her. He hadn't finished setting up the energy pulse, but had gone back to finish the job. She couldn't go back for him, not with those creatures there, and he did have a gun, but leaving him alone seemed so wrong. It was against everything she believed in.

She had no choice but to get back to the surface and warn Stepan and the general. If the creatures made it through the door, they would all be in danger. She looked one last time towards the direction of the control room, hoping to see the captain running up to meet her through the darkness. There was nothing.

She stumbled up the steps towards ground level, squinting in the bright light of day. As she reached the top, she heard a gunshot coming from deep underground. It could only mean one thing: the dogs were out.

Panting heavily, Natalya found the general and Stepan waiting in the main lobby. 'Captain Malinov...' she breathed, 'he's still down there... We were attacked... It was those wolf things, the ones from before... They're down there... I heard gunfire... We have to go...'

General Valentin looked back and forth between the two. 'Wolf things? Are you sure?'

Natalya was already making her way towards the main doors. 'Yes, the last time we were here, we were chased by the same creatures. Whatever they are, they're down there now and any minute they'll be up here. When they are, I'd rather not be.'

Stepan was already heading towards the main doors with Natalya.

Valentin paused to stare in the direction of the stairwell. He knew only too well what Natalya was referring to, and felt another knock of betrayal as he realised that the captain had not followed his orders to destroy the creatures. Not only had they survived, but also they had escaped their confinement. With the predator weapon loose, Malinov was now very likely dead. There was no way of knowing if he had succeeded in his task, but they needed to get far away from this place, and as quickly as possible. The general said a mental goodbye to his second in command, and followed outside, closing the main doors behind him.

The glade was filled with its usual eerie calm. The surrounding forest absorbed every sound, every breath of wind, leaving nothing except a dead silence. Straight away, Valentin knew that something wasn't right. He knew this place. He had even begun to feel at home here after all these years, but there was something missing, something he couldn't quite identify.

As the group approached the truck, Valentin realised what was wrong. In a single, fluid motion, he swooped around to the back of the vehicle and clambered inside. From within, all was quiet. The generator for the counter-wave transmitter had stopped.

The small black box looked the same as it always did. He turned his attention to the generator. There was plenty of fuel; nothing seemed to be obviously wrong. Through the panic filling Valentin's mind, his steady logic started to emerge. The generator had stopped and yet they were all still unaffected. It could only mean one thing: C-1 had been deactivated. Being so close to the centre of the energy pulse had fried the electronics of the generator and counter-wave transmitter, but that didn't matter. The mission had been successful and the equipment was now redundant.

'It's worked! The captain must have done it!' Valentin called out. 'The transmitter and the generator have cut out, but we are still the same. That can only mean that the energy pulse was effective.'

'Really? Is that it? I didn't feel anything,' said Natalya.

'That's it,' replied the general, clambering out of the back of the truck. 'All that's left is for us to get out of here.'

'And we're waiting because?' Natalya started as she climbed into the cab, still clutching the rucksack and rifle.

Stepan jumped in too, but Valentin hesitated before pulling himself into the driver's seat.

He turned to the building they had just left. 'Thank you, Captain,' he said quietly, making a salute. Once inside the cab, he reached around the steering wheel and turned the key. Nothing happened. He let go, then tried again. Still nothing. Leaning back in his seat, he began to examine the ignition.

'In your own time, General,' Natalya said.

'It's not starting. It's totally dead. Not even a glimmer; it's as if the battery has…' Of course, it wasn't *just* the generator and counter-wave transmitter that had been fried by the energy pulse. 'Unless anyone has a spare battery, we're not going to get this truck going… Come on, we can't stay here…' he said, as he opened the door to get out.

'So where do we go now?' Stepan began. 'Even if C-1 has deactivated, it's not going to help us here. We're still miles from any safe zone. There's no way we'll make it on foot.'

'I agree,' replied Valentin, 'we need to make our way to the closest safe zone, due south. In the meantime, we need to find another mode of transport. There may be a working vehicle in town, but even if the electronics are fried there too, push-bikes will be better than nothing until we find something better.'

They hopped down from the cab one after another, all keeping a watchful eye on the main building. Natalya passed the backpack to Stepan, who filled it with what food supplies he could gather from the cargo area.

'How far are we from the safe zone, General?' asked Natalya.

'Based on the predicted range of C-1 from Luga, I would estimate, six hundred kilometres.'

Natalya let out a sigh. 'That's a whole lot of pedalling. Let's start by getting out of here.'

The trio jogged towards the edge of the clearing, passing over the embedded metal track that marked the gap in the chain-link fence.

'There used to be a gate here,' Valentin said to no one in particular. 'What I would give to be able to close it now.'

The sound of doors being smashed open caused all three to spin round. Back at the main building, five dog-like creatures exploded out of the double doorway, driven into a frenzy by the scent of new prey. Nobody uttered a word. There was no breath left for talking.

Natalya quickened her pace, but the rifle swung wildly across her back and slammed into her shoulder with every step. Stepan was also now breathing hard. Once the creatures had their scent, they wouldn't be able to outrun them for long. Hiding in the woods would be useless; they would be sniffed out in no time. They could stand and fight, although the creatures were fast and strong, and they were outnumbered, but maybe she could help their odds. Taking the rifle in her hand, Natalya crouched down on one knee and levelled the barrel. A loud crack echoed around the clearing as her first shot discharged.

One of the creatures flew back, landing in a heap. The remaining four spun around to the direction of the sound. Natalya ejected the spent casing and prepared to fire a second round. The creature that had fallen was climbing back to its feet.

Natalya fired again, hitting the same beast once more. It hit the ground hard as the rest of the pack scattered.

Valentin crouched next to her. 'Good shooting, but we need to go now. There's no way you'll take down the whole pack.'

'At least that's one less,' said Natalya as she rose to her feet.

'Come on, we need to move,' Valentin urged, and began running.

Natalya glanced back towards the building. The creature she had hit had gone. 'What's with those things?' she breathed. 'I had two hits. It should be down for good.'

'You slowed them down, showed them we're dangerous. That's good, but actually killing them may not be so easy.'

With thundering footsteps, the three continued to run through the evergreen forest.

'If we can't kill them...' panted Stepan, 'and we can't outrun them... then what's left, General?'

The general carried on running in silence, the sound of his breathing becoming steadily heavier.

'Can we... out climb them?' Stepan tried again. 'Dogs and wolves can't, so if we made it up the trees the creatures wouldn't be able to follow.'

Valentin heaved another gulp of air. 'That is true, but look at the forest.'

The tree trunks surrounding them were smooth. Even the first wispy branches were way out of reach, and far too weak to support any weight.

From behind them, the sound of faint snarling was unmistakable. Through the darkness of the forest, five predator weapons barrelled along the access road after them.

Natalya could see that Stepan and Valentin were struggling to keep up the pace. 'You two go on ahead,' she shouted. 'I'll catch up.' She crouched again with the rifle. She tried to search for the one she had wounded earlier, but the creatures were all moving normally. Natalya forced a slow breath and fired. The shot missed. The round hit the ground between them kicking up a small plume of dust. She reached to prepare the next shot, but the creatures had already reacted to the danger, scattering into the trees.

She sprinted to catch up with Stepan and the general. They were just arriving at the next clearing. Natalya had pace to spare and caught up with them quickly. Just ahead of them, to the right stood the pink building that she thought was a guardhouse. It looked sturdy. Its windows were intact; although, how much force they would be able to withstand was another question.

'I'm going ahead to try the door,' she gasped, speeding through the tall wild rye grass.

The sprint had taken its toll. By now, Natalya was also finding it hard to breathe. She stumbled up to the front of the building, and threw herself against its heavy door, trying the handle. It barely moved. She took a deep breath and tried again. The others were approaching, their eyes wide through exhaustion. Natalya tried once more, throwing all the strength she could summon into the handle. Still there was no movement, not even a creak. She fell back. It was useless; there was no way she could open it.

Valentin was next to arrive, the general's red face looked fit to burst as he managed to speak. 'This building always locked… Door reinforced… Never get in…'

Natalya nodded. 'Any other ideas?'

The five creatures had reassembled and made their way into the clearing, sniffing the air before fixing their hunger-filled eyes on their desperate prey.

Valentin spoke as quickly as his breathless body would allow him. 'No matter what we do… they'll keep coming… They're relentless. We won't outrun them. Stepan's idea is our only chance. They cannot climb…' a coughing fit caused the general to bend over double.

'But like you said, how do we get into the trees?' asked Natalya. 'The branches don't come down anywhere nearly low enough.'

Valentin's head was still low as he took in desperate gulps of oxygen. Without looking up, he waved his hand vaguely across the other side of the track. 'Not the trees...'

Natalya followed the line of the general's swinging arm. A few metres into the forest stood the precarious twisted metal of the old transmission tower.

37

The creatures bounded toward them, travelling even faster, sensing their fear. Their jaws snapped wildly at the air in anticipation of their next kill.

Natalya threw the rifle to the ground and grabbed the old general by the arm, hauling him upright. Stepan was approaching, shining sweat cascading down his pained red face. He was quickly reaching the point of total exhaustion.

'Come on!' she yelled at him. 'This way.'

Stepan didn't have time to stop. He changed direction to follow, but his legs were nearing their limit. He stumbled forwards, arms flailing through the air.

The tower stood just a few metres away.

Natalya used all her strength to push the general into a run, as she caught Stepan by the hand to right him. Heaving at his arm, she broke into a sprint. He stumbled again, his legs giving way, but Natalya held his balance. The yelps and growls from the pack behind grew as the distance between them closed ever smaller.

'Go…' breathed Stepan. 'Please… just go… I'm done.'

'No chance, you're not leaving me again,' Natalya yelled back at him.

'I can't make it…'

'Shut up and run. Not another word, just run.' She gave his arm another tug as they approached the edge of the forest.

Valentin reached down to draw his Makarov pistol as he ran. Glancing over his shoulder, he took aim and fired two rounds. Both hit the skull of the lead creature. Deep red gashes appeared in its bare skin, yet the creature didn't slow. The general turned again, this time targeting its legs. Several more shots found their target under the short fur. It stumbled a little for a few steps before righting itself to regain its previous stride.

Valentine threw away his empty weapon and grabbed at the first rung of the twisting ladder, pinned into place by rusted rivets to the framework of the tower. As he heaved himself up, the metal groaned as it accepted the man's weight.

From the front of the pursuing pack, the lead creature howled as its prey began to climb out of reach. Travelling at full speed, it launched itself towards the generals' legs, flying through the air, clean over the heads of Stepan and Natalya, just as Valentin heaved himself another step higher. He felt the creature touch his feet as its head drove between the rungs he had been standing on seconds before.

Its head stayed anchored by the ladder as the momentum of its heavy body carried on wrapping around the outside of the frame, causing it to yelp loudly as its neck twisted into an impossible angle. The bottom of the ladder gave way, and the beast dropped. It hit the ground hard, and for a few seconds lay stunned, long enough for Natalya and Stepan to surge past, and grab at the flailing ladder.

As the three climbed, the animals beneath surged around the base, jumping up at them and snapping at the air. Globules of white foam flew from their rancid jaws. The general had been right: they were unable to follow. They climbed higher as the creatures below howled in frustration.

Natalya chanced a quick look down. The creatures had moved slightly away from the base of the tower. One ran forward, building speed before coiling its body and launching itself towards the leg of the tower. The metal groaned, as the whole structure was sent into an ominous sway.

The trio clambered on, following the ladder's winding path around the great structure, through the branches and pine needles of the surrounding trees. Sunlight greeted them as they broke through the thick canopy.

At the summit of the ladder was a small metal platform, but it was designed for radio transmission equipment, not people. There was no shelter from the elements, or railings for support. The area was two metres square, only just large enough for them all to sit in a triangle and hang on, thirty metres in the air. They reached it just as the pack launched a second attack on the base of the tower, sending it into another lurching sway.

The forest below them stretched out for miles in all directions rolling over the hills of the land. A perfect sea of faultless green. The creatures below were out of view, but each quiver of the tower reminded them they were still waiting.

'They won't stop.' Valentin began. 'They won't give up.'

'That's reassuring,' Natalya said. 'You seem to know more about these creatures than anyone. Do they have a weakness?'

Valentin shook his head. 'We spent years perfecting them. They were our project to design the perfect predator. I could understand the benefits of such engineering, but the project was Malinov's. He was the head of development. As far as I know, they have no weakness.'

'Well, how wonderful that your hideous experiment was successful. So what do you suggest we do from here?' Natalya said.

The tower surged again. Its sway felt greater now they were at the summit. A gust of frozen wind whipped up around them as the three found themselves grabbing at the platform for balance.

'I ordered them to be destroyed. I knew the danger they posed. I would never turn them loose.'

'Well, that's great, General, because I would hate for them to escape, and then be cornered by them. Maybe next time you could do the job yourself—'

'Natalya, this isn't helping,' Stepan interrupted. 'We need to think this through.' He turned to Valentin. 'You say they won't leave, but do they sleep?'

'No,' Valentin replied. 'They become dormant for brief periods, but never sleep. They can go for weeks without water and even longer without food – they can even survive Arctic temperatures. And, they have no fear.'

The tower groaned again as a huge surge from beneath sent the top part bending through the air. It centred itself again, but the platform was no longer level.

'This tower might not last much longer, if this keeps up.' Stepan began.

Natalya shuffled closer to him, placing her arm around his waist, moving her head closer to his. 'You know that I would have trashed your apartment in days, don't you?'

Stepan smiled. 'I'd have liked that,' he said, tilting his head to rest on hers.

As the time passed, they sat in silence. The cold deepening as the hours passed by. The creatures were relentless, and between the attacks below and the swirling wind above, it seemed as if the tower was in constant motion. With each movement, the metal screeched and strained, growing ever weaker, becoming ever closer to its inevitable downfall.

38

Over the previous twenty-four hours, Anomaly Border Control command had monitored everything it possibly could. The European Union has commissioned the ABC agency to create an adequate perimeter and to maintain containment of the Affected Zone.

The construction of a great barrier to circle the entire area had already begun. It would be in two parts. One in mainland Eastern Europe, travelling through the length of Poland and most of the Ukraine. The second spanning the width of Finland. Once constructed, the combined barrier would span a total length of over two thousand kilometres, becoming one of the largest man-made structures ever built.

ABC command had already gathered vast databases from scans, probes, and satellites, all in hope that somewhere there would be a clue that might lead to a method of controlling the situation. Overnight, the Affected Zone had become the closest monitored area on the planet. A few hours ago, every sensor had gone off the scale. A huge energy surge had burst from coordinates deep within the area. Shortly after, the mysterious electromagnetic wave transmission that had been resonating out of Luga had halted. The Affected Zone was no longer active. Two reconnaissance helicopters had been dispatched to investigate. One was on course for Luga city, the other to the location of the unknown energy pulse.

The pilot of the Mi-17 twin-turbine helicopter was approaching its destination.

'ABC base, this is Ranger One.'

'Go ahead, Ranger One.'

'Erm… you're not going to believe this, but I have eyes on survivors.'

Three figures, balanced on a tiny platform at the top of a huge, swaying transmission tower, had seen the helicopter and were waving as enthusiastically as they dared.

There was a long pause before base replied. 'Please repeat your last transmission, Ranger One.'

'I have eyes on survivors: three unaffected survivors. Request permission for immediate evacuation.'

Another long pause.

'Permission confirmed, Ranger One. Proceed with immediate evacuation.'